# PRAISE FOR THE
# STEEL BROTHERS SAGA

*"I'm dead from the strongest book hangover ever. Helen exceeded every expectation I had for this book. It was heart pounding, heartbreaking, intense, full throttle genius."*
**~ Tina at Bookalicious Babes Blog**

*"Proving the masterful writer she is, Ms. Hardt continues to weave her beautifully constructed web of deceit, terror, disappointment, passion, love, and hope as if there was never a pause between releases. A true artist never reveals their secrets, and Ms. Hardt is definitely a true artist."*
**~ Bare Naked Words**

*"The love scenes are beautifully written and so scorching hot I'm fanning my face just thinking about them."*
**~ The Book Sirens**

# BREATHLESS

**STEEL BROTHERS SAGA**
**BOOK TEN**

# BREATHLESS

## STEEL BROTHERS SAGA
## BOOK TEN

WATERHOUSE PRESS

*This book about the Steels' little sister is dedicated to my own little sister, Louise Betcher Staab.*

*Sissy and Flaxie forever!*

*And the Betcher girls are not high maintenance!*

# PROLOGUE

I am the person standing at the magazine rack in the convenience store, nose in *Sports Illustrated*...one eye on you.

I am the person at the gym with a towel around my neck, never making eye contact with anyone, my legs pumping the pedals of a stationary cycle...one eye on you.

I am the person walking along the street who stops at the antique shop to peer in the window at the collection of baseball cards. Through the reflection of the glass, I have one eye on you.

I am here.

And I am watching.

# CHAPTER ONE

**Marjorie**

*I'm happy to be doing this. She's my best friend.*

I repeated the mantra to myself as I tore romaine lettuce for a Caesar salad. Again as I mashed potatoes, adding cheddar, sour cream, and crumbled bacon. Again as I carefully spooned the mixture back into the potato skins and placed them in the oven. And once again as I salted and peppered the round steak, preparing it for the skillet.

I loved to cook. As much as I'd tried to fit in around the ranch that was a quarter mine, I'd finally admitted it. My brothers had control. Joe loved tending to the cattle. Talon was king of the orchard. Ryan made the vineyards sing while creating perfection in a wine bottle.

I wasn't needed on the ranch. I'd have taken off to Paris to study but for my best friend in the world, Jade Roberts Steel, my new sister-in-law. According to my other new sister-in-law, Dr. Melanie Carmichael Steel, Jade was experiencing hyperemesis gravidarum, a fancy name for really bad morning sickness—the kind that incapacitates a pregnant woman.

Not fun.

Add to the ingredients that Jade and Talon had just adopted two troubled little boys, ages ten and seven, and that their housekeeper, Felicia, had gone on an extended leave to help her ailing mother. Mix well, and what do you get?

Auntie Marj to the rescue.

I was happy to help. Truly, I was.

Jade was the best friend a woman could ask for and had been there for me more times than I could count. And Talon was my brother—my brother who had been to hell and back, largely because of me.

*It's not your fault, Sis. No one blames you.*

Words all three of my brothers had drummed into my head.

They were right. I knew that. I couldn't help being conceived. Being born. It hadn't been my choice.

Still, the fact remained.

But for my conception and birth, Talon wouldn't have been taken. Wouldn't have been beaten, tortured, and worse as a ten-year-old child.

I bit my lower lip and opened the door to the refrigerator. The cool air always helped, for some reason. When I found myself strolling down this ugly path, a chill on my skin reminded me not to go there.

Melanie had initially suggested a rubber band around my wrist. I was supposed to pull on it and sting myself when I had these unwanted thoughts. Problem was, the thoughts had been so overwhelming that I'd ended up with a swollen and bloody wrist that was still a little tender to the touch.

Since I spent so much time in the kitchen, Melanie then suggested a whiff of cold air. It helped.

A little.

At least it didn't lead to self-mutilation.

I laughed aloud.

Self-mutilation.

Mel—I was the only one who called her Mel—knew my horrible secret. She'd apologized profusely about the rubber band idea once I'd told her. I'd sworn her to secrecy, and as a therapist, I knew she'd never give me up.

Even Jade didn't know...and I told Jade everything.

Almost.

Anyway, Mel had offered free therapy, guided hypnosis, anything in her arsenal to help me deal with everything my family had been through, but I wasn't ready.

Not yet.

Not while Jade needed me to be strong while she was struggling.

I couldn't crumble. Jade had always been there for me, and I'd be there for her now.

"Hey, Auntie Marj."

Donny, one of my new nephews, scurried into the kitchen. He was a beautiful little thing with blond hair and green eyes, so different from all of us Steels. We were all dark-haired and dark-eyed. Of course, he was now a Steel. Or he would be, as soon as the adoption was finalized, which was supposed to happen within a month. Donny was more talkative than his older brother, Dale. Poor Dale had taken the brunt of the abuse to spare his little brother, and he had a lot to work through. They both did.

But Donny could always put a smile on my face. Despite being imprisoned and horridly abused for several months, he was a happy kid. At least he seemed so to me.

"Hi, sweetie."

"I'm hungry."

"Supper will be ready in a half hour."

"Where's my dad?"

"He's on his way."

"And Miss Jade?"

Donny had taken to calling Talon Dad easily. He'd grown up without a father. Calling Jade Mom was coming more slowly. Dale and Donny's biological mother, Cheri Robertson, had committed suicide after her boys were taken, though the boys didn't know that yet. Talon and Jade had told them she'd died in a car accident.

"She's in bed."

"Throwing up again?"

"I'm afraid so."

"That baby in her belly is making her awful sick."

"Yes."

"Maybe we should get the baby out."

"No, we can't do that."

"But if it's making her sick..."

I sat down at the kitchen table and pulled Donny onto my lap, placing a kiss on his sweet-smelling head. "She and your dad want the baby very much. So even if it makes her sick, she's going to stick it out until it's time for the baby to be born so you and Dale will have a little sister or brother."

"I hope it's a boy," Donny said, smiling. "What do you want it to be, Auntie Marj?"

"It doesn't matter. As long as it's healthy."

"I suppose." Donny hopped off my lap. "Can I have a drink of water?"

"Sure thing." I rose and got him a cup out of the cupboard.

He filled it at the refrigerator. "I'm going to go play with the doggies." He trotted out through the sliding glass doors onto the deck, where Roger, Bo, and Beauty were napping.

Not for long. Donny would have those dogs up and

running and fetching in no time. The kid was full of energy.

I sighed. Being here was good for me. With all the commotion, I barely had time to think those horrible thoughts.

Except that now I was thinking them again.

I walked over to the refrigerator, but before I opened it, a knock sounded on the front door.

I quickly wiped my hands on a dish towel, walked through the kitchen and foyer to the door, and peered through the peephole.

My heart jumped.

Bryce Simpson.

Bryce was my brother Joe's best friend. I'd known him ever since I could remember. Both he and Joe were thirteen years my senior, and I'd never thought of him as anything but Joe's buddy...until he and I had almost shared a kiss after I'd babysat his young son, Henry, one time.

I'd followed him to check on the sleeping baby, and we'd smiled down at his angelic face. Then we'd turned to one another. My heart had stampeded as he leaned toward me, his gaze meeting mine and making me melt. I lifted my face to meet his lips.

We got closer...

Closer...

Had I stopped it? Or had he? I couldn't quite recall. At any rate, a million things had happened since then, and I hadn't seen him or Henry since Ryan and Ruby's wedding a couple of months ago.

I knew one thing, though. Bryce Simpson was no longer just Joe's best friend. Now he was the tall and muscular man with sandy-blond hair and blue eyes that made my heart beat a little faster.

Many times, I'd imagined the kiss that hadn't happened.
Many times, I'd wished it had.
My skin prickled.
I wanted to see Bryce.
I wanted to see him badly.
I opened the door.

# CHAPTER TWO

**Bryce**

"Hi, Bryce."

Marjorie Steel.

Damn.

I remembered when she was born. I remembered a pink-faced baby, a cute toddler, a gawky preteen.

I remembered a hot eighteen-year-old going off to college.

I remembered telling myself she was no longer jailbait.

Then I remembered thinking my best friend would pummel me for even having that thought.

That particular thought was tame compared to what I was thinking now.

She was five feet ten, model gorgeous, and those deep brown eyes could melt me with just a look.

Plus, she was great with my son. What a plus.

Damn again.

I wanted her.

But I was a fucking mess. I couldn't even take care of my own son. He was with my mom, and though I was living with them, I'd hardly been hands-on lately. Thank God for my mom. And thank God for Henry. Henry had saved my mom after she'd found out the truth about my father.

Henry had given her a reason to stay sane.

He'd given me a reason as well, but with Mom taking care of him—*needing* to take care of him—I'd been free to wallow in the mess that had become my life.

Marjorie widened those gorgeous baby browns. "Bryce?"

Oh, yeah. I hadn't said anything yet. I cleared my throat. "Is Tal around?"

"He should be here any minute. You want to come in?"

"Yeah. Sure." I stepped into the foyer. "I went to Joe's first. No one answered."

"He and Melanie went into town for dinner."

"Oh." I cleared my throat again.

"We're going to eat soon. I'm making pepper steak and twice-baked potatoes. There's plenty. Would you like to stay?"

As if on cue, my stomach let out a roar.

Marjorie smiled. "Is that a yes?"

"I can't. I just need to talk to Talon. It's important."

"Tal's been working all day. I can guarantee you he won't be in any mood for talking until his belly is full. Come on." She walked toward the kitchen of the large ranch house.

I had no choice but to follow. My appetite hadn't been great lately, but I couldn't deny my hunger as I inhaled the rich beefy scent.

The kitchen table was already set, a clear vase filled with yellow flowers resting in its center. She removed the vase and set it on a nearby counter.

"These get in the way when we eat, but I love to have them around me while I'm working in the kitchen."

"What are they?"

"Lilies. Asiatic lilies. The light yellow are my favorites, and Jenna rarely has them."

"Jenna?"

"The florist in town." She busied herself adding another place setting. "I make a ton of food these days. Even though Jade hardly eats a thing, Talon and those two growing boys eat like maniacs."

"How's Jade doing?"

"Sick as a dog, the poor thing. She's resting now, but she's a trouper. She spends time with the boys every day, and I make sure she eats enough to keep going. Doctor's orders."

"I don't get it. Melanie wasn't sick at all."

"Pregnancy is different for every woman, apparently. Mel got lucky. By the way, did you hear the good news?"

"What news?"

"Melanie got her amnio results back. Everything is normal, and they're having a boy."

I smiled. The amniocentesis had been on Joe's mind. Melanie was forty years old, an age where things could go wrong with pregnancy. "Why didn't Joe tell me?"

"They just found out this afternoon. That's why they went into town for a celebratory dinner."

"That's great news. Really."

"I know. I'm so happy for them. I just wish Jade felt better."

"Yeah. Makes me happy to know I'll never have to go through it."

She scoffed. "You men don't know how lucky you are."

I nearly scoffed back at her, but I held it in. I didn't feel particularly lucky these days. Discovering that my father was a pedophilic psychopathic rapist had that effect on a guy.

"Where's Henry?" Marjorie asked.

"He's home with Mom."

"You should bring him by. I miss him."

"With this brood keeping you busy?" I forced a laugh.

"How could you?"

"Because he's adorable and I love him," she said, her tone serious.

"I've been letting him stay with Mom mostly," I said. "It's good for her. He's keeping her from thinking about...other things."

"Oh. Yeah. I guess I get it."

"How's your mom?"

She sighed. "The same."

Daphne Steel lived in a mental institution in Grand Junction. Marjorie and her brothers had recently relocated her from California, once all the threats to her had been removed. Long story. She lived in an imaginary world where Marjorie was named Angela and she was still a baby.

I wasn't sure what to say. Daphne's prognosis wasn't good. I finally settled on, "Smells great in here."

"It'll be ready soon. I'm going to make a small plate for Jade and then stand over her while she eats it. Make yourself at home. Tal should be here in a few." She quickly filled a plate.

I tried not to, but I ogled Marj's perfect ass as she left the kitchen. I couldn't help myself.

Now what?

I stood and walked to the sliding glass doors leading out to the redwood deck. The younger boy, Donny, ran around in the yard, being chased by two golden retriever pups and Talon's loveable mutt, Roger. He was doing well, all things considered. Bouncing back was apparently easier at seven than at thirty-eight.

I shook my head. How could I even compare my situation to Donny's? He'd been through the hell that Talon had been through—physical and sexual abuse as a young child. Me? I was heading into middle age when I found out my father was a perverted psycho.

Despite my father's disgusting tendencies, he'd never laid a hand on me or my mother. He *had* laid a hand—and other parts—on my best friend's brother, Talon Steel. He'd done worse to my cousin Luke Walker. My father and his two psycho cronies had killed Luke after torturing him.

How Joe and Talon could even look at me eluded me sometimes. If the situation were reversed, I wasn't sure I could be so forgiving. Granted, I'd done nothing wrong. Nothing. And they didn't blame me for my father's actions.

But shouldn't I have known?

My father had been a respected attorney. My father had been the one who welcomed Talon back to Snow Creek as a war hero when he returned from Iraq. My father, who'd also been Talon's rapist when he was young.

I shuddered.

I shuddered a lot these days.

Yet the Steels bore no ill will toward me or my mother. But I did. How could we not have known? Shouldn't we have seen clues? How do you live with a psychopath and have no idea who he truly is?

Pure evil.

That was my father.

Pure evil.

And part of me was frightened beyond words.

Frightened that I was the same as he.

"Bryce?"

I nearly jumped, spinning around.

Talon Steel stood in the kitchen, his hair a mass of unruly dark waves and his cheeks pink with windburn.

"Hey, Tal."

"I said your name three times. You were in another world."

"Just watching Donny and the pups."

"Yeah, he's amazing. So much strength for such a little guy."

"Do you ever worry he'll break?" I wished I could take back the words as soon as I uttered them. Of course Talon worried. We all did.

"I do. But he's getting the best therapy available with Melanie twice a week and with a child psychologist in Denver once a month. Right now, though, Dale is the issue. He's having a hard time opening up to both doctors. At least Donny's talking. Trust me. The more you hold it in, the more it just eats away at you. I've been there."

I nodded. What could I say? We all knew Talon's story... including my father's involvement.

"So what's up?" Talon asked.

I cleared my throat. "I went to Joe's first, but he wasn't home."

"He and Melanie went out."

"I heard. Great news about the baby."

"True. Jade's so young, she doesn't need an amnio. Thank God. This pregnancy has been hard enough on her as it is."

"She's strong."

"That she is. And we both want this baby so much. Can you imagine? Me with three kids? I never thought I'd want children, but when I met Jade, that all changed."

I nodded. Again, I didn't know what to say. I had always wanted children. Indeed, I had a child—a beautiful son I adored. But now I worried constantly. I didn't exactly come from great genes.

Henry was here, and all I could do was hope like hell he hadn't inherited any of my father's mental issues. But that was it for me. No more kids. No more chances of handing down my father's defective brain.

Talon cleared his throat. "Is everything okay? Your mom? Henry?"

"We're fine."

Right. Fine. What a crock. Henry was fine, at least. At a little over a year old, he was way too young to have a clue about the upheaval we'd all been through. Thank God for small favors.

"What's up, then?"

I inhaled, gathering what little strength I had left. "I hate asking you this, but I'm desperate. I need a job, Talon."

"Aren't you—"

I shook my head. I was a financial analyst by trade, and I knew what he was going to ask. "I can't. I can't work at a desk right now. I want to be outside doing physical labor."

"Really? With your background, we could find you a desk position. We could use your brain, man."

I shook my head again, this time more vehemently. "Most of my father's assets have been seized, so I need to be working. But no, Tal. Please. I just want to be a hand. In the orchards, vineyards, with the cattle. Whatever. I don't care. Just put me to work. I want to do a hard day's work and then be too fucking exhausted to think."

"If it's money—"

"Absolutely not. I want to earn my keep."

"You know we'd do anything for you. You and Joe have been friends your whole lives."

"I do know that, though I don't deserve it."

"Look, this is getting to be a broken record, Bryce. None of us blames—"

I held up my hand to stop him. I'd heard it all before. He was right. It *had* become a broken record. "Damn it, Talon, I want to work. I *need* to work. I need to feel like I'm doing something for my son and my mom. I know you don't blame me, and I appreciate it. That doesn't stop me from blaming myself."

"But you didn't do anything."

"No, I didn't, but I should have known what kind of man my father was. I should have figured it out before now."

"You were thirteen when I was taken, Bryce."

A tiny spot on the wall piqued my interest. At least I pretended it did. "Okay. Maybe I couldn't have prevented what happened to you. But later. As a man. I should have seen—"

"All fed!"

I turned at Marj's voice.

She whisked into the kitchen. "Jade ate it all, though she looked a little green. But I think she'll keep it down."

Talon smiled. "Good to hear. I need to go see how she's doing. In bed all day?"

"Most of it," Marj said. "She's a little better now."

He nodded and walked out of the kitchen.

Leaving me without the job I'd come for.

And in the presence of the most beautiful woman I'd ever laid eyes on.

"Ready for dinner?" she asked.

"Uh...sure. Where should I sit?"

"Wherever you want." She set a salad bowl on the table and then went to the door and opened it. "Donny! Dinner!"

The little boy ran inside. "I'm starved!"

"Good." She ruffled the hair on his head. "Go get your brother. Your dad is in his bedroom with your mom. Tell him to come on out and eat too."

He trotted out of the kitchen.

She laughed. "That kid never walks. He trots. It's the cutest thing."

"He's a great kid."

"He really is." Marj bit her lip. "I just can't..."

I walked over to her and placed my hands on her shoulders. Her warmth surged into me, and though I was far from in the mood, my groin tightened. "I know. It's horrible what he went through. His brother too. And Tal."

She nodded, saying nothing, her eyes becoming shiny with tears.

"Hey. Don't. Everything's okay now."

She sniffed back the tears and nodded. "I have to be strong for them. All of them."

Strength. This woman had it in abundance. So much more than I possessed.

I wanted some of it.

Needed some of it.

Needed *her*.

Without thinking, I bent my head and pressed my lips to hers.

# CHAPTER THREE

### Marjorie

Soft. So soft.

I'd dreamed of how Bryce's lips might feel on mine ever since our "almost kiss."

Now I knew. His gorgeous full pink lips were soft, the softest I'd ever kissed.

I parted my own.

Was I being too forward? Perhaps he just meant to give me a—

He swept his tongue into my mouth.

Not too forward after all.

His tongue was warm and probing, and I met it with my own. It was a soft kiss, not urgent, though I could feel the potential. A soft hum vibrated from his throat, warming me all over.

Just as quickly, though, I pulled away, breaking the suction. My family would be trampling into the kitchen at any moment.

Bryce's cheeks reddened. "Fuck. I'm sorry."

"No. Don't be. I... It's just... They're coming in for din—"

Donny clanked in, his older brother, Dale, behind him. "Dad's coming," he said.

I swallowed. The boys wouldn't notice anything. But Talon...

"Hey, guys," Bryce said. "Looks like I'm eating with you tonight."

"Cool," Donny said. "Are you going to make us eat salad again, Auntie?"

I smiled, gathering what was left of my composure, which wasn't much. All I could think about was that kiss and how I ached to finish it.

"You bet I am. It's Caesar salad. You like that."

"Not with the fishies."

"I left the fishies out this time, sweetie. Dale, you hungry?"

Dale nodded. As usual, he didn't say much. At least he was eating, and he'd gained back most of the weight he'd lost while in captivity.

The boys sat down as Talon entered.

"Jade's doing better," he said. "I hate that she's so sick."

"And the doctor says it's all okay?" Bryce asked.

"Yeah. Just really bad morning sickness. It might be another month before she gets any relief. I hate leaving her here all day, but the work has to get done. We all took so much time off with the case, so it's crazy now. I'm really glad you're here, Sis."

"I'd do anything for her," I said. "And you."

"I know. We appreciate it more than you'll ever know. Once Jade is feeling better, you can go on with your plans for Paris."

Bryce stopped with a forkful of salad in midair. "Paris?"

"It was only a passing thought," I said.

"Not a passing thought," Talon said. "You're going to study at Le Cordon Bleu. Joe, Ryan, and I are handling things here. We'll take good care of your quarter. It's time for you to do what you were meant to do. You'll be a master chef someday."

"Paris?" Bryce said again.

"Why not?" Talon said. "Julia Child herself studied there. One day you'll be cooking circles around her."

"Paris?" Bryce said for the third time.

"You hard of hearing?" Talon jibed him.

He let out what sounded like a forced laugh. "Paris sounds great. You'll be a smash there, Marj."

"Nothing is set in stone," I said.

"The hell it's not." Talon took a bite of salad.

Donny and Dale said nothing, just shoveled food into their mouths. My heart broke just a little more. They were still so afraid their food would be taken away.

My brothers had been hounding me to take my cooking more seriously since Ryan and Ruby's wedding. I'd taken a few classes in Grand Junction and had loved them, but right now, I truly felt my place was with my family. They'd all been through so much. I wanted—needed—to be here for them.

And then there was Bryce...

Lord, I wanted to finish that kiss.

*He's too old for you.*

The voices of all three of my brothers chanted inside my head.

Of course, Talon was ten years older than Jade. Bryce was a mere three years older than Talon, making him thirteen years older than I was. Would they really balk at a measly three years?

I jarred myself back to reality. We'd had one tiny kiss, and already I had us walking down the aisle. Truth was, I wasn't in any hurry for marriage, even though within the past year I'd witnessed all three of my brothers find love and tie the knot.

I had to get out of my own head first.

My father had left me when I was eighteen. At the time, I'd thought he'd died. Instead, he'd faked his own death once all his children were of age. I was the youngest and the only girl, seven years younger than my youngest brother, Ryan.

Then there was my mother...

I'd always been told she'd killed herself when I was a baby. I had no memories of her. Until recently. She lived in a fantasy world where I was still a baby and Talon and Jonah were still little boys. Ryan didn't exist in her world...because he was not her biological child.

He was the son of my father and his stalker, Wendy Madigan.

My life was a big mess.

Plus, I had God only knew how much crazy in my genes. My brothers shared the genetic crazy. In fact, Ryan probably had more. His biological mother was a true psychopath. Still, Joe and Tal were having children from their own bodies, and Melanie had assured all of us that if we weren't exhibiting "crazy" by now, we were probably fine.

Still...I worried.

I loved children. Dale and Donny had both wormed their way into my heart in a short time, and Bryce's son, Henry, was an adorable little mini-Bryce with a sweet disposition.

I missed him.

I hadn't seen him since Ryan and Ruby's wedding. Bryce had been around a few times, but always sans Henry. I wasn't sure why.

"Right, Marj?"

I jerked toward Talon's voice. "Huh?"

"Aren't you listening?"

"Sorry," I mumbled.

"No big deal," Talon said. "I was just telling Bryce that we could use his expertise around here, but he's dead set on a job that uses his brawn instead of his brain."

"Oh?" I had no idea what they were talking about.

Bryce chewed his salad.

Instead of saying anything more, I stood and collected the empty salad plates and then brought the meat, potatoes, and green beans to the table. I also set a plate of bread next to Dale and Donny. They both grabbed a slice. Anything to fill up their little bellies.

"Can we talk about this later?" Bryce asked softly.

"Sure," Talon said. "After dinner."

I brought the food over. Talon served the boys first and then passed the dishes around. Bryce took very little, which surprised me. He was nearly as big as Joe, the tallest and most muscular of my brothers, at six feet four.

Something was bothering him, clearly.

I held back a huff. Of course something was bothering him. He'd been through hell just like the rest of us. His father was as crazy as Ruby's. As crazy as Ryan's mother.

Rather than face the consequences of what he'd done, Bryce's father had offed himself, right in front of Joe.

Would things around here ever get back to normal?

I was content most days, helping Jade and taking care of Dale and Donny. Cooking for my brother and his family who had been through so much.

At least my brothers were more than content. Despite everything we'd gone through recently, they'd all fallen in love and found their soul mates. They were deliriously happy.

And I was happy for them.

Truly I was.

I just didn't see that in the cards for myself—at least not anytime soon.

The boys gobbled up their food and were excused. Then Talon, Bryce, and I finished up in silence.

Really uncomfortable and awkward silence.

Whatever Bryce had come to see Talon about, he didn't want to discuss it in front of me.

Made sense. Bryce and I had no connection.

No connection other than a short kiss that I yearned to continue.

But as I looked at him chewing his food in silence, I saw no yearning in his eyes.

# CHAPTER FOUR

### Bryce

Marjorie had cleared the table and went to check on Jade.

Talon turned to me. "Let's go down into the family room for a drink."

A drink. Sounded great. But not in the family room. Not where anyone could hear me. "Do you mind if we use your office?"

"No," he said. "Why?"

"Privacy."

"No one's around but— Oh."

Marjorie. Talon probably had no idea why I didn't want Marjorie seeing my weaknesses, and I certainly wasn't going to tell him how attracted I was to his baby sister. He'd probably want to pummel me. God knew Joe would.

"I'll get us a drink. Peach Street okay?"

I nodded. Normally I was a beer guy, but I loved a good bourbon, and Peach Street was Tal's favorite. He bought it by the case directly from the distiller.

I followed him down and took the drink he'd poured for me. Then he led me down the hallway to his office.

"Have a seat." He indicated one of three leather chairs as he took a seat behind his desk.

"You mind sitting here with me?" A strange request,

considering I was asking for a job on the ranch. But I wanted to be on equal footing with a friend. He was going to grill me, and I didn't want to feel like I was opening up to a potential boss.

"Sure, man." He walked out from behind the desk and sat down in the chair next to me. "What the hell is going on?"

Where to start?

"You know as well as I do that life will never be the same for any of us," I said. "I don't want to get into specifics."

"There's no reason to," he said. "No one knows the specifics better than I do."

Wow. I felt like a douche. Talon had been through the worst of all of us. I never forgot that, but sometimes I got so involved in my own issues that it nudged itself into the back of my mind. I had no idea how to address my self-absorption, though, so I took a long drink of my bourbon, letting its smoky crispness float over my tongue. The smooth burn down my throat felt good. Damned good.

"Let me get right to the point," Talon said. "Joe, Ryan, and I have already discussed bringing you on, and we were going to bring it up sometime soon. But things get in the way."

I stifled a surprised jerk. They'd talked about it? "I get it. I wish Jade weren't having such a hard time."

"You and me both. It kills me. But she and the baby are healthy, so that's the main thing."

I nodded.

"Then we were all on pins and needles waiting for Melanie's amnio results. They came in fine, thank God."

Again, I nodded.

"I'm sorry it's taken a while, but the three of us are on the same page. Even though Ry and Joe aren't here, I know they wouldn't mind me telling you what we've been discussing, especially since you came here today asking for a job. The three of us want you to be a part of Steel Acres, and not just as a ranch hand, Bryce. You have a ton to offer, and we need you."

"That's kind of you to say."

Very kind of him, but it wasn't true. The Steels did *not* need me. They had a first-class, billion-dollar operation that was thriving despite the trauma of the past year. If they truly wanted to bring me on, it was probably out of pity. Pity for me because of what my father had done. What my father had been, and the fact that he'd basically left my mother and me penniless.

"You're worth a lot more to us than a hard laborer, Bryce," Talon continued. "We're prepared to make you a solid offer that includes a profit share."

I widened my eyes without meaning to. A profit share? Even a tiny share would amount to more money than I'd seen in my lifetime. As much as I just wanted to labor—do physical work without thinking—I had an obligation to my son. This could mean everything for him.

I cleared my throat. "That's generous of you. What exactly did you have in mind?"

"I don't want to get into all the details without Joe and Ryan here, but it's an offer you won't be able to refuse." He smiled and took a drink of his bourbon.

"All right. I'll hear you out." I took another sip. "But honestly, Tal, all I really want is to do a hard day's work for a fair wage. I need to help my mom and support my son. I don't want a lot of time for..."

"For what?"

"For thinking, man. I want to work my body so damned

hard that I collapse from exhaustion. Surely you get what I mean."

He nodded. "I do get it. Why do you think I joined the army? Went to Iraq? I was running, Bryce. Running from a bunch of shit I didn't want to face. But you can only run for so long before your legs give out and the past hits you in the gut."

"Look," I said seriously. "I'm not equating your ordeal with what I'm dealing with. It's nothing compared to what you went through."

"Don't do that," he said. "Don't belittle your own situation. Your father turned out to be something horrible, and now you have to live with that."

"But nothing was done *to* me."

"Sure it was. Maybe not the same way it was done to me, but you're going through your own hell right now. Own it, man. Accept it. Only then can you begin to get over it."

I shook my head, chuckling softly. "You're something. You really are."

"I'm just a guy. My past doesn't define me. My father doesn't define me. And your father doesn't define *you*."

I smiled. "Melanie must be a hell of a therapist."

"She is. And she's an even better sister-in-law. She's the best."

"Maybe I'll talk to her."

"She'd be happy to help. Or if you're uncomfortable with her, she can refer you to someone else."

Therapy. We were getting a little off the subject, and I was feeling more than uncomfortable. Talon Steel was everyone's hero. I was a self-absorbed douchebag.

Big-time.

I stood, swallowing the last of my bourbon. "Okay. You

guys are really generous. I'll hear you out. Just call me and let me know when the three of you want to get together. I should probably be going."

"You sure? We can have another drink. Catch up on other stuff."

What other stuff? Ruminating about my father had been my life for the past couple months. Hell, I wasn't even being a father to Henry. I'd told myself on more than one occasion that I was laying off for my mom's sake, that she needed to focus on Henry right now. That was all true, but there was more to the truth.

I was feeling unworthy. Unworthy of being a father. What if I went crazy and turned out like my old man?

No way would I put my little boy in danger.

No fucking way.

I raked my fingers through my hair.

Fuck.

"Another time. Let me know when you guys want to talk." I set the glass down on Talon's desk and walked out of the office.

When I walked past the kitchen, Marjorie had her back to me and was loading the dishwasher. Her dark hair fell in long waves nearly to her perfect ass. Her skinny jeans accented her long and shapely legs. God, those legs... They went on forever. How I'd love to have them around my neck as I pumped into her perfect body...

Damn. I needed to get out of here.

I was in no condition to begin a relationship, and neither was she.

We could have a fuckfest, but Marjorie Steel wasn't the one-night-stand type. Instinctively I knew that. Plus, Joe and I had been friends for over thirty years. I couldn't risk a one-nighter with his baby sister.

I reached toward the doorknob—

"Bryce!" Footsteps sounded behind me.

I turned. Marjorie's big brown eyes seared me. So beautiful. And that body. And those hands. I chuckled. She was wearing rubber gloves, the long yellow kind that my mom used to use while cleaning toilets when I was a kid.

"What's so funny?"

"Sorry. The rubber gloves."

"I just got a manicure yesterday." She cringed a little. "Crap. That sounded so Steel ranch heiress, didn't it?"

"My mom gets manicures sometimes, and she's sure no heiress."

"Something I learned when I started cooking. Kitchen work is murder on my hands, so I use rubber gloves. They're hot and sweaty, but my hands stay silky smooth." She cocked her head. "Why am I explaining this to you exactly?"

"You don't owe me any explanation. I get the gloves. It's just..."

"Just what?"

"Marjorie Steel wearing rubber gloves. It's like the ultimate paradox."

She huffed. "I get the feeling that was an insult."

"Not at all. You're just so beautiful, so glamorous. The rubber gloves are the ultimate contradiction to that."

She swallowed. "You think I'm beautiful and glamorous?"

"I have eyes, don't I?"

She softened and peeled off the gloves slowly. Damn. My groin tightened. Removing rubber gloves, and she made it look like she was on stage, stripping.

Once revealed, her hands were smooth with slender

fingers, nails painted red. Classic and perfect.

Long fingers that could so easily wrap around my bulging cock...

Damn.

Her cheeks pinked. Had she read my thoughts? No. She was reacting to my "beautiful and glamorous" comment.

I cleared my throat. "I have to be going."

"Did you and Talon have a nice talk?"

Did she know what her brothers were up to? Of course she did. She was a quarter owner of the ranch.

"Yeah," I mumbled.

"I hope you'll consider their offer, Bryce. We need you here."

Talon had said the same thing, but it was a lie. The Steels didn't need me. My son did. My mother did.

"I don't actually know what the offer is yet. Tal said he wanted to wait until all three of them could talk to me."

She pulled at the rubber gloves she still held. "Believe me. It's an offer you won't be able to refuse." Again, she echoed Talon's words. "It would be nice..."

"It would be nice...what?"

"It'd be nice to have you around here more." She continued to fidget with the gloves. "That's all."

I nodded. What could I say?

Her bottom lip trembled a bit. Just a bit, but I noticed. *Kiss me. Kiss me.* The slight tremble echoed the words.

I tried to hold back. Truly I did.

To no avail.

My lips came down upon hers.

# CHAPTER FIVE

**Marjorie**

Talon was around somewhere. Probably close. The boys were out back.

Anyone could walk by and see us making out by the front door.

Anyone.

I didn't care. Not in the slightest.

Every part of me became hypersensitive and tingly as Bryce swept his tongue into my mouth. He tasted of vanilla, oak, a touch of caramel. Peach Street bourbon. Of course. Talon had given him a drink of his favorite.

I wasn't a bourbon drinker, but mixed with the essence of Bryce, this whiskey was my new passion. An elixir I wanted more and more of.

When Bryce deepened the kiss, I groaned. It wasn't the bourbon at all. God, no. It was all Bryce. The intense flavor, the fragrance of cedarwood and spice, the powerful pressure of his firm lips on mine...

All Bryce.

All me.

All Bryce and me.

No wonder I'd yearned to complete our earlier kiss. This was heaven. Pure heaven.

Reality hit me like a brick, and I broke the kiss with a smack. Bryce's blue eyes widened, but I didn't explain. I grabbed his hand, looking around quickly, and pulled him out of the foyer, down the hallway to my bedroom. Once we were inside, I closed the door quietly and locked it.

"Marj—"

I quieted him with a touch of my fingers to his lips. "Shh." Then I wrapped my arms around his neck and pulled him toward me, our lips meeting once more.

I'd been ready to take the lead, but I didn't have to. He thrust his tongue into my mouth and kissed me deeply. Passionately. I eagerly returned his enthusiasm, our tongues dueling and twirling.

I'd dreamed of this for so long. So, so long.

Watching all my brothers find love.

Love?

Why was I thinking about love?

This was just a kiss with a man I was very attracted to, a man I'd known since...

*Oh, God...*

*Stop. Need to stop.*

*Don't want to stop...*

I didn't have to. Bryce pulled away, breaking the suction of our mouths.

His eyes seared into mine. They were dark blue and smoky with desire. I touched his cheek, his sandy stubble rough under my smooth fingertips. Rough. Perfect.

He grabbed my wrist, gently removing my hand. "Don't," was all he said.

I bit my lip. The word "sorry" hovered back in my vocal cords, but I couldn't bring it forth. Simple. I wasn't sorry. I wasn't sorry at all.

Finally, I said, "Why?"

He turned away from me, saying nothing.

Nope. That was *not* going to cut it. I grabbed his arm and forced him to turn back around and meet my gaze.

"You wanted that kiss as much as I did, Bryce. Now tell me why you stopped it."

"We're in your bedroom, for God's sake."

"So?"

"Marj, this bedroom used to be painted pink and yellow with a unicorn theme."

He remembered that? I'd painted over those walls over a decade ago and discarded the stuffed unicorn collection before then. I held back a giggle. "Again...so?"

"You were a little girl. You were five when Joe and I graduated high school."

"Once more...so?"

"Do I need to spell it out for you?"

"Don't treat me like a moron, Bryce. I'm not five. I'm nearly twenty-six. I haven't had unicorns on my walls since I was twelve. Look around you. I have white walls with portraits of famous chefs. I'm a grown woman. A grown woman who is more than capable of deciding who she wants to kiss. And by the way, you were kissing me back."

"I'm not denying that."

"You said I'm beautiful and glamorous. You're attracted to me."

"I'd have to be blind not to be attracted to you."

Good. Now we were getting somewhere. I wasn't asking him for anything more than a kiss. I smiled.

"Your brothers..." he began.

"My brothers love you, Bryce. All three of them."

"Maybe so. But they don't want me kissing their baby sister."

I smiled again, in what I hoped was a seductive manner. "It might surprise you to know that I don't ask my brothers' permission before I decide to kiss someone."

"In Jamaica, they didn't like it when..."

"When what?"

"I made a comment about how attractive you were. They all looked like they were ready to set hellhounds on me."

I sat down on my bed with a plunk. "My brothers are protective. Not a big surprise there. But you kissed me back, Bryce, so what is this *really* about?"

He paced around the room, his hands fidgeting in his pockets. "It's about that. It's about a lot of things."

"I'm not asking for forever. Just for a kiss. A kiss we were both enjoying. Or did I read you wrong?" I tensed. What if he said I *had* read him wrong?

"You didn't read me wrong."

Thank God. I relaxed my muscles. "Then what's the problem? And if you say pink and yellow unicorns or my brothers, I'm liable to punch you in the nose."

He laughed. God, he was gorgeous when he laughed. He had a dimple on his left cheek. Just one. A perfect imperfection.

"The unicorns and your brothers are definitely a consideration, but there's a bigger and more important thing." He raked his fingers through his sandy hair. "You deserve better, Marjorie."

"Seriously? You're Joe's best friend. You're one of the best men I know. My brothers love you."

"That's not what I mean. I'm a mess right now. I can't give

you what you deserve."

He was a mess? So was I. I wasn't looking for anything permanent. "All I'm asking for is a kiss."

His eyes burned into me. "What if I can't stop at a kiss?"

My nipples hardened, pressing against my bra. "What if you can't? What if *I* can't? We're both adults here."

"You're not someone I can just fuck."

"What if I'm okay with that?"

At the moment, I just wanted *him*. Wanted to feel his kisses, his lips all over my body, his teeth tugging on my ultra-hard nipples, his tongue probing my most private places.

"I'm *not* okay with that, and I'm not ready to give more than that to you or anyone else right now."

My mouth dropped open. He might as well have stabbed me in my heart. He wanted me. That was clear. He wanted me as much or more than I wanted him.

But he didn't love me. He *couldn't* love me. And he wasn't willing to just fuck his best friend's sister.

I understood.

I didn't love him either, though I was feeling something big—bigger than I'd ever felt. Still, this was only the beginning of whatever could be between us.

But he was saying nothing more could happen. There was no beginning. Just a fuck.

Just one fuck.

I *did* deserve more. I knew that objectively. But I was fighting my own demons, and I wasn't ready for anything more than a fuck either.

All I knew was that I needed those lips around my nipples. I needed them so badly.

I lifted my T-shirt over my head.

"Marj…"

I paid no attention. I unclasped my bra quickly and tossed it over a chair. Then I trailed my fingers lightly over my hard nipples. A sigh escaped my throat. "Please. Please, Bryce."

"Fuck. Why are you doing this to me?"

"My nipples are so hard. They need you. I need you." I gave one a quick pinch, and a jolt arrowed straight between my legs.

"You're so fucking beautiful."

*Please.* The word was again at my lips. But I'd begged enough already. He needed to make the next move. And if he walked away? I'd be embarrassed as all hell. But I had to believe he wouldn't do that.

He didn't.

He walked toward me, reached out, and lightly swept his fingers over one nipple. I drew in a quick breath.

"I won't be able to stop," he said gruffly.

"Who's asking you to?" I stood and began unbuttoning his shirt.

"Damn," he said. "Damn it all to hell."

"Nothing worth damning here." I undid another button. His skin was warm under my touch.

"Marjorie…"

"Shh…" With the last button, I parted the two sides of his shirt, revealing his tanned and muscular chest. The perfect amount of sandy hair scattered across his perfect pecs. I pressed my breasts against his warmth, my own body tingling with desire. Without thinking, I kissed his neck. His silky corded neck. Then I inhaled.

Woodsy. Spicy. Bryce.

"God, Marjorie. Oh my God." He yanked on my hair,

tilting my head back, and then he crushed his mouth to mine.

# CHAPTER SIX

**Bryce**

I had no business being in this room.

Kissing this woman.

Feeling her beautiful breasts against my chest.

No business.

No business at all.

But damn, nothing had felt this good since...

Since fucking forever.

Her mouth was gingery and sweet, and her tongue so soft against my own. I wanted this. Wanted to explore every crevice in her mouth, every inch of her supple body. Wanted to embed myself inside her warmth, escape my life and immerse myself solely in her beauty and her heat.

I had nothing to offer this worthy woman. Nothing at all.

I was empty, so empty. But filling her might ease that. Fuck. My cock strained against my jeans. I was so hard, as hard as I'd ever been. I hadn't had sex in nearly two years. Not since Henry's mother, and that had been a one-nighter that morphed into a quickie marriage that I still couldn't believe had happened. Frankie was a Las Vegas topless showgirl, a hot and sexy redhead with a smoking body. I'd forgotten a condom, but she'd assured me she was on the pill, and we'd had an incredible time. I married her when she showed up at my door a few weeks later, pregnant. A couple months after Henry was born, I caught her fucking a pizza delivery guy—a scene straight out of a bad porn flick. I divorced her and she didn't fight me on custody. In fact, she signed away her parental rights.

That Henry resulted was a true gift, but the actual act that made him hadn't meant a thing to me. No regrets. None at all. I loved my son deeply. But being a solo parent to an infant didn't leave much time for dating or sex, especially when I was also dealing with the truth about my father.

That one-night fuck had enriched me in so many ways, yet, at its base, it was still that—a one-night fuck.

As this would be.

I couldn't offer more, no matter how much I wanted it. No matter how much she wanted it.

The only problem was...in my heart I ached to offer Marjorie more.

So much to think about. So much...

Within a few seconds more, though, all thoughts turned into fragments, leaving me only with feeling. Pure, raw feeling.

Intense feeling, intense desire. Had I ever wanted a woman as much? Ever?

Not that I could recall.

Our chests were fused together, as were our mouths. Her tongue was velvety against my own, her lips soft yet demanding.

She left me breathless.

So breathless that I had to forcefully end the kiss to inhale deeply.

I pulled away, my dick throbbing in my jeans. She gazed at me, her dark-chocolate eyes heavy-lidded. Her cheeks were rosy, and her lips red and swollen from our kiss. And God, her breasts... Perfect in every way. Round and pert and just the right size. Nipples like hard brown berries. Marjorie was long and lean, and her waist indented slightly, leading to narrow hips and long legs still clad in skinny jeans.

I'd seen her in a bikini. I knew what lay under all that denim. Didn't stop me from wanting to rip it off her and ogle that Victoria's Secret body.

"Why did you stop?" She touched her lips lightly.

*I needed to catch a breath* didn't seem like the right thing to say.

"I needed to catch my breath." I said it anyway.

One side of her mouth curled upward into a half smile. "Oh." Then she stalked toward me.

I held up a hand. "Wait."

"Are you kidding? Do we have to go through this again?" She spun around. "Look. No unicorns. This is a woman's bedroom. Not a little girl's."

"Talon is home."

"So? He won't barge into my bedroom. He respects my privacy."

"Shouldn't you...check on Jade? The boys?"

"You said it yourself. Talon is home. I'm here for them during the day, when Talon is working. He's home now. Jade is his wife. The boys are his children. He likes looking after them." She cupped her breasts and held them out to me, as if in offering.

I nearly exploded inside my jeans.

"What's going to happen when Talon sees my car still outside? Won't he wonder where the hell I am? And then he'll see your door closed..."

She huffed and grabbed her T-shirt, pulling it over her

head sans bra. "You know what? Just go, Bryce. Get the hell out of here."

Finally, someone was talking sense. The problem? I didn't *want* to go. I didn't want to go at all.

But I would. Because it was the right thing to do. Because I couldn't offer her what she deserved. I quickly buttoned up my shirt, barely making eye contact with Marjorie.

And I walked out.

# CHAPTER SEVEN

**Marjorie**

He left.

He left, leaving me hornier than I'd ever been. I was so wet, so ripe, so freaking ready.

I relocked my door and shed my flip-flops, jeans, and undies. Then I lay down on my bed and spread my legs.

I rarely resorted to masturbation, but I was so turned on. And so angry.

It didn't take long.

★ ★ ★

The next morning, after feeding the boys their breakfast and taking them to school, I sat in Talon and Jade's bedroom, visiting with my best friend.

"And don't tell me he's too old for me," I said after spilling my guts about Bryce. "You're my age, and he's only three years older than Talon."

Jade had gotten up and showered but still wore her bathrobe and slippers. "I'd never tell you that, Marj."

"He's attracted to me. He admits it."

"Of course he is. Who wouldn't be? That's obviously not the issue."

"He says it's my brothers, but I'm not buying."

"They *are* very protective of you."

"He also says it's my age. He remembers when my room was decorated with pink and yellow unicorns."

"Unicorns?" Jade laughed. "Really, Marj?"

Jade and I hadn't met until college, so she hadn't been privy to my childhood décor. "What was your room decorated like when you were a kid?"

"Well, four walls and the basics. A dresser, a bed, and a desk from the Salvation Army. The occasional poster I found at a garage sale."

I shook my head. "I'm sorry, Jade."

"Don't be."

My heart twisted. Despite being the daughter of supermodel Brooke Bailey, Jade and her father had lived a modest life on his construction salary after Brooke had abandoned them. Brooke, who'd been in a terrible automobile accident several months ago, now lived in a Snow Creek townhome subsidized by Talon and Jade. Brooke and Jade had seemingly made peace, despite Brooke's abandonment of her daughter as a child.

"Just sock me in the mouth when I start playing the 'poor little rich girl,' okay? Promise?"

Jade laughed again. "You know I always do."

"You need anything? Crackers? Water?"

She shook her head. "I'm feeling a little less putrid today. Let's hope it sticks." She stood and shed her robe, reaching for a pair of jeans in her closet. "Bryce is a mess right now, Marj. Just give him some time."

Bryce was a mess. So was I. What would a fuck matter?

Jade went on, "Maybe try to meet someone else in the meantime. Was there anyone interesting in your cooking class?"

"Not really."

"Then get out of this house. Go into town. Get back to the gym. Anything."

"You guys need me here."

She smiled. "We can spare you for a few hours a day. You need to have your own life."

"But the boys..."

"The boys are in school most of the day, and I'm not dead. I can still be a mother even when I'm nauseated twenty-four-seven."

I sighed, the truth ready to pour out of me. "I don't want to meet anyone else, Jade. I want Bryce. It's crazy, I know. Talk about baggage. No job. A psycho father. A needy mother. A kid with another woman. He looks horrible on paper, doesn't he?"

"Talon and his brothers are going to take care of the 'no job' thing, I think. At least they're going to try. But you can't escape the other three."

"I don't want to escape Henry. He's adorable and I love him. But I worry about him. Bryce doesn't seem to be spending much time with him these days. Before all of this came to a head, I never saw Bryce without Henry. Now? He's never *with* him."

"I know. Tal and I have talked about that. Bryce says his mom needs to focus on Henry right now. But what is Bryce focusing on? That's a big reason why the guys decided to offer him employment here on the ranch. But it's not a charity offer. The guys say Bryce is perfect for the job they have in mind."

"You think he'll take it?"

"I don't know. Talon said he talked to him about it a little last night after dinner, but Bryce is adamant that he wants a job as a hand. He wants to do physical labor, which Talon understands. He's trying to escape from his mind through exhaustion."

"If anyone can understand that, Talon can."

"Exactly. But they want to offer him more than that. A permanent position here with a profit share."

"I had no idea. Then again, since college, I've always told them I'm happy being their silent partner." And I loved the idea of Bryce being around all the time. I didn't voice that part, though.

"They would've told you about it before they made the offer. I'm sure."

"Maybe. It doesn't really matter. I trust them to do what's best for the ranch and to look after my interests. Honestly, Jade, before everything went down, I thought about asking them to buy me out so I could go off and learn to cook. I mean *really* cook, like the great ones."

"I'd miss you terribly, but why not do it? Talon always talks about you studying at Le Cordon Bleu. If you don't want to go that far away right now, what about culinary school in Denver? You're so gifted, Marj. You could be one of the great chefs."

"I can't leave right now. I'd never miss the birth of your baby. And you guys need me."

"We love having you here, and yes, we need you, but we'll be fine. You need to live your life. You're almost twenty-six years old. You need to go find your life. You might be a ranch heiress, but you're not a rancher."

"Wait a minute. I worked just as hard as my brothers around here. My father saw to it."

"I get that. You know the business, but it isn't your dream. It never has been. The guys—this place is their blood, their life-force. But you? Not so much."

I couldn't fault my best friend's observation. "I know. Still, this is home."

She smiled. "Home is where the heart is. Your heart may be with your brothers, with me, but you can't fight your future forever."

"I'll think about it," I said, "but I'm not leaving anytime soon. Not until I see your bundle of joy. You're stuck with me for several more months."

"Good enough." She squeezed my arm. "I wouldn't want to go through this without my best friend. Can you believe it? You have two new nephews, and you're about to have two more."

"Well, one might be a niece," I said, patting her still slim belly. "We don't know what's in here yet."

"I know. I just have a feeling it's a boy. We'll see. All I care about is that it's happy and healthy. And that it *never* has to go through the hell its father and brothers have been through."

"It won't." I smiled. "We've got to be due for some good luck in this family about now."

Jade stood. "Excuse me." She placed her hand over her mouth as she walked quickly to the bathroom.

Sick again, the poor thing.

No way was I going anywhere.

★ ★ ★

I was putting dinner on the table when Talon walked in wearing dirty jeans and a tattered shirt.

"What happened to you?"

"Nothing. Just decided to help the guys out in the fields today. Does a body good every now and then."

Interesting. That was exactly what Bryce was after. Talon had come such a long way, but his past still haunted him sometimes. How could it not? At ten years old, he'd been held for two months, repeatedly starved, beaten, and raped.

I tried not to think about what my brother had been through. It messed with my head. Now he and Jade had taken in the Robertson boys, who'd been through much of the same, so I couldn't *not* think about it. In fact, it invaded my thoughts constantly, so I tried to take from it the most positive things I could. Tenderness in handling the boys, and a vision of my brother's endurance.

My brother had the strength of a Titan.

"Dinner's ready, so get cleaned up. I'm going to call the boys, and then I'll take a plate in to Jade."

"You don't have to." Jade entered the kitchen, dressed and looking...well...a little peaked. "I want to eat with my family tonight."

"Hey, blue eyes." Talon pressed his lips against hers.

Jade smiled. "You're a mess."

"I'll be clean in a few. Just a quick shower." He kissed her again and walked toward their bedroom.

Jade sat down at her place at the kitchen table. "Ugh. Now I'm feeling crappy again."

"Go back to your room. I'll take care of things."

"No. Those little boys need me. They need a mother, and I need to be here. Talon needs me. You need me."

"We need you to rest for your baby."

"The doctors assure me that everything is fine. I promise I'll go right back to the bedroom after dinner. I have to do this. Women have been having babies for millennia. This isn't an illness." She stuck out her tongue. "Even though it feels like it sometimes."

"Have it your way." I set the salad on the table.

The boys ambled in.

"You eating with us tonight, Miss Jade?" Donny asked.

"Yes, sweetie. I've missed seeing your face at the table."

He still wouldn't call her Mom. Jade looked slightly disappointed, but she smiled anyway. She was determined to let the boys go at their own pace.

My eyebrows shot up.

*Their own pace.*

Little boys weren't the only creatures who needed to go at their own pace. Was I rushing Bryce?

He'd wanted me last night. The physical evidence couldn't have been faked.

But Bryce was fighting his own demons—demons I understood well.

Many times I'd wondered if I might be headed down the same path as my own mother. Insanity. These things could be genetic, though Melanie insisted that if any of us were going to follow the path of our mother, we'd have shown signs by now.

Bryce was concerned, with good reason.

His father was a complete psychopath—possibly even worse than Ruby's father had been.

Tom Simpson had lived a double life—devoted husband and father, attorney and mayor of Snow Creek by day. Psychotic pedophile rapist by night.

The stuff nightmares were made of.

Nightmares Bryce must have every time he nodded off to—

"Marj!"

I turned. Jade was doubled over in her chair. I rushed to her. "What's going on?"

"I don't know. Get Talon. Please."

# CHAPTER EIGHT

**Bryce**

I signaled the bartender at the dive in Grand Junction. "Another here, please."

He pushed the rotgut bourbon down the wooden bar. It landed right in front of me. The guy was good.

I shot it quickly, letting it claw like fire-dipped tentacles down my throat until it warmed my belly.

Joe had told me about this place. He'd stumbled in one night when he was at his worst and had gotten some really good advice from an old-timer. I wasn't looking for advice so much as an escape. The Steels were bound and determined to make me some kind of honorary brother. I should be flattered. Thrilled.

But I didn't want it. All I wanted was to make an honest day's pay for an honest day of hard labor.

I signaled to the barkeep for another. The glass slid down the wooden bar once more and then stared up at me, the brown liquid swirling.

I turned my head away from the drink. Another man about my age sat at the end of the bar, and a few stragglers sat at tables. A cocktail waitress was taking their orders. She sported cropped platinum-blond hair with black roots. Her face was pretty but worn, but her body... She wore a pink tank top and a denim miniskirt with stiletto sandals. I wondered if she also worked as a stripper. Her legs were muscular and could easily make their way up and down a pole. A decent chest too.

She met my gaze. Her eyes were a striking dark blue.

I smiled and picked up my shot, gesturing to her.

She turned back to her customer.

Okay.

So much for that.

I'd told Marjorie Steel that all I could give her was a good fuck. It had taken every bit of my strength to leave her bedroom yesterday. Every damned ounce.

And now I was getting shot down by a worn-hard cocktail waitress.

Served me right.

I shot my third bourbon quickly.

Only to look down to see the waitress shove a napkin toward me before disappearing into the back room.

*I get off at 7.*

Scribbled underneath was an address in Rosevale, one of the more crime-ridden areas in Grand Junction. About a fifteen-minute drive from the bar.

I checked my watch. Six forty-five. I signaled the barkeep. One more shot, and I'd be on my way.

★ ★ ★

"What's your name, cowboy?"

I gazed at the woman in the denim miniskirt. How she'd beaten me here was beyond me. I'd left my car at the bar and taken a cab. I felt okay, but after four shots, I didn't trust my blood-alcohol level.

"You deaf?" she asked.

I cleared my throat. "Bob."

"Yeah? I'm Alice." She giggled. "Bob is not your name. You don't look like a Bob."

"I *am* a Bob, but you are definitely not an Alice"—I eyeballed the nametag she still wore—"Heidi."

"Okay, fine. We'll play it your way. Come in, *Bob*."

I entered the modest studio apartment. The queen-size bed in the corner was neatly made, and my gaze zeroed in on it.

That was where I'd fuck this woman.

My groin was tight.

"You want a drink, Bob?"

"Sure. Bourbon if you have it."

"I do. Not crazy about it myself, but I keep everything on hand." She walked into her kitchenette and pulled a bottle out of a cupboard.

"What are you having?" I asked.

"I don't drink."

"Really? And you work at a bar?"

"Precisely why I don't drink. I smoke a little weed, though. You want some?"

I shook my head. "Never enjoyed it."

She handed me the bourbon in a half-pint mason jar. Cute. "You mind if I have a little? Just helps me unwind. Get in the mood."

"Uh...sure. Whatever."

She pulled out a black jar from her refrigerator and then grabbed a pipe out of a drawer. "Make yourself at home."

Again I eyed the bed. We both knew why I was here. If I

took a seat there, we could move forward quickly.

But I couldn't do it. I sat down on the love seat across the room and set my drink on the end table.

"Wait," she said. "Let me get you a coaster."

I nodded. Nice. A small place, but she took pride in it. Bed made. Coasters.

She set down the coaster and then sat beside me. She pulled a small amount of weed out of the jar and placed it in the pipe. Then she lit up.

I held off inhaling for as long as I could. I detested the smell of weed. To me, it hovered somewhere between roasting green chilies and blue cheese. I loved the smell of roasted green chilies. I hated the smell of blue cheese. Totally ruined the smoky scent of the chilies.

But I'd come here to get laid, and if a few tokes put her more in the mood, all the better. I'd deal.

The smoke from her pipe rose above our heads.

"So what's your story, Bob?" she asked.

"Just looking for a good time. You?"

"Same." She inhaled, holding the smoke inside her lungs for several seconds.

"How old are you?" I asked.

"Does it matter as long as I'm over eighteen?"

She was way over eighteen. "Just wondering."

"Thirty-three. You?"

"Thirty-eight."

She nodded, taking another toke from the pipe.

"Ever married?" I asked.

"Twice. Both losers. The last one nearly put me in the hospital. Had to get a restraining order."

Shit. What had I walked into?

"You?" she asked.

"Once."

"Got kids?"

"One. You?"

"Nope. Can't. Bad endometriosis."

A little TMI there, but at least I didn't have to worry about knocking her up. Not that I was worried anyway. There would definitely be a condom involved in this little fuckfest.

She set her pipe down, emptying the ashes onto a ceramic plate and grinding them out. Good. The smell would start to dissipate now.

"Here's the deal," she said. "I'll blow you for twenty-five. You can fuck me for fifty, and you can fuck my ass for seventy-five."

I shot my brow upward. She was a hooker? A fucking hooker?

I stood, my groin still tight. "Not exactly what I had in mind."

She let out a raucous laugh. "Kidding, Bob. Just kidding. Do I look like a prostitute to you?"

She really didn't want me to answer that honestly.

"You think any hooker worth her salt would let you into her apartment without seeing the money first? Oh, man. You should see the look on your face!"

"Uh..."

"And by the way, no one fucks my ass, so if that was your plan, you can go quietly."

Hadn't been my plan, but I remained standing. "I think I changed my mind, Heidi."

"Bob, I was fucking with you. Can't you take a joke?"

I was four-plus bourbons in with a hard-on for another

woman. All I wanted was a fuck. This conversation hadn't been part of the bargain.

But she stood, forwardly cupping the bulge in my jeans. "Sure you want to go?"

I wasn't sure at all. The only thing I was damned sure of was that she was a poor substitute for Marjorie Steel.

But she *was* a substitute, and she was willing to let me fuck her.

I walked toward the bed. "Coming?"

# CHAPTER NINE

### Marjorie

"Talon!" I banged on the door of his bedroom. I could hear the whoosh of the shower. I turned the knob on the door and then banged again on the bathroom door. "Talon! I need you!"

The shower shut off, and Talon appeared at the door, a towel around his waist. "What is it?"

"Jade. She's in pain in the kitchen. I'm scared."

"Shit!" He grabbed his robe while I turned away. Then he followed me to the kitchen.

Jade was still doubled over.

"Baby? What's wrong? Tell me." Talon knelt beside her.

"I don't know. It hurts."

Talon scooped her into his arms. "We're going to the hospital."

That meant a trip to Grand Junction. Talon could get her there before an ambulance made it out to the ranch.

"I'm going too," I said.

"You have to stay with the boys," Talon said. "Call Jade's doctor and have her meet us there."

Right.

"Talon, the baby..." Jade sniffed back tears.

"The baby is fine," he told her. "Think good thoughts."

"Tal," I said. "You can't take her to the hospital in your robe."

"The hell I can't."

"Lay her down on the couch in the living room and get changed. I'll stay with her."

"All right. All right." He easily lifted Jade, walked through the foyer to the living room, and laid her down gently before taking off for the bedroom.

"Are you bleeding?" I asked.

"I... I don't know."

"Let's check."

"The boys..."

"I sent them outside for a few minutes. Can you sit up?"

She nodded.

"Stand?"

She nodded again, and I handed her a tissue and then turned my head.

"Marj!"

I turned back to her. She held out the white tissue.

Streaked with red.

"Talon!" I screamed. "Hurry!"

A few seconds later he appeared fully dressed, his hair still dripping wet.

"She's bleeding, Tal. You need to go quickly."

"Damn!" Talon rushed to her. "Did you call the doc?"

"Not yet. I'm on it."

"I don't want to lose this baby," Jade pleaded.

"You won't, blue eyes. Not if I have anything to say about it." Talon scooped her up again and raced toward the door.

"You call me as soon as you know anything!" I yelled.

Talon nodded as I closed the door behind him.

My heart was pounding like a bass drum against my sternum as I called Jade's OB and alerted her.

This was not happening.

Talon and Jade had been through so much.

I couldn't even let my mind go there.

I sat down on the couch Jade had vacated and breathed in. Out. In again.

*Steady, Marj. Steady.*

After a minute or two, I rose.

I had two boys to feed.

★ ★ ★

Two hours.

Two freaking hours ago Talon and Jade had left.

And not a word. I'd forced myself not to call Talon's cell. His attention needed to be focused on Jade. I hadn't called Joe or Ryan either. I had no news.

The boys had taken their baths and were in their bedroom. Talon and Jade had given them separate rooms, but that hadn't worked out. They needed each other right now. They could change bedrooms when they were older.

Eight thirty was bedtime, but they were both fighting it.

I didn't have the strength to force them to go to sleep. The light still shone under the doorway of their room, and Donny chatted, with Dale answering in short sentences. Dale talked the most to his brother, and I didn't want to discourage it.

Besides, I was too worried about Jade to fight them.

I desperately wanted to talk to someone, but the person I always turned to when I needed to talk was Jade.

I still resisted calling Joe and Ryan. No need to worry

them, and Joe and Melanie had just gotten such great news about their own pregnancy.

I fiddled with my phone as I sat in one of the recliners in the large family room.

A little before nine. Early yet. Not too late to call anyone.

Not too late to call Bryce.

His was the voice I wanted to hear. His was the voice I knew could soothe me. But he'd walked out on me.

I sighed. That didn't matter. I needed him, and I knew, though he'd never admit it, that on some level he needed me as well.

My fingers hovered over his name in my contacts.

# CHAPTER TEN

### Bryce

Kissing Heidi was like kissing an ashtray—a sour marijuana ashtray.

I broke away. No need for kissing. I could keep my eyes closed and simply fuck her, pretending she was Marjorie Steel.

I jerked when my cell phone started playing Styx in my pocket.

"Ignore it, babe," Heidi whispered huskily in my ear.

I pulled away, my heart beating faster. "Sorry. It could be my son." I pulled my phone out.

Damn.

Marjorie Steel.

Why would she be calling me? I put the phone to my ear. "Hello?"

"Bryce?"

"Yeah."

"It's Marjorie. I'm sorry to bother you, but I need to talk to someone."

"Is everything okay?"

"No." She sniffed. "Talon took Jade to the hospital. She's bleeding and cramping. It's been two hours and he hasn't called. I have to stay here with the boys. They don't know what's going on. I don't have the heart to tell them."

"Did you call Joe? Or Ryan?"

A pause. Then, "No. I don't want to worry them."

"I'm on my way. You need to call them."

"Okay," she said timidly.

I looked at my watch. "I should be there in half an hour. You call me if you hear anything, you got it?"

"Yeah," she choked out. "Thank you, Bryce."

"I'd do anything for you. All of you," I clarified. "I'll see you soon." I ended the call and shoved the phone back in my pocket.

"What's going on?" Heidi asked.

"I have to go. Family emergency." That had sobered me up quick. So much for the four bourbons. "Damn!"

"What?"

"My car is still at the bar."

"You want me to drive you over there?"

"Yeah, if you don't mind. I'm sorry."

"It's okay. But you owe me." She gave me what she no doubt thought was a naughty, seductive smile.

To me, it was kind of disgusting.

I didn't say much during the short drive.

When she leaned in for a kiss before I got out of the car, I turned, letting her lips brush my cheek.

I wanted desperately for Jade and the baby to be okay, but I was reluctantly thankful for Marj's call. It had stopped me from making a big mistake.

I quickly left Heidi's car, got into my own, and began driving.

★ ★ ★

Marj was waiting by the door and opened it for me before I had the chance to knock. She pulled me inside and fell into my arms.

I kissed the top of her head, inhaling. Her hair smelled like coconut. "Hey. Everything is okay."

She pulled away. "I still haven't heard anything."

"I know you haven't, because you would have called me, right?"

She sniffed and nodded.

"Did you call your brothers?"

"Ryan didn't answer, and Joe... I just couldn't."

I sighed. "They need to know."

"They can know when I have actual news. I can't burden them. They've all been through so much."

"But this is family, Marj. If ever there were three brothers who were there for each other, it's the Steels."

"I know. I know. But..."

"No buts. We'll call them together, okay?"

She swallowed, nodding, but we both jerked when her phone buzzed against her thigh. She pulled it out. "Oh, God. It's Talon."

"You want me to answer?"

She nodded.

I took the phone from her. "Hey, Tal. This is Bryce."

"Where's Marj?"

"She's here. She's upset. How's Jade?"

He paused a moment. "The baby's okay, so far. They saw the heartbeat on ultrasound, and they've got her hooked up to a monitor. The cramping has subsided, but she's still bleeding a little bit. They're going to keep her here overnight for observation."

"Okay."

Marj tugged on my arm. "What's he saying?"

I held my hand up to stop her so I could hear Talon.

"Apparently some spotting during pregnancy can be normal," he said, "and so can cramping. But because of her severe morning sickness, they want to keep an eye on her."

"Good."

"I tell you, Bryce. I've never been so scared in my life."

"Did you call your brothers?"

"No. I assume Marj did."

"She didn't. She didn't want to scare them."

"Just as well. So far, everyone is cautiously optimistic. No need to bother them."

"Talon..."

"Okay. Okay. I'll call them. Tell Marj I'll be home sometime tomorrow."

"Will do."

"Thanks for being there with her. I know her. Jade's her best friend, and she's probably worrying herself into a big mess. How are the boys?"

"I assume they're in bed. You want to talk to your sister?"

"Yeah. Put her on."

I held the phone out to Marjorie. "So far Jade and the baby are fine. He needs to talk to you."

She nodded and took the phone, her facial muscles finally relaxing. "Tal?"

She bit her lip as she listened to her brother for several minutes, only mumbling "okay" here and there. Finally, she said, "I will. You call me if anything changes. I don't care what time it is." Pause. "Okay. Bye."

"You better now?" I asked.

She sighed. "A little. I don't like her staying at the hospital."

"The hospital is the safest place for her right now."

"I know." Her lips trembled, and her eyes glazed over with unshed tears.

"Come here." I pulled her to me in a warm embrace.

She felt so good against me, and my cock hardened. Fuck. She didn't need a horny man right now. She needed comfort.

So that was what I'd give her. I led her through the foyer and down into the family room, where I deposited her on the leather couch and then sat beside her. "The boys are asleep?"

"Yeah. I checked on them right before you arrived."

I eyed the bar. "Can I get you anything? Water? A drink?"

She shook her head. "Just sit with me for a little while, okay?"

"Of course."

She snuggled into me, and without thinking, I placed my arm around her shoulders. She felt so good in my arms, as if everything were right with the world.

Too bad everything was *not* right with the world.

But damn, with this beautiful woman in my arms, I could pretend it was, if only for tonight.

Funny. I was horny as hell for Marj, but the thought of fucking her wasn't in my mind at the moment. I wanted to hold her, comfort her, let her lean on me. I wanted to be a rock for her.

Which was fucked up, really, because I was in no condition to be a rock for anyone. I couldn't even be a rock for my own son and mother. They deserved better.

Marjorie Steel deserved better.

My legs itched. I should leave. I was the last thing she needed.

Yet she'd called *me*. She'd wanted me. She hadn't called her brothers.

I kissed the top of her head once more.

Man, I was a goner.

Why had I tried to ease my ache for her with someone else? I could have fucked Heidi into oblivion, and I wouldn't want Marjorie any less. I'd wanted her since I'd seen how amazing she was with Henry. Yeah, she'd looked like a supermodel in Jamaica, her long, lean body clad in a hot-pink bikini. I couldn't deny she was beautiful or that I was physically attracted to her.

But I was physically attracted to a lot of women.

Marjorie Steel was different.

Marjorie Steel was better.

Marjorie Steel deserved the best.

Unfortunately, that wasn't me.

But she needed me now, so I'd be here for her. I'd hold her as long as she wanted me to. Then I'd leave.

# CHAPTER ELEVEN

**Marjorie**

Snuggled into the crook of Bryce's muscular arm, I inhaled deeply. He smelled like man. Pure strong man. Woodsy and musky and everything I wanted. Everything I needed.

He'd walked out on me previously, and that still stung, but he'd come tonight when I called. I wouldn't throw myself at him again. I'd wait this time. I'd wait for him to come to me. Even though everything in me was screaming at me to kiss him, to touch him all over, I'd wait.

At the moment, I was content to simply be in his arms.

To simply *be* with him.

I let my eyes flutter closed, inhaling once more. Again, he kissed the top of my head, as a father might kiss a daughter.

It was sweet. It was comforting.

I'd take what I could get.

I smiled against his chest when he took my hand in his, first entwining our fingers together and then rubbing my palm with his thumb. The massage felt good. Bryce had such strong hands. Beautiful hands—tan, perfectly square nails, long thick fingers.

Yeah. Long thick fingers...

I squirmed a little.

Nope. I was determined. If a move was to be made, he

would make it. I would not throw myself at him again. That wasn't me, had never been me. I wasn't the forward type.

But I *would* look into his beautiful blue eyes. I needed to, needed to see what was reflected back in them.

I pulled away slightly and raised my head. He gazed down at me with those amazing eyes. Blue eyes had always attracted me. They were so much more vibrant and sparkling than my own boring brown ones. Green were also nice, but blue... When I was younger, I'd gotten some blue contact lenses to change my eye color, but I couldn't stand how it felt to wear them, so I'd reluctantly accepted my brown eyes. My whole family had them, after all, and my brothers were considered the best-looking men in Snow Creek.

I didn't agree, though. As much as I loved my brothers, their looks didn't hold a candle to Bryce Simpson's blond beauty.

His dark-blue eyes, like sapphires. His perfectly sculpted nose that still had a light spray of freckles over it. His high aristocratic cheekbones, his golden stubble. And those full, firm lips, even redder than I—

I jerked.

Bryce's lips were a gorgeous dark pink, but tonight... I rubbed his bottom lip and then looked at my thumb.

Red.

Red lipstick.

"Marjorie..."

"I'm pretty sure you're not a cross-dresser, Bryce."

"Of course not."

"Then exactly what did I interrupt tonight?"

Not that he owed me any explanation. Just because we shared a kiss to end all kisses twenty-four hours ago. I gulped down the uneasiness in my throat. I had no hold on Bryce Simpson. No hold at all. Yet I felt like he'd been unfaithful to me.

"Nothing. You interrupted nothing."

"You're wearing lipstick."

His cheeks pinked a little, but he offered no explanation.

I certainly wasn't about to demand one, even though inside I was screaming. *How could you? How could you?*

None of my business. None of my damned business.

Except that it was. It was because I cared about this man, wanted this man.

*Still none of your business, Marj.*

I pulled farther away from Bryce so that his arm was no longer around me.

"Marj..."

"It's okay." I gulped. "No big deal. You must have been reaching for lip balm and mistakenly picked up your mom's lipstick. Happens all the time." I tried to sound serious, but my voice came out pretty curt.

"It's not my mom's lipstick."

Damn! He couldn't even let me think for a minute that he *hadn't* been making out with another woman?

"She meant nothing to me, and I—"

I shook my head, stopping him with a gesture. "Really. I don't want to know."

"Nothing happened."

I yearned to interrogate him, but I stopped myself. *None of my business. None of my business.*

I dropped my mouth open, feigning surprise. "Really? A kiss obviously happened. That might mean nothing to you, but it doesn't mean nothing to me."

"It didn't mean anything with her. For God's sake, I left as soon as you called me."

"I interrupted you?" I held back a huff. "Sorry to cramp your style."

"You didn't cramp anything." He raked his fingers through his hair. "Shit. This is coming out all wrong. I'm all wrong."

"I grew up with three brothers, Bryce. I'm well aware of how men are. You don't stop at a kiss."

"What?" He shook his head, his forehead wrinkled. "Your brothers are gentlemen, and so am I. We'd never force—"

"That's not what I meant."

"Sure as hell sounded like it."

I'd stepped in it this time, especially considering the type of man Bryce's father had turned out to be. He *had* forced men, women, and children, including my own brother. Open mouth, insert foot. I was being a spoiled brat. Spoiled little ranch heiress. I felt like a piece of shit.

*Repeat this to yourself, Marjorie. You have no hold on Bryce Simpson. You have no hold on Bryce Simpson. He's allowed to kiss whomever he wants. He's allowed to do any...*

I couldn't finish, not even in my head.

Bryce stood. "I need to go."

Shit. Not at all what I wanted. I inched toward him. "Please, don't. I don't want to be alone in this big house tonight."

"The boys are here."

"You know what I mean. They're asleep, and if I'm alone with my thoughts..."

"You'll worry about Jade. Tal says everything looks good."

"But what if—"

"Marj, don't do this to yourself." He shuddered slightly.

Only slightly, but I noticed. If he hadn't been with another woman five minutes ago, I'd think he wanted to reach out to me. Hold me like he had been.

"Can't you stay? We have"—I cleared my throat—"plenty of room, as you well know."

"I should get home. Henry."

"He's with your mom. Plus..."

"Plus what?"

What the hell? We were both thinking it. "Plus...weren't you planning to spend the night with lipstick woman, anyway? You'd have been out all—"

He pulled me to him, smashing our chests together. "You want to know what lipstick woman was?" He grabbed my hair in his fist and yanked it back, forcing me to meet his gaze. "She was a substitute. A piss-poor substitute at that. A substitute for what I really wanted."

My heart thundered inside me, the beat radiating out to my fingertips. "Wh-What do you want?"

"You fucking *know* what I want, baby."

I closed my eyes, waiting for his kiss.

A kiss that didn't come.

I opened my eyes.

His own were full of torment.

I couldn't help myself. I cupped his cheek, letting his sandy stubble scratch my fingertips.

"Damn it, Marjorie," he said gruffly.

"Take it, then. Take what you want, Bryce."

# CHAPTER TWELVE

**Bryce**

*Take it, then. Take what you want, Bryce.*

If I were stronger, her sweet coconut scent wouldn't entice me.

If I were stronger, her trembling pink lips wouldn't set my loins on fire.

If I were stronger, those sweet nipples protruding through her tight T-shirt wouldn't be my undoing.

If I were stronger, I'd do the right thing.

If I were stronger.

If...

I stroked her rosy cheeks, her skin like silk beneath my rough fingertips, and I pulled her face to mine, our lips meeting.

She opened, her smooth tongue melting against my own. She tasted of a hint of lusty red wine, a touch of mint, a sweet sensation that had my senses spinning.

I was going to hell for this. Surely I was going to hell. I had nothing to offer this wonderful woman. I had nothing to offer this baby sister of my best friend.

That last thought should have stopped me. Should have had me breaking the kiss and running toward the door.

But it didn't.

No.

Nothing would stop me now.

This would happen, and it would be amazing.

Damn the consequences.

Damn the fallout.

Damn everything—everything except Marj and me and this amazing kiss.

Our lips still smashed together, I explored her silky neck with my fingers, and then her lean shoulder and upper arm, lightly brushing the fabric of her short sleeve upward. I trailed down her arm, circling her wrist and then entwining her fingers with mine.

I groaned into her mouth.

This felt so right.

It was wrong, but so right.

With reluctance, I broke the kiss to inhale a necessary breath.

Breathless again.

She always left me breathless.

Then I pressed my lips to her soft cheek, her jawline, the curve of her neck, the soft part of her shoulder that was exposed.

Tonight my lips would explore every inch of Marjorie's body. Every fucking inch. My cock was hard as a rock in my jeans, and I absently pushed it against her belly, craving more and more of her.

Damn the consequences.

Damn the fallout.

"Bryce."

Her voice was a soft sigh, a careless whisper in the night.

I groaned again and nipped her neck, not giving a damn if I left a mark.

In fact, *wanting* to leave a mark.

Yearning to mark her as mine forever.

Damn the consequences.

Damn the fall—

"Auntie Marj?"

I jerked my lips away from her neck and looked up. Donny stood at the top of the small staircase that led to the large family room and bar.

Marj turned toward the little boy quickly. "Hey, sweetie. What are you doing up?"

"I had a bad dream."

Talon and Joe had told me about the boys and their nightmares. They were coming less and less frequently, and they tormented Dale more often. Tonight, though, apparently little Donny was affected.

Marjorie pulled away from me, not missing a beat. If Donny had noticed what we were doing, he didn't let on. She took the little boy's hand and squeezed it. "Let's get you some water. Then I'll read you a story. Would you like that?"

He nodded, trotting along at her side.

I drew in a breath, trying to will my cock back to normal size but having no luck. As much as I wanted Donny to sleep peacefully, I was slightly thankful for the interruption. I could fix this mistake I'd been about to make.

As if she'd read my mind, she looked over her well-kissed shoulder, arching her eyebrows. "Make yourself at home. Don't even *think* about leaving."

I sat back down on the couch with a thud. "Now what?"

*Leave. You should leave.*

*Absolutely.*

Somehow, though, I stayed glued to the couch.

My head spun a little, though not from the drinks I'd had earlier. They'd long worn off.

No. This was Marjorie Steel's doing.

The woman made me crazy. I didn't know up from down when I was with her. And damned if I didn't enjoy it.

*She's your best friend's sister.*

*She's thirteen years younger than you are.*

*You remember when she was born.*

*Pink and yellow unicorns.*

*You're a mess, Bryce Simpson.*

*You have no business getting involved with anyone, especially not Marjorie Steel.*

*She means something to you.*

*Don't hurt her.*

Over and over, I played through the myriad reasons Marj and I could never happen. Every single one, and I even invented a few for good measure.

And still I remained glued to the damned couch.

I sighed. Fact was, I wasn't leaving.

I didn't want to leave.

"Damn the consequences and damn the fallout," I said aloud.

I rose and walked up the stairs into the kitchen where I poured myself a glass of water and downed it. Then I stood, leaning against the granite countertop on the island.

*I am not my father.*

A mantra I'd repeated since I'd discovered who he truly was.

All the men, women, and children he'd abused...and Tom Simpson had never once laid a hand on me—his only child. He hadn't abused my mother either, as far as I knew. I felt certain she'd have told me by now if he had.

In a warped way, I'd come out of this smelling like a rose. I was truly lucky.

I felt anything but.

I was determined not to lose myself to self-pity. I had no reason to pity myself. I'd been through nothing. *Nothing.* Talon Steel had been through everything. That little boy Marj was currently comforting had been through everything.

Me?

Nothing.

Yes. I was the lucky one.

How fucked up was all of this?

My feet seemed glued to the tile floor. No way was I leaving, even though I knew I should. *You're thinking too much, Bryce.*

No shit.

I'd done nothing but think since the whole thing with my father went down.

Time to stop thinking.

Take what Marjorie Steel was offering me.

Feel, instead of think, for a change.

I laughed out loud. Had I really intended to fuck a pot-smoking cocktail waitress earlier this evening? Had I really been dense enough to think someone like Heidi could erase Marjorie Steel from my mind? Or at least ease my ache for her?

Sometimes I was so obtuse.

I might have gotten my rocks off, but I'd still want Marj.

My balls might no longer be blue, but that aching emptiness inside me? It would still be there in abundance. Only one woman could ease that ache.

I smiled when Marj walked right past the kitchen to the stairs leading to the family room. She whipped her hands to her hips. "Seriously, Bryce?" she said aloud.

She thought I'd left. I was almost amused.

I cleared my throat loudly.

She turned back toward the kitchen with a jerk.

"Donny okay?" I asked.

She nodded, walking toward me. "Good news, actually. The nightmare wasn't about his ordeal. He was worried about Jade and the new baby." She wrapped her arms around my neck. "I'm glad you didn't run off."

"I probably should have. I'm not sure you know what you're getting into, little girl."

"Stop the little girl bullshit. We both know how old I am."

I opened my mouth to respond, but she placed two fingers against my lips.

"If you mention unicorns, I might just knee you in your misters."

I couldn't help laughing at that one. In fact, the laugh was damned near boisterous.

I felt good here. I felt good around Marjorie Steel.

And I hadn't felt this damned good in a long time.

I lowered my lips to hers.

# CHAPTER THIRTEEN

### Marjorie

Those lips. Those wonderful firm and manly lips.

I'd been kissed many times, but Bryce Simpson was in a league of his own.

I hadn't expected him to still be here once I'd tucked Donny back into bed and read to him. I was certain he'd take the opportunity to run like hell, as he had the previous night.

But he'd stayed this time. And he was kissing me.

Our lips slid together, our tongues twirled, and my knees buckled. Not to worry. Bryce's strong arms kept me steady as we explored each other's mouths with ferocious desire.

This was more than a kiss.

So much more.

I wanted to hold on to him forever, kiss him forever. Kiss him until lipstick woman was no longer a memory.

Too soon, he broke the kiss.

I arched my brow and met his gaze.

"What if Donny wakes up again?"

"Then I'll comfort him again. He already sort of saw us kissing. He knows you. What's the big deal?"

"It's just—"

"You're looking for an excuse again."

"No. Yes. Hell, I don't know." He stepped back awkwardly.

"I came over here because you called me. You were upset. I didn't think—"

"Didn't think we'd end up making out in the kitchen?"

I laughed a little. "Making out" sounded so juvenile. Like making out in the car as teenagers. I wanted to do a lot more than just make out with Bryce.

"Actually, I figured we'd end up exactly where we are," he said. "Which is why I shouldn't have come at all."

"But you did."

"Because you were upset, Marj. I didn't come here to take advantage of you."

"Who's taking advantage? I'm giving you the advantage."

"You're Joe's little sister."

"Yeah, I know." I rolled my eyes. "And you remember pink and yellow unicorns on my wall. I've heard it all before, Bryce. It's beginning to sound like a broken record."

"You're not understanding me. It's more than just you being Joe's little sister. Right now I'm just...so messed up in my head."

"Don't you think I understand better than anyone else? I've been through the same hell you have."

"Your father might've made some mistakes in this lifetime, but he never committed the heinous crimes my father did."

I wanted to say something, but words eluded me. We both knew what horrible atrocities Bryce's father had committed not only against my brother but also against countless others.

Finally, I said, "You are not your father, Bryce."

"I know that. I really do know that."

"You don't sound too convinced of it, though."

"It's just... I feel like some parts of me are missing. Like I can't give a woman my whole self right now."

I understood those words better than he knew. I was a mess myself. "Bryce, I'm not asking you for a commitment."

"You don't understand. You're Joe's little sister."

"There goes the broken record again."

"What I mean is... I can't just...have sex with you. It wouldn't be right."

"Don't just have sex with me, then."

"I'm not up for anything else right now, Marj. I wish I were. Truly, I do. I just don't have it in me. I may never have it in me."

"If my brothers can get through this, so can you."

"Your brothers are three of the strongest men I know."

"And you don't think you're as strong as they are?"

Bryce paced around the kitchen, his hair a mass of sandy-blond waves. "I'd like to think I am. I wish I were."

"Are you attracted to me?"

He chuckled at that one. "Can't you tell?"

"Tell you what. Let's just be two people tonight. We won't be Marjorie and Bryce. We'll be two lost souls who come together. We don't even have to say each other's names."

He regarded me then, his gaze scanning my body from top to bottom. My nipples hardened.

"Can you *do* that?"

"I can do that. The question is, can you stop seeing the little girl who once had yellow unicorns on her wall?"

"God, I want you so fucking much."

"Then take me. Take what I'm offering. Just for tonight. No names. Just two people who need each other."

He stepped toward me then, grabbing me. In an instant, his lips were back on mine, this time more feral than before. He thrust his tongue deeply into my mouth, exploring every crevice of it, running it over my teeth, my gums, the inside of my cheeks, all the while twirling it around my own. My skin prickled, and a flaming arrow shot right into my core. My pussy was on fire. Already I could feel the wetness. My nipples ached for him. My whole body ached for him.

And still we kissed.

Our mouths still fused together, I began moving backward, leading him out of the kitchen and down the hallway into my bedroom. He took over the lead, opening the door and pushing me inside, and then he closed the door quietly.

And still we kissed.

I finally pulled away and inhaled a desperate breath. I gazed into Bryce's blue eyes, and I ached at the pain and sadness I saw in them. If I could take away that pain and sadness for one night, I would. Yes, I wanted this for my own reasons, and I wanted it for much more than one night. But now, this particular time meant even more to me. I wanted to ease his pain, take away everything that had ever hurt him. I touched my palm to his cheek.

"Bryce..."

"Shhh." He turned his cheek and kissed my palm. "No names, remember?"

Right. No names. My idea. My stupid idea, because now, I wanted more than anything in the world to hear Bryce say my name, to tell me he wanted *me*, Marjorie.

I'd made my bed, though.

No names.

Tonight I would give this man my body.

Tomorrow I'd deal with the consequences.

# CHAPTER FOURTEEN

**B r y c e**

No pink walls. No unicorns. No posters of food and chefs. This was a stranger's room—a beautiful stranger who had invited me in. Into her room...and into her body.

The stranger had long dark hair, warm chocolate-brown eyes, and dark-pink lips. She was tall, with perfectly shaped tits, narrow hips, and long slender legs—legs I imagined resting on my shoulders while I devoured what was between them.

The stranger gazed at me, her hand on my cheek, and her eyes—was it my imagination? Or were those lovely warm eyes shadowed with a touch of sorrow?

I didn't know why that surprised me. She had been through just as much as I had.

*Stop.*

We were just two strangers helping each other through a rough time. Period.

I reached forward and caressed her cheek. Her skin was warm beneath my fingers, and I trailed my index finger over her jawline. I traced her swollen lips, and she puckered, kissing the tip of my finger.

Should I let her take the lead?

*Stop.*

We were strangers. I'd take the lead. I always took the lead in a sexual encounter. I pulled her red T-shirt over her head. She wore a white lace bra, hard nipples protruding through the satiny fabric. I flicked one, and her short gasp morphed into a moan.

"Take off your bra," I said, my voice even lower than usual.

She obeyed me, unclasping the back and letting it fall off her shoulders onto the floor.

Her breasts were plump and perfectly formed, the brown nipples at attention. I'd seen them before—

*Stop.*

We were strangers now. This was all new to me.

I pulled her to me and kissed her again, hard, unsnapping her jeans at the same time. Once I had unzipped them, I thrust my hand inside, finding the paradise between her legs. I groaned. God, she was wet. Slick and wet and warm. My cock strained, still bound by my jeans and boxers. With my other hand, I led her palm to my bulge.

I broke the kiss and pushed her gently backward until her knees met the back of her bed, and she sat down. I removed her flip-flops, jeans, and panties—God, she was hot—in record time. I inhaled. Already I could smell her arousal, musky and sweet. She was shaved, her pussy bare—a delight for my gaze.

"Are you going to get undressed?" she asked.

I stood, torn. Part of me wanted to be naked as she was, our skin melting together. The other part wanted to remain clothed, remain in control, do whatever I wanted to her and enjoy the feeling of my cock straining against rough fabric before I let it loose to plunge into her.

Control was overrated. I trailed my lips to her ear and nibbled on the edge. "Unbuckle me, honey. Please."

Again, she followed my command, removing my belt and

then unfastening my jeans. She pushed them over my hips and exposed my black boxer briefs, my hardness thrusting outward. I removed the rest of my clothes quickly. Her gaze followed my every move. She liked what she saw.

Good.

I quickly grabbed a condom out of my jeans and then threw them back on the floor. I stood before her, my cock fully at attention. She opened her legs, teasing me. I couldn't stop my gaze from dropping to her beautiful pussy. Dark pink and glistening, it beckoned me. And I knew. Before I could go any further, I had to taste her.

I dropped to my knees, and again a battle warred inside me. Part of me wanted to just stare at her for a moment, take in the beauty of her private parts. The other part of me wanted to dive right in.

As much as I wanted to get those soft folds against my tongue, I took the moment. I looked. This would be the only time, so I gave my eyes the feast they desired.

Pure beauty. Pure shining, glorious beauty.

Once my eyes had enough, my mouth was more than ready. I slowly slid my tongue along her wet slit. She fell back on the bed, moaning. She tasted like heaven. Musk and apples and heaven. I pushed her thighs upward, positioning those gorgeous legs over my shoulders, something I had dreamed of many times.

*Stop.*

Strangers. Hadn't dreamed of it. We were two strangers. We'd never met before.

I dived back into that luscious pussy, sucking and kissing.

"Yes, yes," she sighed. "Feels so good. So good."

I continued to ravish her. Couldn't get enough. Everything

about her pussy enticed me. The beauty, the taste, the way she ground against my mouth. The soft sighs coming from her throat, the mumbled words I didn't hear yet understood.

I moved away for a moment, teasing her with nibbles on the inside of her thighs, which were coated with dew.

She was on the edge. She wanted to come, and damn, I wanted it too. I'd give her an explosive orgasm, and I wasn't going to stop at just one. I wanted this strange and beautiful woman to come and come and then come some more—first all over my face and then all over my cock.

"Yes, please," she moaned.

I gave her clit a hard suck, and then I thrust my long tongue as far as I could into her wet channel.

"God, yes!" Her pussy walls shuddered around me, coating me with her juice.

I reveled in her climax, sucking more honey out of her, and when her contractions began to subside, I pushed two fingers inside her.

"That's right, baby. Come. I want to make you feel good. I want to make you feel nothing but good."

I thrust some more, and she undulated her hips, grinding against my mouth.

"You like that? You like my fingers inside your hot pussy?"

I clamped my lips around her clit, and she flew into another orgasm and then another. When she finally came down from that one, she grabbed two fistfuls of the blanket covering her bed.

"You. Need you. Inside me."

I hadn't yet paid any attention to her beautiful breasts. I wanted to explore every inch of her body with my lips and my fingers, but I couldn't deny her plea. I ripped open the condom package and rolled it onto my hard dick. Then I rose above her, my knees on the bed.

And I thrust inside that sweet pussy.

Fuck.

Home.

Home sweet home.

Even with the rubber barrier between us, I knew this was home.

Home inside this stranger.

Except she wasn't a stranger.

*Stop.*

I forced the thought from my head.

Stranger.

Stranger.

Stranger.

*Not the sister of your best friend. Not the most beautiful woman you've ever laid eyes on. Not the woman who can ease your aching emptiness.*

Simply a beautiful, giving stranger.

No names. No information.

Just two strangers passing in the night.

I was inside a beautiful stranger, sating a need and a desire.

Nothing more.

I pulled out and then plunged back into the beautiful warmth of this stranger, this stranger who was giving of herself. Her warmth clamped around me, milking me, making me want her all the more.

This stranger.

How I wanted her.

This stranger...

Until—
"Oh, God! Bryce!"

# CHAPTER FIFTEEN

**Marjorie**

"Damn!" he grunted. "Can't. Can't stop."

"I don't want you to stop." I kissed his salty neck covered in perspiration. "Feels too good. Don't stop."

He was so big, so demanding, stretching me, and the burning stretch had never been so amazing.

"Supposed. To be"—he panted—"strangers."

Strangers. Right. Couldn't think about that right now as he was thrusting back inside me, nudging my already sensitive clit.

Fuck strangers. This was Bryce Simpson, the man I wanted more than anything. I would not apologize for using his given name. He had demons. Who didn't? Who knew more about demons than the Steels? All of us, including my new sisters-in-law, especially Ruby.

"Don't stop," I said. "Please don't stop"—*pause*—"*Bryce.*"

A sound escaped his throat. Not a moan or a groan or a sigh. No. This was more like a growl. A growl from an animal. An angry animal.

He increased his pace, fucking me hard and fast, and as he nudged that secret part of me, I flew into another orgasm, my whole body throbbing and tingling, stars bursting from my core and imploding back to my pussy.

I resisted the urge to yell. The boys' room wasn't adjacent to mine, but I still had to be careful.

"Why?" he grunted. "Why?"

"Why what?" I said between gasps.

"Why"—*thrust*—"can't"—*thrust*—"we"—*thrust*—"be"—*thrust*—"strange— Fuck!"

He pushed into me so deep, I was sure he touched my heart. So sensitive were my walls that I felt every single pulse of his cock as he released.

Every. Single. Pulse.

We lay, our bodies joined, for several moments, until he finally rolled away, covering his eyes with his arm.

"Damn," he said.

Was that a good damn or a bad damn? I had a hunch it was both.

I leaned over, propping myself up on my arm. His face was covered in perspiration, his blue eyes covered by his arm. I gently moved his arm back to his side.

"Look at me, Bryce."

His eyes remained closed.

"Damn it. Look at me."

He slowly opened his eyes. "I'm sorry."

"Sorry for what?"

He simply shook his head.

"Hey." I kissed his salty forehead. "Let it go. Just for tonight. Let it fucking go." I nudged his other arm and snuggled into his shoulder. "Let it go."

★ ★ ★

The alarm on my phone blared at seven a.m.

I was already awake. My sleep wasn't great these days, although in Bryce's arms, I'd slept better than I had in months.

He shot up at the sound, his eyes wide and disoriented.

"Just the alarm." I rose from the bed. "I need to get the boys up for school. Stay here as long as you want."

"What time is it?"

"Seven."

"Shit."

"What?"

"I have a meeting at nine."

"Where?"

"Here. With your brothers."

"Talon's still at the hospital with Jade. I'm sure they're going to reschedule your meeting." The mention of Jade made my pulse quicken. I hurriedly checked my phone. No texts or missed calls.

I exhaled.

Good. No news was good news.

"I need to get out of here," Bryce said, standing. "What if the boys see me?"

"What if they do? You're a family friend. They know that. You being here is no big deal."

He scanned the room. "Yeah. I suppose. Right."

I wrapped my robe around my shoulders and secured it with the fabric belt. Then I walked toward a still-naked Bryce—he was magnificent—and touched his upper arm. "Hey. Everything's fine. Trust me."

He lowered his gaze, not meeting my eyes. "This... It was... It was great. It was amazing."

"I'm glad you think so. I agree."

"But Marjorie—"

I smiled. "You said my name."

"I know."

"You didn't say it at all while we were making love."

"Because we were supposed to be strangers. And that wasn't..."

"Wasn't what? Making love? Just a fuck?"

He still didn't meet my gaze. "That's right. It was just a fuck."

# CHAPTER SIXTEEN

**B r y c e**

I finally looked up. She stared at me, her lips parted. I had no idea what she might be thinking.

All I knew was that I was the lowest of the low. A pig. A shithead. An asshole douchebag.

I'd fucked my best friend's baby sister.

And hell, I'd loved it. If I didn't leave now—right fucking now—I'd do it again. Even in a long matronly bathrobe, her hair a messy disarray, Marjorie Steel was the most beautiful thing I'd ever laid eyes on.

Already my cock had stirred and was at half-mast, a fact that wasn't lost on her, judging by her gaze.

Marjorie cleared her throat. "Have it your way. I have two boys to take care of." She slid on a pair of slippers and left the bedroom.

I breathed a sigh of relief. Not that I wanted her to leave, but now I wouldn't be ripping the robe off her and throwing her back onto her bed.

Damn.

She'd been great—everything I'd imagined and more. Her body had been created to sheathe mine, and she was so responsive to my every touch. Her kisses made me feel like a teenager in the back of my old truck again.

She'd been a baby when I was a teenager...

Yeah, that still got to me some, but the real problem was me.

Just me.

I was fucked up, and a woman like Marjorie Steel deserved so much better.

But as fucked up as I was, my cock was full-on hard just thinking about her. I sighed, gathered my clothes from the floor, piled them onto a chair, and then went into her attached bathroom.

Time for a shower.

And not a warm one.

★ ★ ★

I was dressed in the same clothes I'd worn the night before. No big deal. Only Marjorie had seen me. I texted Joe quickly to see if our meeting was still on this morning. He said yes, it was, and that he'd checked in with Talon, who'd said Jade was doing fine and that the rest of us should go ahead and have the meeting without him. Marjorie hadn't been back to her bedroom, which I thought was odd. Finally, I opened the door to her room quietly and eased out at about eight thirty a.m.

No sign of the boys. No sign of Marjorie either. Perhaps she had driven them to school. I remembered how well Joe and his brothers had liked riding the bus all the way from the ranch. Meaning, they hadn't.

I couldn't avoid her forever, and I certainly didn't have time before my meeting at nine to go home and change.

But how would it look, when Joe and Ryan arrived, finding me already here?

I jerked when I heard bustling at the door. I walked out of the kitchen, and there was Marjorie, obviously coming back from... Where? If she'd taken the boys all the way into town to school, she wouldn't be back yet. She wore a fleece jacket and sweat pants, her feet clad in old sneakers.

She shed the jacket and hung it on the coatrack in the hallway.

"You still here?" she said, not meeting my gaze.

"Yeah. I have a meeting with your brothers here at nine. Remember?"

"I heard from Talon," she said. "Jade is going to be okay, and they'll be home later today."

"Yeah, me too. Joe and Ryan decided to still have the meeting with me."

"I'll make you guys some breakfast."

"Joe and Ryan probably already ate."

She laughed softly, not really smiling. "Trust me. I know my brothers. They're bottomless pits. They'll want breakfast. You want coffee?" She walked into the kitchen.

I shoved my hands into the pockets of my jeans, shuffling my feet on the area rug between the hallway and the kitchen.

Marjorie laughed—sort of. "I get it. You want to go outside and sit in your car and then come back in once Joe and Ryan have arrived so it doesn't look like you've been here all night." Her tone was sardonic and a little hurt.

I cleared my throat. "No, that's not what I was thinking."

"It's written all over your face, Bryce. You do know as soon as they drive up, they'll see your car, right?"

I opened my mouth to respond, but she quieted me with a gesture.

"Don't even start, for God's sake. Just sit down at the table and let me pour you a cup of coffee. Did you ever consider the fact that maybe you got here before they did? Maybe you're excited to hear their proposal?"

Again, I said nothing and sat down at the table as she instructed. A few seconds later, a steaming cup of black coffee was thrust in front of me.

"I'm going to take a quick shower. When my brothers get here, just tell them you let yourself in. I'll even tell them I left the door unlocked for you. Got it?"

I nodded, feeling like the world's biggest asshole.

"Also, tell them I'll make some breakfast when I'm done."

I nodded again. Then I simply sat, taking a sip of coffee that burned my tongue, and waited. Waited for two of the Steel brothers to show up for our meeting. And I knew, as soon as they saw my face, they'd be able to tell I'd fucked their little sister.

I'd made such a big mistake.

As much as I wanted to, though, I couldn't bring myself to regret what had occurred. In fact, as much as I knew I wasn't ready to offer Marjorie Steel anything close to what she deserved, all I could think about was getting back into her bed.

Which meant only one thing. Even though I needed the work, I had to turn down whatever the Steels were about to offer me. I couldn't be around Marjorie. Our need for each other was too great. I would never be able to resist her, so the only choice I had was to stay away from her.

Far, far away from her.

I looked up when the door opened. A few seconds later, Jonah Steel, my best friend in the world, walked into the kitchen.

"Bryce, you're early. What's wrong with this picture?" He laughed.

Not too obvious. I'd never been known for my punctuality.

"Just interested to hear what you guys want to talk to me about."

"I thought Tal filled you in a little."

"He did." I cleared my throat. "But I'm still curious. About the details. You know."

Joe smiled. "We're hoping to welcome you aboard here. Ryan should be here soon. Is there any more coffee?"

I cleared my throat again. "I don't know. Marjorie poured me this cup and then excused herself to go take a shower. She said she'd make us breakfast when she was done."

"Great. I'm starved. We'll call this second breakfast, like the hobbits do. My first breakfast was at five thirty. So how are you holding up?"

Nothing like getting right to the point. *Oh, I'm a huge mess. Such a huge mess that I took advantage of your baby sister last night. Right in the room that used to have unicorns on the wall.*

Yeah. Couldn't really say that.

"I'm good."

"Your mom still okay?"

"The same. Henry helps a lot. She's pretty much taken over." I sighed. "I miss him, actually."

"You're his father. Take back the reins."

"She needs him right now. And he adores her."

"He adores you too. Don't stop being his dad just because his grandma needs something to focus on."

I nodded. What else could I do? I didn't want to tell Joe that I was so much a shadow of my former self that I didn't feel I could be a father to my son. What if I turned into my own father? No, couldn't even begin to go there. I could never put my son in harm's way. I'd leave him first.

"It's working for now, Joe. I'm doing the best I can."

"I hear you asked Tal to make you a hand around here."

"I did."

"And that's when he told you about what we were considering."

"Yeah."

"I get it, Bryce. You want to work your body to a pulp so you can forget everything that went down, if only through exhaustion. But buddy, it won't work. Been there, done that."

"With all due respect, your father wasn't a psychopath."

"Maybe not, but he sure fucked up as a dad."

"Please." I scoffed. "Don't compare our situations."

"I'm not. But take a look. Be thankful. You're strong and healthy, and you have a strong and healthy kid. And whatever else your father did, he was around for you when you needed him, and he never abused you."

"That's supposed to make me feel better?" I stood. "Christ, Joe. Give me a break."

"Hey. Sit back down." He gestured. "I didn't mean to cross any line. No one knows better than I do the guilt of being the one who *wasn't* abused."

I nodded. Joe was right. He'd harbored immense guilt for decades over not accompanying Talon that fateful day.

By my psycho father and two other equally psycho dicks.

"Luke, Joe. And all those other kids. Names I'll never know. Colin Morse. My father destroyed them. Why not me?"

"I don't know. I wish I had answers. All we can do in this life is play the hand we're dealt. It is what it is."

"Am I supposed to feel lucky?"

Joe took a sip of coffee and paused a moment. Then, "I don't know. I often thought the same thing. I never felt lucky, though."

"I don't either."

"It took a while, but I learned to focus on the good. I learned that Talon didn't blame me for what happened to him. He never did. And no one blames you for what your father did."

"But the guilt, man. How do you let go of that?"

"A lot of soul searching." He smiled. "And the love of a good woman helps."

The love of a good woman...

Marjorie. She was as good as they came. And the best woman in the world deserved someone whole.

That was not me.

"You lucked out. You got a good woman who is also trained to help you through the crap."

He laughed. "You think I married Melanie to have a live-in therapist?"

"No. That didn't come out right. I'm sorry."

"It's okay. I lucked out in a lot of ways with Melanie. I don't deny it. But I married her for love. True love. Not her talents and abilities. Not her intelligence. Not her amazing body and blond beauty, either. We fell in love. Simple as that."

"I'm not ready for a relationship," I said.

"That's cool. Just take things one day at a time. Talk to Melanie if you need to. Or she can recommend someone else if you're uncomfortable talking to your best friend's wife. But you need to do something, Bryce. Don't take this the wrong way, but you've gone downhill."

I sighed. "Now why would I take that the wrong way?"

"Come on. You and I don't mince words. We never have."

I nodded. "True."

"Remember our wedding in Jamaica? You were in a great mood for those couple days."

"There was a nude beach, and I had a buzz going the whole time," I said truthfully. "It hit me harder about a month later. I think I was numb at first, you know?"

"Yeah, I get it. Like I've said before. Been there, done that. But you've got a son. And even if you didn't, you've got a life, man. You're *alive*."

"And so many others aren't because of my father."

"True. There's no sugarcoating it. But *you're* not dead, Bryce, so here's my best advice, whether you want it or not. Don't live your life as if you are."

I opened my mouth, though I had no response. Thankfully, I was interrupted by Ryan Steel ambling into the kitchen. "Hey, I'm not that late, am I?"

"We were early," Joe said.

A few seconds later, Marjorie arrived, her long dark hair hanging in wet waves. She sauntered in barefoot, wearing her trademark skinny jeans and fitted T.

My breath caught. Always breathless around this woman.

She regarded her brothers and laughed. "Yeah, yeah. I know. You're hungry. Eggs, toast, and Canadian bacon will be ready in five."

"You're a gem," Ryan said.

"And don't forget it! You're just lucky I love cooking."

"We never forget that, Sis," Ryan said jovially.

Ryan Steel had always been jovial, always had a smile on his sculpted face. We'd all found out recently that he was actually a half brother to the other Steel siblings. Still, though, his old personality shone through as if nothing had occurred.

Of course, he'd *also* found love. With Ruby Lee, a former police detective, who was the daughter of the one man who might rival my father for being the worst psycho in the world.

Reality hit me like a brick. All the Steels, including Marj, had been through just as much, or more, as I had, and they were still functioning, not allowing themselves to sink in the quicksand of self-pity.

They were better than I.

Another reason I needed to turn down whatever they were offering.

I eyed Marjorie's perfect ass as she fried eggs at the gas cooktop. Marjorie. She was the main reason I'd turn down the Steel brothers.

I had to stay away from her.

If I didn't, I'd hurt her.

Her brothers would never forgive me.

And I'd never forgive myself.

# CHAPTER SEVENTEEN

### Marjorie

My back was burning. I actually felt Bryce's blue eyes on me as I cooked breakfast for him and my brothers.

Maybe it was my imagination. Maybe he wasn't feeling what I was feeling.

What we'd shared couldn't be one-sided, could it?

Yeah, he didn't want my brothers to know. I understood. I didn't want them to know either. Not yet, anyway. It was too new. Telling anyone, even Jade, would make it seem slightly less exciting.

Except that I was both excited and sad.

Bryce had made it clear this had been a onetime deal. I supposed it was up to me to change his mind, but why should it be? I'd already been forward, which was usually out of my comfort zone. Of course, never had I wanted anyone as much as I ached for Bryce Simpson.

Truth be told, I'd been attracted to him since I was a kid. He'd been around all the time, being Joe's best friend and all, and his blond-haired and blue-eyed handsomeness was such a striking contrast to the dark hair and eyes we Steels possessed.

I finished the eggs and flipped the slices of Canadian bacon. I divided the eggs among three plates and then buttered the slices of whole-grain toast. Then I started another pot of coffee while I waited for the Canadian bacon to finish.

The guys were talking, mostly Joe and Ryan, but every once in a while, Bryce piped in. I went back in time in my mind once more. Bryce used to be nearly as jovial as my brother Ryan. When I was a kid, he was always smiling and laughing. He'd been good for Joe, who was on the quieter side. Though I was too young to remember, apparently Joe had been as boisterous as Bryce before Talon had been taken. Bryce must have done a lot to pull Joe out of his funk during that difficult time. Of course, no one but the family, excluding me, even knew Talon had been taken. Had Joe confided in Bryce? I had no idea. They were as close as two men could be, as close as Jade and I were. I would have told Jade everything, but perhaps male friendships were different.

I'd had my own issues with my brothers over them not telling me about Talon until last year. Sure, they were trying to protect me, but I was far from a shrinking violet. I hoped I'd proved that by now.

I certainly harbored my own guilt. Talon's abduction had been orchestrated by Ryan's birth mother, a crazy bitch who'd been obsessed with my father. The reason? Finding out my mother was pregnant with me.

But for me, my brother wouldn't have gone through hell.

No, I didn't blame myself, not objectively at least. But I had at first, and I possessed the scars to prove it. Several talks with both Jade and Melanie had helped me see the truth, but still a smidge of guilt remained. It would always be there.

It was a part of me, just like Joe's guilt would always be a part of him.

I had to learn to live with it. Assisting with Talon's family was helping. I'd grown to love Dale and Donny, and Jade was my all-time bestie. Plus, I was getting to know my middle brother. He'd always been elusive, having been gone so long with the military. I'd always been closer to Joe and Ryan.

Maybe I'd tell Bryce about my feelings of guilt. If I had the chance, that was. He didn't seem to want anything to do with me now.

But again, he'd been so vibrant before. Even if Bryce had known about Talon when he was younger, he certainly hadn't known of his father's involvement. None of us had.

I finished up the Canadian bacon and slapped it on the full plates. I turned and forced a smile. "It's ready." I brought two plates over and set them in front of Joe and Bryce.

Ryan lifted his brow.

"I only have two hands, Ry. Sheesh." I brought him his plate.

"Just kidding, Sis. But why do those two bozos rate higher than I do?"

"They were closer," I said, forcing my smile again. "I made another pot of coffee."

Joe held up his cup. "I'll take a hot topper."

Then Bryce stood. "I'll get the coffee. I'm sure Marj has other things she'd rather be doing than feeding us."

Ryan laughed. "Are you kidding? She *lives* to feed people."

"Right," I said, again with the forced smile. My brother was teasing, of course, but his words irked me. "Thanks, Bryce. I do have some things to do." I walked swiftly out of the kitchen.

In truth, I didn't have much on my plate today, but I relished the chance to escape. With Felicia gone, I was also doing the laundry, but I'd just completed it two days prior. We'd hired the rest of the housework out to a maid service that came once a week, which worked fine for me. I was an atrocious housekeeper.

Since Jade was still at the hospital and the boys were at school, I was off the clock for now. Though I was tempted to curl up with a good book and escape thoughts of Bryce Simpson, I decided instead to go into town. I'd take Jade's advice and get back to the gym. I hadn't gained any weight, but I was getting a little soft. Ryan's wife, Ruby, had given me some pointers for my workouts. That woman had an amazing body, all toned and muscled but still beautifully feminine. In fact, maybe I'd give her a call and see if she wanted to accompany me. She'd quit the police force when they wouldn't give her time off to go after her father, and though she was toying with opening up a PI business, she hadn't yet. For now, she was helping Ry with the wine business.

I quickly dialed her cell, but she answered with a text that she was tied up in a meeting all morning. So much for that idea.

Off to the gym by myself, then. I grabbed my workout bag and headed out.

★ ★ ★

Holy smokes, was I out of shape! A half hour on the elliptical about did me in. I showered quickly, and changed, and then went next door to get a raspberry smoothie. I sat down at a small table and checked my phone, trying not to think about Bryce.

I wasn't having much luck, until—

"Marjorie."

A voice I recognized. I looked up. Colin Morse, Jade's ex-fiancé, who I'd known since college, stood at the opposite end of my small table.

I swallowed. I had no idea what to say.

"Mind if I sit down?" he asked.

"Sure. Go ahead." I avoided his gaze.

Colin had been held captive, tortured, and raped by Bryce's father, Tom Simpson. Joe had rescued him, but Colin's father, instead of being grateful, had threatened Joe with criminal charges, saying Colin was ready to name Joe as his captor.

Joe didn't bite, however, and Colin came clean.

He hadn't deserved his fate, but I was still pissed he was ready to blame my brother. Plus, he'd left Jade humiliated at the altar. I couldn't turn him away, though. I'd never turn away a rape victim.

He sat down.

"What are you doing in Snow Creek?" I asked. This ought to be the last place on earth he'd be hanging out. He was abducted here, after a run-in with all three of my brothers.

"How's Jade?" he countered.

So much for him answering my question.

"She's good." Did he know she was pregnant? I had no idea. None of his business anyway.

He sighed. "Do you know how many times I've thought about how much simpler my life would have been if I hadn't chickened out the day of my wedding?"

Okay, this time I wasn't holding back. "Look, Colin. I'm sorry for what you've been through. Truly I am. But if you think I'm going to let you off the hook for leaving my best friend totally humiliated, think again."

"Still the same Marjorie Steel," he said. "You don't take shit from anyone."

"Especially not people who hurt my friends."

"I was your friend once."

"Jade trumps you, I'm afraid."

Then I felt like a horrible person. Maybe he was looking for someone to talk to. I wasn't the right person, but I could at least be nice. Maybe suggest he get help. But first I needed to know why he was here.

"What are you doing here, Colin?"

He didn't respond right away. Just took several sips of his green smoothie. It looked like pea soup in a clear plastic cup. Yuck.

"Trying to help myself, so to speak," he finally said.

"How?"

"By taking back my life. Facing the place where I was kidnapped."

"How is that supposed to help you?"

"Hell if I know. It was my father's idea."

His father? The one who'd been ready to extort money from my brother? Great.

"Have you thought about getting some real help?"

"What do you mean?"

"I mean seeing a therapist, Colin."

He huffed. "My father says that's only for cowards. Weaklings."

*Well, your father is a supreme douchebag.* Seriously, it was on the tip of my tongue.

"So he thinks you should be helping yourself. Facing the music."

"Yeah." He cleared his throat. "In a manner of speaking."

"In other words, 'get over it.' Right?"

He nodded.

His hair was growing out nicely. Tom had shaved his head. Colin had always been handsome, with blond hair and greenish eyes.

"Colin," I said, "what exactly did your father think of you running out on Jade that day?"

"He told me I was a coward."

Shocking.

"And were you?"

"Well...yeah."

"You're putting me in a weird position here," I said. "I don't want to give you an excuse for what you did to Jade, but frankly, your dad is being a dick."

He didn't respond.

"Sorry if I crossed a line there." But I wasn't sorry at all.

"It's okay."

I rolled my eyes. "Look. You need some real help. It's not a weakness. It's strength."

"Jonah's wife is a psychiatrist, right?"

"Yeah. But I don't think she'd be the right fit."

"Why not? I hear she's the best."

"She is. But you're forgetting that your esteemed father tried to pin your abduction on Joe. Little conflict of interest there."

He stared at his pea glop in a cup. "I really just want to talk to Jade. Can you arrange it?"

"That's why you came here? Not to 'face the music'?"

"Well, both reasons, actually. I wasn't sure how to go about seeing her, but running into you here was kind of like kismet."

I shook my head. "Trust me, Colin. Nothing about this was kismet. Since when do you even use the word kismet?"

"Since my life was ripped away from me by Tom Simpson. Facing death has a way of making you think a little differently."

"That makes no sense. If you believe in kismet, you must believe it was kismet that you were taken."

"No. Of course not! And could you keep your voice down?"

People in the small smoothie shop were looking our way. Colin was an adult. His name hadn't been kept out of the papers. Everyone in Snow Creek knew their once-esteemed mayor, Tom Simpson, had brutalized the young man sitting with me—if they recognized him, that was.

"Sorry." And I was. He didn't deserve the fame after what he'd endured.

"Can you arrange it?"

"For you to talk to Jade?" I shook my head. "Sorry."

"Please?"

"She's married now. To Talon."

"I know. The *first* guy to nearly beat me to a pulp."

Oh, no. He was so not going there. "And then you pressed charges, got him dragged off to jail. Do *not* compare my brother to that degenerate Tom Simpson," I said through clenched teeth.

"Why not? Don't you worry about Jade?"

I opened my mouth but then counted to ten in my head.

Seriously. All the way to ten. And still I wasn't sure I wouldn't say something I might regret later.

Colin had no idea what Talon had been through. The same as he had been, only at age ten instead of twenty-six and for a longer period of time.

"You need to stop talking about my brother right now, or this conversation will end."

"I'm just—"

I held up my hand. "Don't."

He sighed. "Fine. Will you arrange for me to talk to Jade or not?"

"Not," I said.

The door to the small shop opened.

"Hey, Marj. What are you doing here?"

Talon.

Talon had entered the shop.

This would not end well.

# CHAPTER EIGHTEEN

### Bryce

I cleared my throat. "Your offer... It's extremely generous."

It definitely was. I'd take over as chief financial officer for the Steel Corporation at a very nice salary with full benefits, and the package also included a two-percent profit share in the business.

Yes, extremely generous.

"You're the best man for the job," Joe said. "There's no one I've known longer and trust more."

I nodded, a huge lump forming in my throat. I'd sworn I'd turn down whatever they offered. I'd sworn I'd stay away from Marjorie Steel. But once I heard the magnitude of the offer, I realized I had other considerations. Important ones.

I had a son. I had a mother. If I didn't take this offer for them, I'd be a selfish bastard. My father had killed himself, so his life insurance hadn't paid. Plus, he'd left next to nothing in their joint accounts. As for his *other* accounts? The FBI had confiscated everything.

We sat in Talon's office. He and Jade still hadn't gotten back from the hospital, but Joe and Ryan had gotten texts saying they were on their way. Joe sat behind Talon's large mahogany desk, and Ryan sat next to me in another of the very comfortable leather chairs facing the desk.

"We'd like you to start pretty much immediately," Ryan said. "You can have a couple weeks to wrap up any loose ends, if you need it."

What loose ends? I hadn't been working. I'd asked Talon for a job as a ranch hand just two days ago. I needed the work. I needed money. What little my mother and I had would soon run out.

I rubbed small circles into the palm of my hand. "I'll need some time to think about it."

"What is there to think about?" Joe asked.

"Just some...things."

"We've known each other our whole lives," he said. "What aren't you telling us?"

"I'll be happy to leave the room if you want to talk to Joe in private," Ryan offered.

"No, no. That's not it," I said. "I just have a lot to think about."

Joe regarded me, his forehead wrinkled. For a moment, I thought he was going to ask what I had to think about again, but then he seemed to change his mind.

"We've all had to deal with parents who turned out to be something other than we thought," Ryan said. "Or who turned out to be someone different altogether."

Ryan's birth mother, Wendy Madigan, had been the mastermind behind the entire Future Lawmakers Club when our parents were in high school. She was just as psychotic as my father.

Ryan continued, "Melanie has assured me that if I were going to turn out like my mother, I'd know by now. Ditto for you, man. You're not your father."

I nodded, saying nothing. Ryan's mother had been a

horrible person. She had not, however, been a rapist and pedophile. Those two things haunted me all the time.

"We wouldn't be offering you this if we didn't think you were the best man for the job," Joe said. "The fact that you're my oldest and best friend has nothing to do with it."

"Really?" I asked.

"Only in that I know I can trust you," he said. "Anyone else, we'd have to vet."

Again, I said nothing.

"Look," Ryan said, "I get what's eating you. Do you hold my mother's crimes against me?"

"Of course not!" I said. "But you weren't raised by your mother."

"I see," Joe said. "Look. Your father raised me as well."

"Brad Steel raised you."

"He turned out to be kind of a dick—"

I opened my mouth, but he stopped me with a gesture.

"I'm not comparing the two. Your father was far worse. I get it. But I knew him nearly as well as you did. He took us on overnight fishing trips, for God's sake. He raised me just as my father raised you. Both men were significant in our lives, but their actions don't define either of us, Bryce. You're a smart guy. You know that."

Yeah, I knew that.

Objectively, I knew all of it.

The problem was that I wasn't thinking objectively.

I had two issues.

Dealing with who my father truly was and its effect on my life.

And Marjorie Steel.

I couldn't be around Marjorie. I wouldn't be able to resist

her, and she deserved better than a man who could only offer her emotionless fucks—or rather, a fuck full of emotion that I couldn't let mean anything. Yeah, I had feelings for Marjorie Steel. Strong feelings. But a lifetime relationship wasn't in the cards for me. I certainly couldn't bring more children into the world—not with the faulty genes I carried.

Problem was, I'd already brought a son into the world, a son I loved dearly and whom I had an obligation to.

A son I'd spent far too little time with the last couple months.

I told myself it was because my mother needed him more than I did. Truth was, I needed him just as much right now. More importantly, he needed me. No matter how afraid I was to be a father, he needed me. His mother had abandoned him, signed away all her parental rights.

He was mine.

My son, my responsibility.

I stood, clearing my throat. "Thank you for your trust in me. I need to talk to my mom, but I will most likely be coming on board."

Joe stood, walked around his desk, and grabbed me in a bear hug. "That's great, man. We're all really happy about your decision."

"My *tentative* decision," I said.

"Yeah, whatever." He pulled back, smiling. "We'll get the paperwork ready."

Paperwork. I nearly told them to hold off, that my decision wasn't final yet, but I didn't. This was what I had to do for my son.

Ryan patted me on the back. "You want to stick around until Tal gets back? It shouldn't be long."

I shook my head. "I have some things to take care of. But tell Talon thanks, and I'll be in touch."

I left without saying anything more.

★ ★ ★

"Where's Henry?" I asked my mother upon entering our modest house in the heart of Snow Creek.

"He just went down for his morning nap," she said. "But he fussed. He'll be down to only one nap per day soon."

I went into the nursery and kissed my son on the forehead, pushing his downy yellow hair to the side. Time for a haircut soon. His first one.

I'd missed so much of his life since I'd found out the truth about my father. I vowed not to miss any more.

Of course, taking the job with the Steels would consume a lot of my time. Which was okay. My mother still needed her grandson, and I needed to start earning a paycheck. A very big paycheck, if I took the Steels' offer.

"It sounds amazing," my mother said after I'd given her the details.

"We can even move onto the ranch if we want to," I said. "They're offering us use of the guesthouse." Which would be close to Marjorie. The ranch was a big place, though. I could still stay far away from her most of the time.

"This is our home." My mother gestured around our modest living room.

"Yeah. But this home has a lot of shitty memories, don't you think?"

She sighed. "I've been trying to focus on the good memories. We had many."

"We did," I admitted. "All while Dad was leading a double life."

My mother swallowed. "That never leaves my mind."

"I've been thinking. We could rent this house out. The rent would pay the mortgage, which will be paid in full soon. Then we could continue to rent it out."

"Who would want to live here? And if we sell, who would want to buy it? The whole town now knows who and what your father was."

She had a fair point.

My mother seemed to have aged five years in the past several months. I definitely had a few more gray hairs myself. It didn't help that when I looked in the mirror, a younger version of my father stared back at me. Normally, that would be a good thing. My dad had been a very handsome man. All I saw now, though, was the monster he truly was.

Yes, I saw a monster in the mirror.

Consequently, I avoided mirrors like the plague.

"All right, Mom. We'll stay here in town."

"On the other hand," she said, "I wouldn't mind leaving. Everything in this house has a memory. Mostly good memories, but memories that have soured. Really soured."

"I know." God, how I knew.

"Maybe we *should* move to the ranch," she said. "But seriously, they can't just be giving you a house."

"No. I mean, yes, but it's part of the compensation package should I choose to accept it. I won't own it, but reasonable rent would be deducted from my compensation."

"You don't feel like this is charity?"

"No. I thought so at first, but they do need a CFO, and I am qualified for the job."

"They already have a CFO."

"He's retiring."

"So good timing, then."

"Seems so."

"What do we do with this place, though? If we can't rent it or sell it..." She darted her gaze around the room.

"We try to rent it, I guess. If that doesn't pan out, we try to sell it. And if that doesn't pan out, we keep it empty."

"What about squatters?"

"In a small town like Snow Creek?" I shook my head. "I doubt we have to worry about that. Plus, eventually someone new will move here looking for a place to live, and they won't know or care that a monster once lived here."

"From your mouth to God's ears." My devout mother crossed herself. "You do what you think is right, Bryce. Thank you for including me in your plans."

"Of course, Mom. We need each other right now. I'd never let you flounder alone."

"I don't want to be a thorn in your side. You're still young. You can still have—"

I quieted her with a gesture. "You and Henry are my family. Nothing else is in the cards for me. I've accepted that. Besides, I'm thirty-eight years old. I'm too old to start a family now."

"That's silly, Bryce. I know you've taken care of me *and* Henry for the past couple of months, but I'm your mother, not your child. I appreciate all you've done since your father's death, but you don't have to take care of me."

She was kind to say so, but finding out her husband of forty years was a psychopath living a double life had taken its toll. My mother was a strong woman, but I couldn't ask her to live alone.

"You'll come with Henry and me wherever we go," I said.

"Not if it means you're sacrificing having a real family. I won't do that to you." She sniffed back a sob. "I can't. Not after everything. You deserve happiness."

"Who says I'm not happy?" I forced a smile.

"I see it all over your face. You're not moving forward, Bryce. You need to do that."

"I think that's what taking the job with the Steels is all about."

"That's something to earn money, to occupy your mind. You can't run forever."

"I'm glad your therapy is helping you, Mom."

"That's not coming from my therapist. That's coming straight from me."

"I have no desire for a relationship or more of a family than you and Henry. Trust me. Don't you think if I wanted those things I'd have found someone long before now?"

"Not necessarily. You just haven't met the right woman."

I couldn't help a small chuckle. No use arguing with my mother. She was, after all, my mother. "Look. This is what I need right now. I need to provide a home for my son. And for my mother."

"I'm not your responsibility, Bryce. Henry is, it's true. But I am not."

Before I could dispute her words, my cell phone buzzed.

# CHAPTER NINETEEN

### Marjorie

"Shit," I said under my breath. Then I smiled. "What are you doing here?"

"Jade wanted a smoothie before we went home, so I—" He glared at Colin. "What are *you* doing here?"

Colin seemed to shrink in his chair. And he seriously wanted me to arrange for him to speak to Jade, when he couldn't even look her husband in the eye?

Still, I needed to cut him some slack. Colin had been through hell since his last altercation with Talon.

"You going to answer me?" Talon pressed.

"Just getting a smoothie."

"With my sister?"

"It's a free country," he said. "She happened to be here, so I joined her. We used to be friends in another lifetime."

"Tal..." I hedged, looking away. My brother knew well what had happened to Colin. He of all people should take a bit of pity on him.

He seemed to understand, thank goodness. "I'll get Jade her smoothie." He walked to the counter.

"Still want me to try to arrange for you to talk to Jade?" I asked sarcastically once Talon was out of earshot.

"Well...yeah."

"My brother is shooting at you with his eyes," I said. "Don't forget what you did to his wife." Though honestly, it all seemed insignificant given what both Talon and Colin had been through. Still, I had no great love for the man across from me. Pity, yes. Love? No way.

"Jade's a big girl. Isn't it her decision who she talks to? Or does she let that animal control her?"

Now I was angry. He'd definitely crossed a line. "Look. I know you've been through hell, but Talon is my brother. If you want my cooperation, you'll stop the name calling. He treats Jade like a queen. Much better than you ever did."

"I doubt that."

"Yeah? He showed up to their wedding."

That shut him up.

He stood and handed me a business card. "Please. You can reach me here. Let Jade know I really do need to talk to her." Then he walked out the door.

Talon returned holding his smoothie. "Good riddance."

I said nothing. I was having a push me-pull you ambivalence about Colin. He'd been a jerk, no doubt, but he hadn't deserved what Tom Simpson put him through.

"You need a ride home?" he asked.

"I've got my car. How's Jade? I didn't want to ask in front of Colin. I'm not sure he knows she's pregnant."

"She's okay. Still nauseated, but that's nothing new."

"What did the doctor say about the bleeding and cramping?"

"Apparently it can be normal in the first trimester, but if it happens again, I have to take her right back in. In fact, he wants to see her every week now instead of every four weeks, which is fine with me."

"I'll be able to drive her to Grand Junction."

"No way. I'll be taking her myself," Talon said.

I nodded.

"They did an ultrasound, and the baby is growing normally and the heartbeat was fine, so we're out of the woods. For now, at least."

"Thank God."

"I know," Talon agreed. "After all Jade's been through with this pregnancy so far while Melanie's has been nearly symptom-free. If she'd lost this child..."

"Don't go there," I said. "She's fine."

"I know. And she's young. We have all the time in the world to have kids. But still..."

"I know." I stood. "Can I see Jade?"

"If you want. Aren't you going home from here?"

"I have a few errands."

"Okay. Come on, then. She's in the car."

I followed my brother to his car that was parked around the corner. Jade sat in the passenger seat. She smiled when she saw me. Talon got in and started the engine, and Jade rolled down the window.

"Hey," I said. "How are you feeling?"

"Can you believe a smoothie actually sounded good to me?" She took the plastic cup Talon offered. "I'm just so relieved."

"We all are," I said.

"Maybe this is a good thing," she said. "I'm feeling a little bit better morning sickness-wise."

I eyed her.

"Just trying to look on the bright side. God knows we all need to be doing that these days."

"True enough," I agreed. "I've got a few errands to run. I'll check in on you when I get home, okay? Unless you need me now?"

"Don't be silly. Your brother's been hovering over me like a hawk. I'll be fine. I need to go home, see my boys—"

"They're at school," I reminded her.

"Right. I've got pregnancy brain." She laughed.

"I can grab them from school on my way home if you want."

"No. Let them finish the day. I'm just being a little overly emotional."

I smiled. "I think you're entitled."

Talon revved the engine a little.

"That must be my cue to let you guys go." I leaned in and kissed Jade's cheek. "I'll be home soon."

They drove off toward the ranch.

I didn't actually have a lot of errands, just a stop to pick up some of my favorite moisturizer that had run out a few days ago. That would take five minutes.

I stood right in the middle of downtown Snow Creek, Colorado. A sweet little town—or so we'd all thought, until we learned our mayor and my esteemed uncle, our city attorney, had been leading double psycho lives. You'd miss it if you took a long blink while driving through. I was parked on a side street. Parking on the main drag was almost always impossible. The small gym where I'd worked out was a few buildings down from the smoothie shop. Only a block away began the residential area, and who should live right on that first block?

Bryce Simpson.

The Simpson house.

I could walk there in less than five minutes. I could knock

on the door. Bryce would be home, unless he was still at our house meeting with Joe and Ryan. I checked my watch. After one o'clock. Surely he'd be home by now.

My feet itched to move.

But he'd made his position very clear. He might be attracted to me, but he didn't want a relationship.

I was twenty-five years old. Still young. I didn't need to find "the one" anytime soon. I didn't need to have kids anytime soon. I had two nephews, and soon I'd have two more. I could be a doting aunt and not have any of the actual responsibility.

Could I be satisfied with a purely sexual relationship? Even if I could, would Bryce be open to it? He'd probably spew a bunch of "I can't just fuck my best friend's sister" crap at me.

I touched my lips lightly. I could still feel his passionate kiss, still feel his lips on my body, still feel his erection inside me, easing the empty ache.

Again, my feet twitched. So easily I could let them walk the block and a half to Bryce's home. So easily I could knock on that door, look into those sparkling blue eyes, see how much he still wanted me.

And he'd want me. Sex and passion like we'd shared doesn't always happen, and it sure hadn't been one-sided.

I sighed.

And then I let my feet move forward.

# CHAPTER TWENTY

**Bryce**

Not a number I recognized. I nodded to my mother and walked away from her to take the call.

"Hello?"

"Is this Bryce Simpson?"

"Speaking. Who is this?"

"Ted Morse, Mr. Simpson."

Morse. Right. The big-time banker father of Colin Morse, my father's final victim.

I cleared my throat. "What can I do for you?"

"You can meet with me. I have information you're going to want."

He did? "Why don't you tell me over the phone? I'm listening."

"This is sensitive information."

"So? I assure you my phone is not tapped."

"How can you be so sure? The FBI is probably watching everyone associated with Mathias, Wade, Madigan, and your father."

I moved my phone away from my ear and stared at it. Was I bugged? Could a cell phone be bugged? I had no idea. Morse was probably pulling my leg, but could I take that chance? I put the phone back to my ear. "I doubt that."

"Trust me. The Feds are always listening. I won't speak of this over the phone."

"Well, if they *are* listening, they now know you have information for me."

No response.

Did this guy think I was stupid?

"This conversation is over," I said, ending the call.

Yeah, hanging up was immature, but I had enough on my mind. First, the Feds had no reason to be watching me. I was not my father, and my father was dead and cremated. Second, the case was closed. All the masterminds behind it were dead, and the human-trafficking ring had been busted. The kids and women had been rescued and returned home.

The end.

The fucking end.

All that remained was the fallout for people like me.

"Fuck you," I said aloud to my phone before stuffing it back into my pocket.

Then a knock on the door. I walked back toward my mother in the living room, just as she was opening the door.

"Marjorie! How nice to see you. Won't you come in?"

"Thank you, Mrs. Simpson." She entered.

"Please, it's Evelyn. What can I do for you?"

"I was in town, so I wanted to stop by and see how you all are doing."

"We're taking it one day at a time, as I'm sure you are as well."

Marj nodded. "How is Bryce? And Henry?"

"Bryce is fine," I said, entering the living room. "And Henry's napping."

Marj reddened a bit. "Hi there."

"To what do we owe the pleasure?" I asked.

*Shit. Really, Bryce? Did you really just say that? Since when do you speak like an aristocrat?*

"Just in town going to the gym," she said. "Thought I'd see how you, Henry, and your mom are doing."

"We're fine," I said dryly.

"Would you like to see Henry?" Mom asked. "He should be awake by now, and he's probably hungry."

"I'd love that," she said, "if you don't mind."

"Sure. Come on back to the nursery."

Marj followed my mom down the small hallway as I looked around. Our humble abode was nothing compared to the sprawling Steel ranch house. Talon and Jade lived in the biggest house on the ranch, the one the Steels had grown up in. Joe had long since built his own home and didn't want to move back into the main house. Ryan had lived in the guesthouse behind the main house—where I'd be moving if I accepted the offer—until he and Ruby married. They now lived in their own place on the ranch.

No, I wasn't embarrassed about my home. Only embarrassed that, at thirty-eight years of age, I didn't have my own.

I truly had nothing to offer Marjorie Steel, who was used to having everything. She was heiress to one quarter of the Steel fortune.

All the more reason not to have a relationship with her.

I could take the Steels' offer, live in the guesthouse with Henry and my mom. I'd be damned close to Marjorie Steel, though.

Damn.

Damn.

Damn.

I walked toward Henry's room.

"He's gotten so big!" Marjorie squealed as my mother pulled a smiling Henry out of his crib. "And still such a good disposition too."

"He's the easiest baby in the world," my mom said. "Bryce was a handful. He had colic and was always wailing. But this little guy"—she cooed—"none of that."

For a reason unknown to me, I was slightly embarrassed when my mother told Marjorie I'd been a handful as a baby. Nearly four decades ago and certainly nothing I had any control over. Still, I warmed a bit in my cheeks.

*Ridiculous. Get over yourself.*

"Hi, sweetie," Marj said to Henry. "Do you remember me? I took care of you a couple times."

Henry rewarded her with a sloppy grin.

"Well, look at you!" Marj exclaimed. "You've got your top front teeth! You're such a cutie!" She turned to my mother. "He's so beautiful."

"Looks a lot like Bryce at that age. Towheaded and those amazing blue eyes." She sighed. "Just like Tom."

Marjorie tensed a bit but didn't say anything.

"Mom..." I began.

"There's no denying it," my mother said. "I don't mean to make either of you uncomfortable, but Bryce, you look so much like your father did at your age. I have an old photo of Tom as a baby around here somewhere. Put his, Bryce's, and Henry's baby photos in a row, and you'd swear you're looking at identical triplets born three generations in a row."

"Genetics are amazing," Marj said. "Just look at my dad and Joe. And Talon, for that matter, though Joe resembles my dad the most. We just found out Melanie is having a boy, so I wonder if the same thing will happen or if the baby will come out blond-haired and green-eyed like his mama."

"A boy! Little boys are just the best, aren't they, Henry?" my mom said, kissing Henry's cheek. "How is Melanie doing?"

"She's great. She's had a nearly eventless pregnancy, which is amazing for her age."

"Forty isn't that old," my mom said. "I'd love to see forty again."

"I know, and Melanie looks ten years younger, but her doctors say that forty is old in the reproductive world. This may be her and Joe's only chance for a biological child."

"Oh, goodness. Well, then, I'm thankful it's been so easy on her. And Jade?"

"Not as easy," Marj said. "But she's hanging in there."

"I was sick as a dog when I was carrying Bryce," my mother said. "But the outcome is always worth it."

"How is Jade doing now?" I interjected, feeling I needed to do something other than stare at the three of them as if I were invisible.

"She's good," Marj said. "I just saw her. Talon stopped in town to get her a smoothie."

"Was something wrong?" my mom asked.

"Oh. You didn't tell her?" Marj said.

Why hadn't I told her? My mother loved the Steels.

"Didn't want you to worry, Mom." I quickly filled her in and then realized why I hadn't told her in the first place.

I'd been intentionally keeping Marjorie at a distance, and Jade was Marjorie's best friend. Talking about Jade made me think of Marjorie. Not that I wasn't thinking about Marjorie pretty much twenty-four-seven anyway, but I had to try.

"I'm glad everything's okay with Jade and the baby," Mom was saying. "I'm going to feed Henry his lunch. Would you like to stay, Marj? I was planning to make BLTs with avocado."

Marjorie fidgeted a little. Was I supposed to say something here? Did I look like an asshole if I didn't?

"Yeah, please stay," I said, trying not to sound too eager. Instead, my words came out monotonous, as if I were a robot.

"I just had a smoothie," she said. "I'm not overly hungry, but thanks all the same."

"Oh, no worries. I suppose a BLT is too simple for a world-class chef like you." Mom laughed.

"I hope you're kidding. I love BLTs."

"Of course I was kidding, dear. You know you are welcome here anytime. All of you Steels are."

Again, I felt compelled to add to the conversation. "Of course you are."

Marjorie smiled at me then. A soft smile, behind which I couldn't quite discern the meaning.

"I know you need to get this little guy fed," she said, "so I'll be going. I'm sure Jade will need me at home."

*But I need you here.*

The words were lodged in my throat, yearning to be set free.

But I wasn't ready to acknowledge the truth in them.

I would never be ready.

# CHAPTER TWENTY-ONE

**Marjorie**

What a mistake that had been. I couldn't get out of the Simpsons' house quickly enough. Away from Bryce, the human icicle. He'd done a one-eighty from the heat we'd shared. Now he was cold as a tit on a boar, which frightened me.

Not in a scary way, but I was frightened for his son. I hoped he could show his son the love he apparently couldn't show me.

I scoffed aloud as I opened my car door. Love? What Bryce and I had shared had nothing to do with love. I might be having serious feelings for him, but they obviously were not returned. Not in the slightest. I had the sinking feeling they never would be.

I had to be okay with that. Right now, Henry was way more important than I was. He needed his dad, and if that meant I stayed away from Bryce, so be it. Of course, if he took my brothers' offer and moved into the guesthouse, that endeavor would be difficult.

But I'd do it. I had to. For the baby's sake.

And speaking of babies, I needed to get home and take care of Jade. But first I'd pick up the boys from school. It was a little early, but it seemed silly to make them ride the bus out to the ranch when I was here in town. Plus they'd be anxious to hear how their mom was doing.

★ ★ ★

Two little boys in tow, I arrived back at the main house on Steel Acres Ranch. Donny went running in to see Jade. Dale, always quiet, walked in with me.

"How was school?" I asked him.

"Okay," he said.

Dale was in fifth grade and Donny in second. They'd been through hell, and the family as a whole—with Dale's and Donny's input, of course—had decided to keep the boys' ordeal quiet. The FBI had plenty of evidence to put everyone involved—everyone who wasn't already dead—behind bars, so there was no need to drag the boys through any more horror.

They were both getting the help they needed, however, unlike their father. My father had kept Talon's ordeal so quiet that my brothers hadn't been able to get the help they needed to deal with it when they were young. My dad had had his reasons—reasons he ended up dying for—but it had cost Talon, Joe, and Ryan. I thanked God my brothers were all healing and content now.

They'd all found true love, as well, and that helped too.

True love.

It seemed so elusive.

At least it was with Bryce Simpson. I knew what I needed to do. Get out there, like Jade had said. But not now. I was staying until Jade had safely given birth, and probably for a few months after that, unless Felicia returned or they hired a nanny.

So I'd be celibate for the next several months.

Not an issue.

At least that was what I kept telling myself.

"You want a snack?" I asked Dale.

He nodded. "I'll get it myself."

"Okay, sweetie." I'd found it best not to hover with Dale. He seemed more content to be quiet and alone, and Melanie had assured me that was fine. Just let him be who he was, and he'd come around. He was most likely more of an introvert than his brother even before they'd been taken.

Jade was in her bedroom, sitting up, with a smiling Donny next to her babbling about his day at school. They made a beautiful picture. Jade was only my age, and she had an instant family. She was reveling in it. She adored those boys, and she was a born mother.

"Hey, Marj," she said. "Thanks for bringing the boys home. I have some exciting news that I was just telling Donny."

"What's that?"

"Talon just got a call when we got home. The boys' adoption will be final next week. We all need to go to Grand Junction and appear in the judge's chambers, and we want you to come as well."

"What for?"

"To be the boys' godmother, of course!"

"What's a godmother?" Donny asked.

"A godmother is just another person who loves you as much as Daddy and I do." Jade gave him a hug.

I laughed. "And a godmother is another person who gives you presents."

"So then I have three mothers?"

"That's one way to look at it," Jade said. "Your mommy in

heaven, me, and Auntie Marj."

"Cool! We should tell Dale. I'll go get him." He scrambled off the bed.

"He's in the kitchen having a snack," I said. Then, when Donny was gone, I turned to Jade. "I'm honored. Really."

"Who else would I choose? I want you to be the baby's godmother as well."

Warm emotion rolled through me.

But Jade continued, "If I can carry the child to term."

"Hey." I patted her hand. "Where did that come from? Tal says everything is fine and what you went through is normal."

"I know. I'm scared, though. Like majorly freaked-out scared."

I hugged her, wishing I could think of something more comforting. All I could think of was, "You're the strongest woman I know. You *will* get through this, and we'll all have another wonderful addition to the family."

She let out a sarcastic chuckle. "Me? Strong? I got humiliated at the altar, and I got over it. That's not strong. Melanie. Ruby. They are strong women."

I certainly couldn't disagree. My two other sisters-in-law had both been through hell. Melanie had been kidnapped and left to die in a locked garage with a car running, and Ruby had survived an attack by her father and had been on her own since she was fifteen years old. They were amazing.

But so was my best friend.

"You can't compare yourself to them."

"I can. And look at Melanie now. She's forty and is gliding through pregnancy. I'm at perfect childbearing age, and I'm having every problem in the book. I can't do anything right."

I pulled back and met her blue-eyed gaze. "Where is this

coming from, Jade?"

"I don't know. Well, yeah, I do. I talked to my mom on the way home from the hospital, to fill her in, and she told me how easy I was to carry."

I had no great love for Jade's mother, ex-supermodel Brooke Bailey. Merriam-Webster could have replaced the definition of "self-absorption" with a photo of Brooke, and it would be completely accurate. Seriously. Knowing her, she'd gushed about how amazing she'd felt—and looked—while carrying Jade, her only child. If she were in the vicinity at the moment, I had no doubt I'd punch her square in the nose.

"First, Brooke was younger than you are when she was pregnant with you. And second, who cares? You are *not* Brooke Bailey. I talked to Evelyn Simpson earlier today, and she said she was sick as a dog carrying Bryce. She was probably about your age when she was pregnant."

"She was younger, I think."

"See? I'm truly sorry this has been rough for you, but you *will* get through it, and then you'll have three beautiful children."

She groaned. "And then I'm done. I can't go through this again, Marj. Three is good."

"You may change your mind when you hold your baby."

"I don't know. I sure hope you don't have to go through this when you get pregnant."

"Not something I need to worry about for the near future." Or ever, it seemed like sometimes.

"Still nothing with Bryce?"

"Nope. I saw him today, and he couldn't have been more frigid toward me."

"Give him time."

"Time?"

"Well...yeah. He's been through just as much as the rest of us, and maybe more, in a way. He's just not ready right now."

"Not ready? I slept with him!" I blurted out.

Jade's blue eyes went wide. "Oh. My. God. When?"

"Last night."

"While I was at the hospital?"

I nodded.

"Well...?"

"It was amazing," I said dreamily. "I've been around the block a few times, and I've never experienced anything like being with Bryce."

"That's great!"

"Not so much. He couldn't wait to get out of here this morning. Except he couldn't, because he was meeting with Joe and Ryan. I got up to feed the boys and take them to the bus, and then I escaped here as soon as I could. He could hardly look at me, Jade. I felt like a pariah."

"But...during?"

"The fucking?"

"I was thinking lovemaking, but yeah."

It had felt like lovemaking, but I was determined not to get caught up in euphemisms. Not when he'd run like hell afterward. "He was attentive, sweet, everything wonderful you could imagine."

"Wow."

"That's it?"

"I'm just surprised," she said. "Not that the fucking was good, but that he hightailed it out of there. Bryce is a warm person, from what little I know of him."

"He is," I agreed. "Or was. A lot like Ryan, you know?

Always joking and laughing. That side of him seems to have taken a hike."

"Coinciding with learning the truth about his father, I'd guess."

"Well, of course, and I understand that. I just thought..." I stopped. What had I thought? Fact was, I hadn't really been thinking at all. I'd let my horniness be my guide, and so had he.

"You thought what?"

"Nothing. Maybe I was just in the right place at the right time. Truth is, I was determined to show him I was no longer the little girl with unicorns on her bedroom walls."

"I think you've done that."

"I thought I had too."

"Methinks unicorns are no longer the issue," Jade said.

"Then what is the issue?"

"Bryce himself. Maybe he doesn't want to saddle you with an instant family?"

"But I love Henry."

"True, and he knows that. But there's his mother, too. She's become totally dependent on him and Henry."

"I have no problem with his mother."

"You say that now..." She shook her head. "Talon was an angel while my mom was living here, but I know she got on his nerves."

"Evelyn is not Brooke Bailey. In fact, she's the anti-Brooke."

"True again."

A thought speared into my mind. Had Talon mentioned Colin to Jade? I didn't know. I'd check with him before I mentioned to her that I'd run into him at the smoothie shop. The last thing I wanted was to upset her while she was still freaking out about the pregnancy.

Donny returned, dragging Dale with him. That was my cue to leave. I needed to talk to Talon.

# CHAPTER TWENTY-TWO

**Bryce**

I joined Henry and my mother for lunch and then told her I was going for a walk to think about the Steels' offer.

Truthfully, I just wanted some alone time. In between daydreams of Marjorie, I'd been ruminating on the call from Ted Morse. What the hell did he want? If he was gunning for money, he was barking up the wrong tree. I didn't have any. The Steels had the deep pockets in this scenario, and neither they nor I owed the Morses anything.

I wasn't responsible for my father's actions.

Still, I gulped.

Ted's son had been through something unthinkable at the hands of my old man.

If I had anything close to Steel money, I'd consider giving something to Colin. But his father? Hell, no. He'd tried to frame my best friend for my father's crimes. He'd get nothing from me.

I walked along, peering through the windows of the shops on Main. I stopped at the flower shop. In the window was a bouquet of the yellow lilies I'd seen on Marjorie's kitchen table. I stood there, overwhelmed by the urge to buy flowers for her. I resisted, shoving my hands in my pockets. I didn't have money to spend on expensive flowers, and I didn't have the emotional strength to get involved with anyone—especially Marjorie Steel, who deserved everything in the world.

I wandered by the tattoo shop. I was ink free, but I'd often thought of getting one. Definitely not a phoenix. A dragon, maybe. Or an eagle. Absently, I turned the handle on the door and walked in.

"Hey," a multipierced young woman with spiky black hair greeted me. "Can I help you?"

"Just thinking. Do you have any design books I can look at?"

She pointed to a table where several thick books sat. "Knock yourself out."

I picked up the thickest book and sat down, plunking it on my lap. I thumbed through the pages quickly, waiting for something to catch my attention.

Something did.

Not a tattoo I'd consider getting, but the phoenix Ruby's father had on his forearm, the very tattoo that had both tormented and saved Talon during his months in captivity. Theodore Mathias had gotten the tattoo years ago, using the name Milo Sanchez.

I quickly turned the page. I couldn't deny it was a fascinatingly beautiful tattoo, but to the Steels and to me, it meant so much more than that. It was a symbol of an evil man, a man we all wished we could forget.

Maybe a tattoo wasn't such a good idea after all. I had no idea what image I was looking for. Most probably went into a shop already knowing what they were looking for.

If only I could find something that could negate my father.

Could negate...

I slammed the book shut. This was stupid. Completely

stupid. A tattoo wasn't some magic charm that could fix my life.

Maybe it was time to talk to someone. Really talk to someone. I put the book back on the table and walked out. As I opened the door, I met a familiar gaze.

A gaze that was only familiar to me because of my father. Colin Morse.

His hair had grown out from the shaved head my father had given him. I cleared my throat. "Excuse me."

Colin cringed but held his ground.

Just what I didn't need. Another reminder of how much I resembled that psychopath who'd sired me.

What to do? Escape? Or say hello? Or say I'm sorry my father put you through hell?

Nothing seemed right. This innocent young man not yet three decades old had been brutalized beyond my imagination.

At the hands of my father.

He said nothing, just froze, the door still open, staring at me. Did he know his father had contacted me? Did he know what it could be about? I wanted to ask him all these things, but the words lodged in my throat.

"Hey!" the girl behind the counter yelled. "Shut the door, will you? It's freaking cold outside."

The weather was actually nice for early February, but Haley—as her nametag said—was wearing a black camisole crop top, no doubt to show off the triple piercing in her belly button.

I stepped back in and allowed Colin to pass. "Sorry," I said to Haley. Then, to Colin, because I felt like a fool not acknowledging him, "Getting a tattoo?"

He nodded.

"You Colin?" Haley asked.

He nodded again.

"Come on in. Trevor's ready for you. You're a virgin, right?"

I swung my head around and stared at Haley.

"Yeah," Colin said.

"A virgin?" I couldn't help asking.

"Virgin skin. Never tatted," Haley explained.

"Oh." I nodded. "I guess I'm a virgin too."

"Did you see anything you liked?" she asked.

"Not really. Nothing stood out to me."

"Well, you think about it." She nodded to Colin. "Follow me."

I should leave. I should walk right out that door. But I couldn't. Everything in me forced my body to immobility.

I wanted to know what Colin was having tattooed on his body. Where he was having it tattooed on his body. And why he was doing it here, in Snow Creek, the home of his brutalizer.

Once Colin had disappeared into the back, Haley returned. "You still here?"

"Yeah."

She lifted her brow. "And...why?"

"Curious," I said.

"About what?"

"About which tattoo Colin is getting."

"You a friend of his? Because he didn't say one word to you."

"Not a friend, exactly. An acquaintance."

"Then what do you care?"

I didn't have a lot of money to spare, but I pulled out a twenty-dollar bill from my wallet and pushed it toward Haley.

"Just tell me what he's getting."

She took the money and slipped it beneath her crop top. "Sure. It's not like we have a tattoo artist and client confidentiality thing. You didn't need to pay me."

Fuck. But I didn't ask for the money back. "So?"

"It's something he designed himself. Pretty artistic, actually." She pulled out a piece of paper and slid it over to me.

I held back a gasp.

It was a skull. A skull missing the entire left side of the cranium. All in black except for the eyes of a snake slithering out from the break. I'd seen similar images, but the snake usually had red eyes.

Not this one.

Blue eyes.

Like my father's.

Like mine.

Underneath were words in block letters.

*Save Yourself.*

# CHAPTER TWENTY-THREE

**Marjorie**

I found Talon in his office, on the phone. He motioned me in, so I sat down across from his desk. The chair was warm.

Was this where Bryce had sat earlier?

Maybe, but the warmth had nothing to do with that. It had been hours ago. God, I was being so ridiculous.

Talon ended his call. "Is Jade okay?"

I nodded. "The boys are with her, so I left. I need to ask you something."

"What?"

"Did you tell Jade about Colin?"

"No. Crap. Did you?"

"No. I wanted to ask you first."

"Good. I don't want anything upsetting her right now. She's still freaked out about possibly losing the baby." He sighed. "Frankly, so am I."

"You won't lose the baby."

"There are no guarantees, Sis, and she's had a tough time."

"I know. It doesn't help that Brooke has been in her face, telling her what an easy pregnancy she had."

Talon ruffled his fingers through his hair. "That dumb bitch! Sorry. I know she's my mother-in-law, but damn."

"She's a piece of work," I agreed. "Jade is trying so hard

to have a relationship with her, but Brooke just has no clue how to be a parent."

"No shit," he said. "I'll take care of Brooke."

"Talon..."

"For God's sake, Marj. I'm not going to do anything to her. Jade is determined to have a relationship with her, and I support that. But Brooke needs to focus on her daughter for once in her life."

"Preaching to the choir here, Tal."

"I'll take care of it."

"In the meantime, I feel I should tell you. Colin wants to talk to Jade. He wants me to arrange it."

"Yeah. Not going to happen."

"I figured that's what you'd say. Apparently that's why he's in Snow Creek."

"He could pick up a phone."

"He seemed to want to see her in person."

"He doesn't have her number anyway," Talon went on. "I plan to keep it that way."

"Tal, you of all peo—"

"Stop right there. I've no love lost for Colin Morse, but I get it. I'm the only one who probably truly gets it, other than my sons." He winced. "God."

"Tal, don't."

"It's okay. You can't hide. Melanie taught me that. But Colin and Jade have a past, one that ended with her heartbroken and humiliated. He can stay the hell away from her."

"I tend to agree."

"Why did he come to you?"

"I'm not sure he meant to. He happened to come into the smoothie shop while I was there. And..."

"And what?"

"We used to be friends, Tal. He was engaged to my best friend. I thought he was a good guy. I've known him since freshman year of college. I was as surprised as Jade when he didn't show up for their wedding. That wasn't like him."

"Well, I'm glad he didn't show up. Or Jade and I wouldn't have met."

"Me too. You and Jade belong together. But still..."

"Look, he got cold feet. He's not the first guy to be an ass on his wedding day. And now—especially now—he has regrets. Hell, he had regrets when he showed up here and I gave him a fucking black eye."

I cleared my throat. "Not your finest moment."

"Maybe not, but I have no regrets. He deserved it for hurting Jade."

"That's not why you did it, Tal."

He chuckled. "You're right, Sis. I did it out of jealousy. In the heat of the moment. And I got tased and locked up for it."

"You did."

"Why are you telling me this? Do you think Jade should talk to Colin?"

"I don't know, honestly. I just know that at one time, Colin was a good guy, and now, after all he's been through..."

"He doesn't deserve mercy just because he's been through hell. I never got a shred of mercy."

"Talon, no one knew. You didn't want mercy."

"No, I didn't. Did you think that maybe he doesn't either?"

I scratched my head. "No. I honestly didn't think of that."

"Did you think maybe he's blaming Jade for what he's been through? If she hadn't started a relationship with me, none of this would have happened."

Now I felt like a dolt. "No, I guess not."

"Don't blame yourself. But trust me. When you go through something traumatizing, you play the 'what if?' game a lot. I did it for years."

"I'm sorry, Tal."

"Don't be."

"But you have an outlook that I don't."

"And Sis, I'm glad you don't."

I nodded, biting my lip. "Do you think Colin sees Jade as something from his former life, a life he's desperate to cling to?"

"Something like that. I don't know. I'm guessing. But it makes a certain amount of sense, don't you think?"

I couldn't deny it. "So rather than allow him to see Jade, who is part of his former life, he needs to deal with the life he has now."

"Yup. And this is coming from someone who didn't deal with his own shit for decades. That's way too long, by the way."

I nodded. Nothing to say to that. Poor Talon had suffered without help throughout the majority of his life, and I'd been ignorant of everything until only several short months ago.

He went on, "I don't want anyone fucking with Jade's emotions right now, and that's what Colin would do. That's what Brooke is doing. I'm putting a stop to it. Jade has enough to deal with at the moment."

I nodded again. "I get it, and I agree. Colin won't see Jade."

"Or talk to her."

"Right. I have his number." I pulled out the card he'd given me at the smoothie shop.

"Give it to me. I'll make sure he's blocked on Jade's phone, just in case he has her number."

I handed it to him.

It was the right decision. For Jade.

But something invisible swept over the back of my neck. Colin wasn't going to disappear. Something was going to go down.

This wasn't over.

# CHAPTER TWENTY-FOUR

**Bryce**

I'd flipped through that damned book, waiting for a design to speak to me, and now one was screaming my name.

Colin's design.

This was the tattoo I wanted.

How sick was that? This image was no doubt born of the damage my father had inflicted on its designer. So why the hell was it speaking to me?

"He designed this himself?"

"That's what he says." Haley shrugged. "It's not like we check copyrights and trademarks here. Someone wants the Coke logo, that's what we give them."

"Someone actually wanted the Coke logo tattooed on their body?"

"Sure. We don't ask questions. We just do the work."

"How much does a tattoo cost?"

"Depends. Usually a minimum of about three hundred."

Had I heard correctly? "Dollars?"

"No. Three hundred potatoes." She rolled her eyes. "Of course dollars. Jeez."

That settled that. No tattoo for me, at least not today. Mom and I needed to be frugal until I started earning income.

Speaking of income, I had no choice but to accept the

Steels' offer. To do otherwise would make me a selfish ass. I'd just have to stay far, far away from Marjorie.

With her in the main house and me in the guesthouse, it wasn't going to be easy.

I took out my phone and called Joe.

★ ★ ★

Dinner with Joe and Melanie at the best restaurant in Grand Junction wasn't how I'd planned to spend the evening, but Mom insisted I go. I deserved it, she'd said, for taking the Steels' offer and making a better life for my son.

Melanie radiated health and energy, her blond hair lustrous and thick around her shoulders and her cheeks a rosy pink. She'd just entered the third trimester of her pregnancy, and she was ravenous, devouring a sixteen-ounce hunk of prime rib.

"I can hardly keep up with her," Joe said, laughing.

"Please," Melanie said, having just swallowed. "The day I have your appetite is the day I weigh three hundred pounds."

"You've hardly gained any weight at all that I can see," I said truthfully. "Except your belly, of course."

"Ha!" she said. "I'm just good at hiding it. I'll be hitting the gym big-time with Ruby after the baby is born."

"You'll look perfect as always," Joe said, his gaze upon his wife.

Love. God, they were so in love it was almost sickening.

I was truly happy for both of them, but being in close proximity with all the Steel brothers, who were as pussy-whipped as all get-out, wasn't going to be the easiest thing to deal with, especially not while I was lusting after their baby sister.

"We figure you can start next week," Joe said. "That'll give you a few days to get settled."

"Hold up," I said. "It'll take some time to move everything to the ranch."

"Don't worry about that. We're hiring movers. You and Evelyn won't have to lift a finger."

I twirled my mashed potatoes with my fork. "We still have to pack."

"They'll handle that."

"I'm perfectly cap—"

"Yeah, yeah, yeah. We know you are. But we're happy to do this. It's a write-off, you know?"

I sighed. "Look. I'm not complaining, but you're making this too easy on me. I'm beginning to feel like a charity case."

Joe shook his head, and the emotion in his brown eyes was almost...hurt. "None of us think of you that way. We've been through this."

"I know, but—"

"No buts. You accepted the offer. We need you, and if we can make the change easier on you in the process, we want to do it."

I opened my mouth to respond when my phone buzzed. I looked down. Shit. Ted Morse again.

"Do you need to take that?" Joe asked.

"I'm not taking it. It's Ted Morse."

"Colin's dad?" Joe furrowed his brow. "Fucking bastard."

"Jonah," Melanie admonished. "This is a nice place."

"Sorry. But you know what I think of that asshole."

"Jonah!"

"He's right," I agreed. "The guy tried to have him framed."

"I get it," she said. "I don't disagree. Trust me."

"What the hell does he want?"

Melanie just rolled her eyes, apparently tired of arguing about language in a rather quiet upscale restaurant.

"He called me this morning. Said he had information for me and wanted to meet."

"And you said..."

"Hell, no. Sorry, Melanie."

"It's okay. I give up," she said.

"I told him to give it to me over the phone, but he said the FBI might have tapped us."

"The FBI? The case is settled."

"That's what I told him. Then I hung up."

Joe shook his head. "He's looking for a payoff. The guy's a mercenary if I ever met one."

"Then why call me? I don't have anything."

"Maybe he got wind of our offer."

"How would he be able to do that?"

"I have no idea, but I think I'll have those PIs, Mills and Johnson, check out our houses just in case. They're expensive but worth every penny. They can check your place too."

"You don't need to. Especially if we're moving."

"Why don't you just meet with him?" Melanie asked.

"Because he's just looking for cash," Joe said.

"You're most likely right," she said, "but what if he actually has some information? Couldn't he ask for cash over the phone?"

"Good point," Bryce said, "and he's got to know I don't have any money."

"I don't buy it," Joe said. "He's up to something."

"If he is," Melanie said, "don't you think it's better that we know exactly *what* he's up to? You and Bryce could meet him together. Take Rosie with you."

I laughed. Rosie was Joe's Glock 23 that was almost always strapped to his ankle.

"Not a bad idea, actually," I said. "My first instinct was to ignore him, but I have to admit I'm curious."

"I don't trust the man," Joe said.

"I know that. With good reason." I took a sip of my bourbon. "I don't trust him either, but if he's right, and the Feds are still watching all of us, we need to know why."

"He's bluffing," Joe said.

"Then let's call him on it," I said.

Before Joe could answer, the server popped by to take our dessert and coffee orders. Once we'd ordered, I said, "Excuse me for a minute. I'll go out into the lobby and return his call. I'll see if I can get anything out of him."

"You sure?" Joe asked.

"Yeah. Your lovely wife convinced me." I smiled and stood.

Once I found a quiet corner in the lobby, I returned the call.

"Ted Morse."

"Bryce Simpson returning your call," I said curtly.

"Change your mind about meeting me?"

"I did. Tell me where and when, and I'll be there."

"Let's get one thing straight. I'll be talking to you and only you. Don't bring any brawn with you."

I was a little offended. He didn't consider me brawn? I could take him out with a look. "Brawn? You mean the Steels?"

"Those three are animals."

"Jonah Steel is an animal who could have had you arrested for extortion," I reminded him.

"You think that scares me? I have the best attorneys in the business."

"And you think the Steels don't?" This guy was a trip. He might be worth millions, but the Steels had passed a billion.

No response.

"You're well off. Why you thought it was a good idea to try to blackmail the Steels is beyond me."

"They hurt my son."

"Talon gave him an ass whooping."

"For trying to see his fiancée."

"His *ex*-fiancée," I reminded Ted. Words lodged in my throat. *That was nothing compared to what my father did to him.* I didn't say it. I couldn't. But it was true. So very true.

"You know what I think, Ted?" I said. "I think you blame me for what my father did to Colin. I can almost understand that, being a father myself. So why are you helping me? Why do you want to give me information? Something here stinks big-time."

He paused a few seconds. Then, "This isn't over. The Feds are asking questions. Asking me questions because I won't allow them to talk to my son."

"Your son is an adult. You have no say in who talks to him."

"I've held them off so far, but the bust on the island wasn't completely successful. My son isn't safe. You're not safe, Simpson. And neither are the Steels."

# CHAPTER TWENTY-FIVE

**Marjorie**

Jade was feeling better, so after getting the boys off to school, I drove to Grand Junction to visit my mother. I tried my best to get to the center once a week, but with Jade and the boys needing me, I didn't always make it.

My mother, with a wrinkle-free face and only a few strands of silver in her nearly black hair, looked beautiful as always. Also, as always, she carried around her realistic infant doll—a doll she was convinced was actually me.

"Hi, Mom," I said as cheerfully as I could.

"Shh," she said, rocking the doll. "I need to get Angela down for her nap."

I nodded. What did she think when I called her Mom? I had no idea, but she never argued the point. Since Dale and Donny had appeared in our lives, they had become young Joe and Talon to her. Ryan no longer existed in her mind, as he wasn't a child of her body.

Ryan had come to see her once. After all, she'd been his mother for the first seven years of his life.

He'd never returned.

It was too painful for him.

It was painful for all of us. We'd all thought her dead until recently.

Daphne Steel laid the doll in the bassinet beside her bed. Then she turned to me. "What brings you here?"

"I just wanted to see how you're doing."

"The usual. The boys are at camp again. I miss them."

Her doctors had told us it was best to play along. "Yes," I said. "I do too."

"But Brad came by."

I stopped myself from jolting. I didn't want to upset her. She'd never mentioned my father since his death months ago. "Did he?"

"Yes, he did. It was nice to see him. He's at camp with the boys most of the time. Such a good father."

I had a few bones to pick with that one, but I didn't voice them. Brad Steel hadn't been the ultimate father, though he had stuck around until I turned eighteen. He'd kept secrets from us, though. Major secrets, not the least of which was that he and our mother were both alive. He'd also kept Talon from getting the help he needed after his abduction.

I could never forgive my father. But my mother? Her insanity was not her fault. She'd been driven to it by my father and his actions.

"When did Father come by?" I asked.

"It was just yesterday, I think. He looks different."

"How?"

"His hair has gone gray, mostly. But you know, he's getting older. We all are." She smiled and then cocked her head to the side.

Looking at my mother was like seeing myself in thirty-plus years. I was the only child who resembled her. Joe and Talon both looked more like our father, and of course Ryan had no genetic relation to her.

My mother spoke again. "He seemed shorter too. But you know, we shrink as we age, right?"

"How much shorter?"

"I don't know. I could look him right in the eye."

Odd. My father was at least six inches taller than my mother. I definitely had some questions, but I didn't want to confuse her.

"Are you sure it was Dad?"

"Of course. Who else would it be?"

Who else indeed? I'd ask the nurse on duty later. "Would you like me to read to you?"

Reading was often how we passed our time. She lived in her own little world, so she didn't understand anything I told her about Joe, Talon, and me or what was actually going on in our lives. She didn't know they'd gotten married and were both expecting children.

"That would be nice," she said. "Let's read Austen today."

My mother loved Jane Austen and Charles Dickens. We'd already gotten through *Emma* and *Great Expectations*. Now we were working on *Oliver Twist* and *Pride and Prejudice*. Funny how she always remembered which book we were reading.

I picked the book up off her table, sat down, and opened it.

Before I could begin, though, a nurse came in. "Time for your medication, Mrs. Steel."

"Could it wait? This lovely lady was just about to read to me, and the pills make me so sleepy."

"I suppose I can give you another fifteen minutes." The nurse smiled.

"Wait," I said. "Could I speak to you for a moment?" I nodded toward the hallway.

"Of course, Ms. Steel."

"Excuse me, Mother. I'll be right back." I followed the nurse into the hallway.

"Did a man come to see my mother yesterday?" I asked her.

"I'm sorry. I didn't work yesterday. But you can check the visitors' log when you leave."

"Perfect. Thanks." I would do exactly that.

★ ★ ★

"I'd like to see who visited my mother in the last week," I told the desk clerk after the nurse had come back to give my mother her meds.

"Name?"

"Hers? Daphne Steel."

"Okay." He grabbed a clipboard. "Uh...looks like her last visitor was Marjorie Steel last week."

"That's me."

"There you go, then."

"She said she had a male visitor yesterday."

"Not possible. Every visitor has to sign in."

I tapped my fingers on the counter, biting my lower lip. My mother could easily be mistaken. She was mentally ill and lived in her own little reality. She could have imagined a male visitor.

Yet something nagged at me. If she were going to imagine a male visitor, wouldn't she imagine someone she knew? She *said* it was my father, but she also said he didn't look like himself.

"Can you tell me which aide was assigned to her yesterday?" I asked. "The nurse I talked to today said she was off."

"Uh...sure." He brought up a different screen on his computer. "Lori was here in the morning, and Barry for the late-afternoon shift. Mary Ann was on night shift, but we don't allow visitors at night."

"Is there any way I can get in touch with Lori and Barry?"

"I can't give out personal information. Sorry."

I twisted my lips. "All right. When will they be back on duty?"

"Lori is here now. She just clocked in."

"Great. May I see her?"

"I'll call her for you. Go wait in the lobby."

"Sure. Thanks."

I took a seat in the small waiting area. A few minutes later, a round middle-aged woman greeted me.

"I'm Lori. Are you Ms. Steel?"

I stood and held out my hand. "Marjorie, please. Thank you for talking to me. I understand you were on duty yesterday, caring for my mother?"

"Yeah. Mrs. Steel is never any problem."

"I'm glad to hear that. I do have a question, though. I just saw my mother, and she says she had a male visitor yesterday. A man with gray hair?"

"Not while I was on the shift, ma'am."

I truly hated it when older people—or anyone, for that matter—called me ma'am. "She says it was my father, but my father is deceased. And he never had more than a few strands of gray hair."

"I don't mean to upset you, Ms. Steel, but she probably imagined it."

"She definitely could have, but wouldn't she have imagined my father as she remembered him? She even said he'd grown shorter. How does that make any sense?"

"She's not well, ma'am."

Yeah, yeah, yeah. I knew all that. And I had to remember that she saw Dale and Donny as young Joe and Talon, despite the fact that the boys were green-eyed and blond. Still, something niggled at me. "Do you know when Barry is coming in?"

"I only keep track of my own schedule. You can ask at the front desk."

"Okay. Thank you for your time, Lori."

"No problem." She smiled and walked out of the waiting area.

After finding out Barry would be in the next day for the afternoon shift, I left. Jade and the boys would be needing me.

I jumped when my phone dinged with a text message from Talon.

*Come home. We need to talk.*

# CHAPTER TWENTY-SIX

**Bryce**

I squirmed in my seat like a high school boy. Marjorie was on her way home to join in the impromptu meeting at the main ranch house. Joe, Talon, Ryan, and I sat in Talon's office discussing my phone call with Ted Morse. He'd hung up after the ominous statement that none of us were safe.

"He's bluffing," Ryan said.

"That's my take too," I said, "but we still need to look into this. I have a son. Tal, you have two kids, and you and Joe both have one on the way. They can't be in harm's way."

"Agreed," Joe said.

I'd argued with them when they'd suggested bringing Marjorie into this discussion. She was so young, had been through so much already. Why worry her more? But they'd ultimately overruled me. She was their sister, after all. Their sister, and nothing to me.

Even I didn't buy that one.

Especially not when she knocked softly at the door and entered after Talon's, "Come in, Sis."

She walked in, looking so effortlessly beautiful as always. Her long dark hair was pulled into a high ponytail, and she wore skinny jeans, short cowboy boots, and a light-green tank top with lacy straps. Man, did those lean, muscled arms look great in a tank. And her chest...

My groin tightened at the sight.

She walked in stoically. "I'm feeling a little like the odd man out here, no pun intended."

"Some stuff might be going down."

"You're telling me. I was visiting Mom this morning."

"How is she?" Joe asked.

"Same," Marjorie said. "But she claims she had a male visitor yesterday. A guy with gray hair who she says was Dad."

"Gray hair?" Talon said.

"Yup. Apparently Dad got shorter too."

"Well, we know it wasn't Dad," Ryan said. "He's dead. We all witnessed it."

"Maybe she imagined it?" Talon said.

"She could have," Marj said. "But if that were the case, wouldn't she have imagined him as he looked the last time she actually saw him?"

"So you think someone was actually there."

"There's no log of anyone visiting her. I checked. But someone must have been there, someone she could describe, even if she thinks it was Dad. You know, how she thinks the boys are you two"—she nodded toward Talon and Joe—"even though they're blond?"

"Okay," Ryan said. "This all just got weirder." He then explained to Marj about the phone call I'd had with Ted Morse last night.

Marjorie's eyes widened, and her beautiful face paled a bit. "Wow," was all she said.

"We all know Ted Morse is a mercenary," Talon said. "And a dick. He'll say whatever he needs to say to make a buck."

"I went to school with Colin," Marjorie said. "The Morses

are hardly hurting for cash."

"That doesn't mean they don't want more," Joe said. "Some people are always looking for an easy way to add to their coffers. I've seen a lot of this since I took over the beef ranch. Plus, the bastard is willing to resort to extortion, as I know firsthand. He's not a good man."

"I know." Marjorie shook her head. "But Colin is. Or at least was."

"Good men don't usually leave their fiancées at the altar," Joe said.

"True," she said. "And he regretted it, which makes me wonder if..."

"Damn," Talon said. "If Ted had something to do with that as well."

"Right," she said.

"I guess I owe him thanks, then," Talon said. "If Jade had married Colin, I wouldn't have her now."

"It's just conjecture," Marj said. "I could be totally wrong. He told me his father called him a coward after he ditched the wedding."

"Yet it kind of rings true, doesn't it?" Joe said. "That Ted might be behind it somehow?"

"Yeah," she said. "It kind of does. And Colin wants an audience with Jade."

"Which he's not getting," Talon said dryly.

"I don't know, Tal," Joe said thoughtfully. "Maybe Jade should talk to him."

"When she's in the middle of a difficult pregnancy? You'd be hard-pressed to convince me when she's in perfect health."

"What if his father *was* behind him not showing up to the wedding? Maybe he wants to tell her that." Joe rubbed at his chin. "Maybe he has some knowledge of what his father might be up to."

"No way," Talon said. "No fucking way."

Marjorie stepped up then. "I've known Jade a lot longer than you have, Tal, and you're not giving her enough credit. She's as strong as they come. She won't let Colin upset her. She won't do anything to put this pregnancy in jeopardy."

"You don't have to tell me how strong my wife is," Talon said.

"Then let Colin talk to her," Ryan said.

"Fuck you, Ry," Talon said, standing. "If Theodore Mathias rose from the dead and wanted to talk to your wife, would you encourage it?"

"Easy, bro," Joe said.

"First, that psycho did way worse to Ruby than stand her up at the altar," Ryan said. "The situations aren't even close to equal. But trust me. If Ruby wanted to talk to her father, I wouldn't be able to stop her."

"You think I should let Jade decide," Talon said with reserve.

Marjorie stood then and faced her middle brother. "Do you even hear what you're saying, Tal? Of course it should be Jade's choice. Jade is your wife, not your child. This is *her* decision."

Talon regarded me then. "What do you think?"

Way to be put on the spot. "I'm not a member of this family. I don't get a vote."

"Hold on again," Marj said. "The only person who gets a vote here is *Jade*. Jesus."

"Bro, you've been an honorary Steel from day one," Joe said. "Plus, you're the one Ted Morse has reached out to. Of course you get a vote."

"Do you people even hear me when I speak?" Marj said.

God, she was beautiful when her temper flared. Her cheeks and lips had darkened to a light crimson. Her hands were balled into fists.

Visions of our night together speared into my mind. Her lips and cheeks had been that same color. And her body...

"Well, Bryce?" Joe said.

"Marjorie is right," I said.

"Thank you. At least someone else in this room has some sense." She didn't meet my gaze, though.

"If your wife was in the middle of a difficult pregnancy—" Talon began.

"I don't have a wife."

"If you did, you'd be as protective as I'm being."

"Maybe so. But she's her own person, and so far she hasn't had a word of say in this."

"She doesn't even know," Marj said. "I agreed with you, Tal, at first. Best not to rock the boat where Jade's pregnancy is concerned. But if Ted Morse is up to something, Colin might know what it is. Right now, he's vulnerable and will be especially so around Jade. We could learn something."

"But..."

"She's strong, Talon," Marjorie said.

"I know that."

"We all understand your need to protect her," Joe said. "Ry and I feel the same way about our wives, right?"

"Of course," Ryan agreed.

"Christ. Fine." Talon relented. "But it's up to her. If she says no, the answer is no."

"Of course," Ryan said. "No one wants to force her to do anything."

"She'll be up for it," Marj said. "I know her. Especially if we let her in on what's going on."

"I don't want her worrying," Talon said.

"She's—"

Talon interrupted Marjorie. "Yes, I know she's strong. I'll talk to her."

I jerked slightly when my phone buzzed in my pocket. My mother. "Sorry. I have to take this." I left the office and answered the call.

"Yeah, Mom?"

"Honey, Ted Morse just showed up at our house."

Adrenaline spiked in my gut. I didn't think Ted Morse was a danger to anyone, but I needed to get my son and mother out of that house as soon as possible. "What did he want?"

"You. He said he needed to talk to you about something important. I told him he'd have to come back another time. Henry was crying, and I didn't know what to do."

"And he left?"

"Yes. He said he was sorry to bother me and wanted you to get in touch with him."

"You did fine, Mom. Don't worry. Just lock up and don't answer the door again. I'll be home soon."

"It's okay. Take care of your business. He didn't seem threatening."

"Are you sure?"

"Of course. We're fine here."

"All right. I'll check in with you if things go much longer. Bye, Mom." I walked back into Talon's office.

# CHAPTER TWENTY-SEVEN

### Marjorie

"Speak of the devil," Bryce said.

My body tingled. Yes, just from him walking back into the room. Damn.

"Colin?" Talon asked.

"No. Ted. Apparently he was at my house minutes ago. My mom sent him away."

"He showed up uninvited?" Joe said.

"Yup." Bryce shoved his phone back into his pocket. "And I don't like it one bit. We'll be moving as soon as everything's packed up, possibly before. Ted and I didn't make plans to meet last night. He just said he'd be in touch, which apparently meant he'd show up at my home unexpected and freak my mother out. I should get home."

"Takes a lot of nerve." Joe's words were more like a growl.

"Agreed," I said, just to have something to say.

"If the Feds are seriously still watching us, why would Morse know about it and we don't?" Joe asked. "And why would he show up at your house with them watching? He's bluffing."

"That's my feeling," Bryce said.

"Then what's the priority?" I asked. "Have Jade talk to Colin, or have Bryce talk to Ted?"

"Why not both?" Joe said. "Seems we'll get the most information that way, and if they give us conflicting accounts, we'll know Ted's a fucking liar."

"Or Colin is," Talon offered.

To Talon, Colin was a villain for what he'd done to Jade. To Joe, Ted was the villain for trying to blackmail him.

"Colin will be more accurate," I said.

"You think?" Bryce asked. "Because Colin's been through hell, and he probably blames all of us for that. It was my father, after all, and if Jade hadn't met Talon, Colin wouldn't have been here anyway."

"How is any of that our fault?" I asked.

"It's not. But he's a victim, and he's looking to place blame," Bryce explained.

"Then he's forgetting that I saved his sorry ass," Joe said.

Indeed, Joe had rescued Colin from Tom Simpson. Colin had been near death, and probably would have died but for Joe.

"We're all sorry for what he went through at my father's hands," Bryce said. "He must know that."

"Sure, objectively," Talon said.

"Objectively?"

"Let's just say I get where he's coming from." Talon sighed.

Of course Talon understood. He was in a precarious position. Colin had hurt Jade, so he wanted to hate him. Yet he was also a kindred spirit to Colin in a way, as they'd both been brutalized at the hands of Tom Simpson.

"I'll go talk to Jade," I said.

"I'll go with you." Talon stood.

"And I guess I'll call the elder Morse and set up a meeting," Bryce said.

"I'll be going with you," Joe said.

"He may not be willing to meet with you," Bryce said.

"That's why we're not going to tell him." Joe smiled. "But I don't want you going alone."

"I can take care of myself, Joe."

"You think that's what this is about? You've held your own against me for thirty-plus years."

"Then why?"

"Because he'll fuck with you, Bryce. He'll use your father against you. I'm not going to let that happen. Plus, he and I have history to settle."

I excused myself, Talon following me, to speak to Jade.

She was in her bedroom, dressed and looking better than she had in a while, so that was good news. Talon entered and I followed.

"Hey, blue eyes."

Her face lit up. "Hey, yourself."

"Marj and I need to talk to you."

"Is everything okay?"

"Yeah, fine. But... Crap. You tell her. I'm still not sure I like this idea."

I gave Jade the lowdown on what Ted had been saying and about my visit with Colin at the smoothie shop. "If you talk to him, maybe you can figure out what's going on."

"Sure. I'll be glad to do my part," she said.

"And I'll be with you," Talon said.

"Tal," I said. "He may not be completely truthful if you're there glaring at him."

"He's got to know that anything he tells me will go straight back to my husband," Jade said.

"Good point," I said, "though he might be more willing to talk if you're alone."

"I'm...not sure I want to be alone with him."

"What if I'm with you? He'll see me as much less of a threat than Talon. He and I were friends once."

"No," Talon said flatly. "I'm there, or this isn't happening."

I huffed. "Tal, stop being all Alpha for one damn minute and think about what's best for the situation as a whole."

"My concern is what's best for my wife and child."

"I get that," I said.

Then, from Jade, "Marj is right, Talon. He'll perceive you as a threat."

"I *am* a threat."

"Point made." Jade smiled. "I can handle Colin. I was in a relationship with him for seven years. I know what makes him tick."

"And I'll be there to have her back," I said.

"I'll be fine," Jade said. "Colin has no power over me. He hasn't since I met you."

"I hate that you were with him for so much longer than we've even known each other."

"So? My time with you means a thousand times more than the time with him. And in a way, he led me to you. We owe him, really."

Talon scoffed. "I'll give you some of that. If he hadn't been a no-show for your nuptials, we wouldn't have met. But we owe him squat."

"We owe him everything," Jade said, her eyes soft. "I couldn't imagine my life without you. You're the love of my life, Tal. He never was."

I eased toward the door. This was getting mushy. Jade had already confided in me that she and Talon wouldn't be able to make love for at least a month after the bleeding stopped, but still... "If you'll excuse me. Let me know when you want me to set up the meeting with Colin, Jade."

I crossed the sitting area and closed the door behind me.

And walked straight into the hard chest of Bryce Simpson.

# CHAPTER TWENTY-EIGHT

**Bryce**

My arms went around Marjorie automatically and I hugged her.

I pulled back quickly. "Sorry," I mumbled.

"No worries. Where were you going?"

"Just to tell Talon goodbye and see how Jade is doing."

"You weren't going to say goodbye to me?" she asked.

"Well..."

"You knew I was in there with them, right?"

"Yeah. I mean... Fuck." I warmed with embarrassment. This was ridiculous. I was thirty-eight, not sixteen.

She moved out of my way, gesturing toward Talon's door. "Be my guest, but they were getting pretty lovey-dovey when I left, so don't say I didn't give you fair warning."

She walked down the hallway toward the kitchen.

Well, she'd definitely talked me out of saying anything to Talon.

Joe and Ryan had already left. Why had I stayed again? To say goodbye to Talon? That was such a crock. Talon and I weren't even that close.

I'd stayed to catch another glimpse of Marjorie Steel.

Damn, I had it bad.

And damn, I had to get rid of it.

The Steel brothers had no idea I'd fucked their little sister. Marjorie wouldn't mention it to her brothers. I knew that instinctively.

God knew I wouldn't mention it. All three of them were fiercely protective of her.

Damn. Damn. Damn.

She stood at the refrigerator, eyeing its contents.

How in hell did she look like sex on a stick doing something so mundane? Without thinking, I inched toward her, letting my fingers touch the ponytail that was hanging down her back. So silky. So soft.

She turned abruptly.

I dropped my hand to my side.

*Sorry.* The word was lodged in my throat.

For one good reason.

I wasn't even close to sorry.

I dropped my gaze to her chest. Her nipples were hard and visible beneath the cotton of her tank. From the cool air of the refrigerator? Or from me?

"What do you want, Bryce?" she asked.

"This." I grabbed her to me and crushed my mouth onto hers.

Her lips remained tightly shut as if sewn together. I slid my tongue along the seam, nibbling their full pinkness. Then I trailed kisses to her ear. "Open for me," I whispered. "Please."

"I can—"

I took advantage of her open mouth and plunged in with my tongue. She responded, as I knew she would, her velvety tongue whipping around mine playfully. And then not so playfully.

This was serious. A serious kiss. A kiss that would lead

somewhere—a place I wanted desperately to go...and just as desperately not to go.

My cock was already hard beneath my jeans. I backed her up against the refrigerator door and then ground into her, deepening the kiss.

Her fingers trailed over my shoulders, up my neck, and she cupped my cheeks. Never had a woman cupped my cheeks before, and it was incredibly sweet and hot at the same time.

Then her fingers threaded through my hair, my scalp tingling from the light massage. We kissed, and we kissed, and we kiss—

*Clomp.*

*Clomp.*

*Clomp.*

The unmistakable sound of cowboy boots. She pushed me away, wiping her mouth. Seconds later, Talon was in the kitchen.

There could be no mistaking our swollen lips and red cheeks. Not to mention the bulge beneath my jeans. I turned away from Talon.

If he'd noticed, he didn't let on.

"I'm going to go pick up the boys at the bus stop," Marjorie said.

"Thanks," Talon said. Then, "You know what? Let me do that today. I'm so rarely home in the afternoons. It'll be a nice surprise for them."

"Um...okay." Marjorie didn't meet her brother's gaze.

"What's going on here?" Talon asked.

"Nothing," I said. "In fact, I was just leaving. Good to see you." I walked quickly out of the kitchen.

Damn. Damn. Damn.

HELEN HARDT

Why couldn't I leave her alone? Or why didn't she tell me to get lost?

This was going to be an issue. A big issue.

I left the house and checked in quickly with my mom. She and Henry were fine. Then I got into my car, the Mustang that had been my father's. It was only a year old. My father had purchased it shortly before he died. With cash, I'd found out when I'd processed his estate. The title was in a locked file cabinet.

My father had always handled the bills, and my mother, being an old-school wife, had never questioned where money came from or went.

I hadn't questioned him either.

How had I been so naïve as to not see him for who he truly was?

I could sell this car. Indeed I'd thought about it. But it was brand-new, gorgeous dark highland green, and loaded.

Paid for by...

Yeah, I was definitely selling it. I was surprised the Feds hadn't confiscated it, but they couldn't prove it had been purchased with dirty money.

Maybe it hadn't been, but I couldn't take the chance.

So why had I held on to it this long?

Not because I loved the car, though I did love it. I could easily sell it and buy another that I picked myself. Or, more likely, I could take the money and buy something cheaper. Or I could drive my own damned car, which I also loved.

Could I be trying to hold on to something from the father I knew? The man who'd taken Joe and me camping and fishing? The man who had taught me...how to be a man?

For he had. He'd been a good father to me, and somehow

I had to reconcile that with what I now knew he'd done to innocent people.

Including Colin Morse.

Including Talon.

I sighed.

I didn't know why I did half the things I did these days.

In the rearview mirror, I watched Talon get in his truck and take off to the main road to pick up the boys at the bus stop. He wouldn't be gone long.

I started the engine and looked behind me—

I jolted slightly when the passenger door opened.

Marjorie Steel sat down beside me. "Hey."

"What are you doing?"

"Nice car."

"It was my dad's."

"I know."

Did she really hijack me to talk about the car? I opened my mouth to say as much, but nothing came out.

"What are you doing, Bryce?" she asked.

"I'm going to sell the car," I said.

"You think I'm talking about the car?" She shook her head, perplexed. "I mean what are you *doing*?"

"Leaving. So if you'll excuse me..."

"Cut the crap. You know what I'm talking about." Her lips were beautifully red and swollen from our kiss only moments ago. Her dark eyes were serious.

Shit.

She wanted to talk.

Beware when a woman decided she wanted to talk. It never led to anything good.

"It was just a kiss, Marjorie."

"You really want to go down that road?" She shook her head. "I should have known."

"Does everything have to have some great meaning? Does everything require a conversation?" I huffed. "Women."

"Women? Really? You're going to play that card? You're better than that, Bryce."

She was right. I did know better than that. My mother had been a traditional housewife, but she'd also taught me how to treat and respect women.

And my father had backed her up.

Man. He'd had two distinct personalities. Had he suffered from a dissociative identity? Probably not. He'd just been a major psychopath. Psychopaths were notoriously good at hiding who they were. My father had been a master at it.

"I'm sorry," I said to Marj. "Truly."

And I truly was.

She trailed her finger over my forearm. Just that little contact had me tightening and tensing, in a majorly good way.

Except it wasn't a good way. Not for us. Not now.

"Listen to me," she said, her tone serious. "Don't start something with me that you can't finish."

Her red lips trembled slightly. The urge to touch her, kiss her, take her right here in my father's car overwhelmed me. My cock was throbbing, aching to be set free from confinement.

I'd already told her I had nothing to offer. Nothing to—

*Finish what you start, son.*

Damn! My fucked-up father had given me good advice over the years. Good fatherly advice. What a time for that particular advice to pop into my head.

I'd take what I wanted, what I yearned for.

And I'd finish it.

Once and for all.

# CHAPTER TWENTY-NINE

**Marjorie**

"I can't offer you anything past today," Bryce said to me. "I wish I could. You have no idea how much I wish I could."

"Fine," I said, not caring at the moment whether it lasted past the next thirty seconds as long as I got to kiss him again. "But don't kiss me unless you mean it."

His blue eyes softened. "I've always meant it." He touched my cheek, his fingers making me tingle.

"I can't be your escape, Bryce, no matter how much I want to be."

"I know that. Why do you think I'm trying to stay away? You deserve better, and an escape is all I'm after right now."

"An escape probably doesn't include moving into the guesthouse and working for my brothers."

He was silent then.

"Have you seen the guesthouse?" I asked mischievously.

"A time or two, when Ryan lived there. But I didn't visit him often."

"Want a tour?"

"Now?"

"Do you have somewhere else to be?"

Silence again.

"Start the engine," I said. "We'll drive over."

He sighed and obeyed. "All right."

A few minutes later we parked at the guesthouse. "Come on," I said, opening the car door. "It's still fully furnished. Ryan and Ruby chose all new stuff when they moved into their permanent home."

Yes, still fully furnished. Including the master bedroom.

Not that I was thinking about that...

I unlocked the door and entered. Bryce kept a safe distance behind me. Wow. He was doing everything he could to resist me. I should leave him alone, let him deal with the issues he felt he needed to. I was a nice person. A good person.

But I wanted this man.

Even now, I ached between my legs just being in his presence.

The house was immaculate. After Ryan and Ruby moved out, everything had been cleaned to a spit shine, and sheets and blankets had been changed on all the beds.

It was a sterile environment.

I could never resist dirtying up a sterile environment.

But I wouldn't push it. Bryce would have to make the first move.

"Here we go," I said, gesturing to the left. "The living roo—"

With a thunk, he pushed me against the wall in the foyer and clamped his mouth to mine.

First. Move. Made.

I opened, letting him in and kissing him back deeply. God, his kisses. I'd done my share of making out, but Bryce kissed on another whole level. He fucked with his mouth, made me crazy with his mouth.

Our lips slid together, and soon I was breathless, but I

couldn't bring myself to push away and gasp. I inhaled what I could through my nose as we continued making love with our mouths. When he finally broke the kiss, we both inhaled. Then he yanked on my ponytail, pushing my head back and baring my neck.

He slid his wet lips over the sensitive skin of my neck and upper chest. "So beautiful," he murmured.

I closed my eyes, surrendering to the moment, to our passion.

"I want to kiss every inch of you," he said, his voice humming against my skin.

"Yes," I breathed. "Please."

"Bedroom," he grunted.

I didn't want to move, didn't want his lips to leave my flesh, but I forced myself, knowing the delights that would come. I grabbed his hand and nearly dragged him down the hallway to the master bedroom.

The room was large and airy, and centered on the opposite wall was a king-size bed covered in a masculine brown comforter.

His eyes widened. "God."

"What?" I said, nearly breathless.

"The bed."

"Yeah, it's a bed."

"I can't..."

"Are you fucking kidding me?"

"I want to. You don't even know how much I want to."

"What's the problem, then?"

I expected to hear the same old excuses. I deserved more. Pink unicorns. Baby sister.

Instead, "I don't have a condom on me."

Was that all? "I'm on the pill. And clean."

He inhaled, closing his eyes. "I'm clean too. I got checked after my marriage ended. Thank God."

He pulled me to him and tugged the band out of my ponytail. My hair fell down my back and around my shoulders. "Love your hair. Love every part of you. You're fucking perfect."

I tried not to pay attention to the word "love." He didn't love me. He was just wildly attracted to me, as I was to him. I loved every part of him too, from the gorgeous sandy-blond hair on his head to his muscular calves and oddly beautiful feet.

Of course, at the moment, his legs and feet were covered.

I wanted them uncovered.

"You're perfect too," I said. "Undress for me."

A smile curved his lips upward. "I give the orders here, sweetheart."

I bristled at the husky timbre of his voice, his command. I wasn't submissive. Far from it. I wanted this man, though, and if he wanted me to undress, I'd do it.

But I'd tease the hell out of him in the process.

I shook my head, letting my hair tumble farther. Then I bent over, giving him a bird's-eye view of my ass while I untied my sneakers. Slowly.

His low groan was my reward.

Damn. If he reacted this way to me taking off my shoes...

I kicked the shoes across the floor and then removed my socks just as slowly.

"Fuck," he said gruffly. "Even your feet are perfect."

I'd always hated my feet. My second toe was slightly longer than my first, and because I was so tall, I wore a massive size-ten shoe. But the nails were painted fire-engine red, and regular pedis kept them soft and silky. I smiled.

His compliment made me feel good.

I continued to torture him slowly. I eased the lacy tank top over my belly, pausing for a moment before pulling it over my chest. Another few seconds passed, and it lay on the floor near my socks. I wore a pale-pink bra, no padding. I wasn't nearly as well-endowed as Jade, but I held my own. My nipples ached, their hardness pushing against the pink lace.

"You're killing me." Bryce closed his eyes and inhaled.

I smiled. "You told me to undress. Just following orders, babe."

"Damn." He opened his eyes. "Do you have any idea how gorgeous you are? What you do to a man? What you do to *me*?"

I inched forward slowly and boldly cupped the bulge behind his jeans. "I have a little idea."

"Fuck," he said through clenched teeth.

"I certainly hope so," I teased.

I moved backward again and removed my bra. He sucked in a breath as my breasts fell softly against my chest. I cupped them, sliding my thumbs over my hard nipples. Prickles shot to my pussy still covered by jeans and panties.

"Fuck," he said again.

I did a quick shimmy, showing off my boobs, and then I unsnapped and unzipped my jeans. I wore skinny jeans because they accented my long and lean legs, but getting them off in a sexy manner wasn't really possible. I did the best I could, inching them down as if I were removing stockings and then pulling them off my feet. I stood nearly naked then, wearing only pale-pink cotton undies. I hated thongs. They were uncomfortable as hell.

"Baby, you are the sexiest thing I've ever seen."

Two points for cotton, then. Thongs? Who needed them?

I was so turned on, so wet. I eased the pink panties over my hips until they landed in a puddle around my feet. I stepped out of them. Then I sat down on the bed, spreading my legs slightly.

"Your turn," I teased.

But Bryce had other ideas. He lunged toward me, fell to his knees, and spread my legs. "Need to taste you. Now." He clamped his gorgeous lips around my swollen clit.

I gasped, nearly jumping into climax at the mere contact. He released my clit, thank the universe, and then tongued the inside of me, sucking on my labia—felt so good—and then pushing my thighs upward a bit to slide his tongue over my asshole.

I sucked in another breath. Hadn't been expecting that, and I wasn't sure how I felt about it, but I didn't have a chance to give it any more thought because he went back to work on my pussy. The sweet slide of lips made me shiver and tingle, and when he glided his soft tongue over my hard clit again, I couldn't hold back.

"Bryce! I'm coming!"

His groan vibrated against me, adding to the already spectacular sensations. The climax penetrated every part of me. Every pore, every cell, every tiny molecule within me burst into flames.

"You taste so sweet, baby. So sweet." He thrust a finger inside me. "God, so tight too."

The penetration forced my climax into another dimension. Shapes and colors swirled in my mind, bright pink and neon blue. I grabbed Bryce's head, threading my fingers through his silky hair, and I ground against him, forcing his lips to suck my clit harder, his finger to thrust deeper.

HELEN HARDT

My climax continued, and with every pulse of my pussy, my body burned hotter.

When I finally began to calm, he removed his finger and rose, still on his knees, facing me. "I plan to taste every inch of you, Marjorie Steel. Every last inch." He pressed his lips to mine.

I opened to his kiss, tasting the tang of my own body mingled with his woodsy peppermint flavor. My nipples ached, and I clung to him, rubbing them against the texture of his shirt, savoring the sweet passion of our kiss. When he pulled away to inhale, I trailed my lips over his cheek, letting his stubble scrape my sensitive skin. He moved to my neck, kissing and sucking, and then, finally, he cupped my swollen breasts, lowered his head, and took a nipple into his mouth.

At first he merely slid his lips over it, softly sucking, and the need for more drove me slowly insane. I arched my back, trying to push it farther into his mouth.

"So soft," he said against my skin. "Like velvet."

They were hardly soft at the moment. I smiled, though. He was speaking of the texture of my skin, my flesh. All those years of moisturizing in the dry heat of Colorado summers had been well worth it.

He slid his tongue around my puckered areola, and without thinking, I grabbed his hand and led it to my other nipple.

He smiled against the swell of my breast and then clamped his lips around my nipple and sucked.

I drew in a harsh breath. The lightning bolt spread through me, recharging me, and soon I was geared up for another orgasm simply from him tugging on my flesh.

Amazing. I wanted more. Needed more.

"I'm going to taste every inch of you," he said again with a groan against my flesh. "Every. Single. Inch."

I opened my mouth to respond that he'd better be ready for me to do the same, but his teeth gripped my nipple, and all that came out of me was a long moan.

He pinched the other between his thumb and forefinger, and I arched again, yearning, aching for more.

"I could spend all day on your breasts alone," he said, his voice even lower than normal. "So beautiful and delicious."

Then he dropped his hand from my breast, down to my vulva, and thumbed my clit.

I sucked in another breath.

"Mmm, you like that?" He thrust his finger back into my heat, still working my clit.

When he bit my nipple again, I lost it. The climax hit me with the force of a tidal wave. I'd never been multi-orgasmic. Usually one, and I was done. But with Bryce Simpson? This was number two, and he hadn't even undressed yet.

"God, you're killing me," I panted, my eyes closed. Fragmented images swirled in my head as my whole body pulsed with the orgasm.

"Keep coming, honey," he said against my breast. "We're just getting started."

# CHAPTER THIRTY

**Bryce**

Her flesh was so edible, and her pussy so tight and inviting. I forced another finger into her, expanding her, and she continued to clamp around me as her orgasm continued.

Fuck. She was so damned hot.

More than that, she was beautiful inside and out.

This was a woman I could fall for. Really fucking fall for.

Which meant this had to stop. Now.

Damn. Damn. Damn.

My cock ached. Seriously fucking ached, an ache so profound that I knew it would never end if I didn't release inside her.

God, inside her. No condom. Just me and her, no barrier.

I clenched my teeth.

If I did this, if I let this happen...

Would once be enough? Could I get my fill and then leave, never to have her again?

I'd be living in this house, sleeping in this bedroom.

There'd be memories.

We had to get out of here. Anywhere. Another bedroom. Wherever. I just couldn't have these memories here, in this room. I'd never get over her if I had to sleep here night after night.

When her orgasm subsided and she lay back on the bed, nearly limp, I took the chance I had. I swept her into my arms and carried her out of the master bedroom.

Her eyes snapped open. "What? Where are we going?"

"Somewhere with a bed," I gritted out.

"Uh...we *were* somewhere with a bed."

I didn't answer, just moved to the next bedroom that had a queen bed. I tried not to think about the fact that my mother might be using this room. Or Henry.

No time for those thoughts. I laid Marjorie on the bed, her eyes still wide.

"I don't underst—"

I lay down next to her, still fully clothed, and silenced her with a deep kiss. I didn't expect her to understand my reasoning. I wasn't completely sure of it myself. So I kissed her. And I kissed her. And I kissed her some more, stealing her sweetness and letting it saturate me.

I let my fingers trail over her chest, her breasts, down the small swell of her belly to her vulva and then through her folds still slick for me. My dick was straining against the prison of my jeans, longing for freedom, longing to thrust inside Marjorie's perfect cunt.

But I hadn't tasted every inch of her yet.

"Take your clothes off, Bryce. Please. Let me touch you."

I was tempted, to be sure. So tempted. But if I undressed, she'd go for my cock, and I wasn't ready for this to be over yet. If I was only going to have her once more, I wanted to savor it, relish it, take my time and drive both of us to the brink of insanity.

"Not yet," I said gruffly.

"Please..." On a soft sigh.

"Not yet," I said in a more commanding tone.

"Damn you," she said softly.

I couldn't help a slight smile. I liked being in charge in the bedroom. I liked it a lot. Marjorie Steel wasn't a woman who submitted easily. In fact, her demeanor indicated she'd fight it. If I had the time, I could teach her the joys of submission. I could teach her everything about obedience during sex and the pleasure it could bring to both of us.

But that was a luxury denied me.

We had today. Right now.

I'd take her as she was. After all, why tamper with what was so close to perfection?

I didn't need her to submit to know already how perfect she was. Her skin was fair and milky, her brown eyes warm and mesmerizing and curtained by thick onyx lashes. Her cheekbones were high, her cheeks rosy, and her chin with just the right amount of prominence.

Her neck long and creamy, and her breasts the ultimate size. Her brown nipples were large and begged to be sucked and chewed on. Her abdomen was just round enough, and her narrow hips worked perfectly with her long, thin, but shapely legs.

Her toes were painted bright red, as were her fingernails.

Fucking hot.

Even better than hot though, Marjorie Steel was beautiful. Achingly beautiful.

I lightly trailed my fingers over her cheekbone, down her jawline and neck, over the swell of her breasts, down her abdomen to her firm thighs, stopping at a jagged pink scar marring her perfection.

She shivered at my touch, such a light touch. "Please, Bryce."

I'd ask about the scar later. For now... "Please what, baby?"

"Take off your clothes."

"Not until I'm done touching and tasting every inch of you."

"Damn you!" She fisted the raspberry comforter, her body tensing. "You're not being fair."

"Who said I had to be fair?" I teased. "I like having you at my mercy."

"You're going to pay for this," she said through clenched teeth.

"I certainly hope so." If her fingers and lips could touch every part of me, I'd enjoy the hell out of it. Savor it. Imprint it on my mind forever as the one time I experienced perfection in every way.

I moved back up to her face and pressed my lips to hers in a soft kiss. Her lips parted, and though I was tempted to dive into her sweet mouth, I held myself in check. Now my lips would visit where my fingers had blazed the trail.

I rained little kisses over her forehead, her cheeks, even her eyes when she closed them, her lashes a soft flutter against my sensitive lips. Then I trailed to her ear, kissing the lobe and then nibbling on it. She shuddered beneath me, and when I stuffed my tongue into her ear canal, she groaned.

"Bryce... Oh my God."

I moved to her other ear, teasing it as I had the first, and then kissed her lips again, sliding down her chin to her creamy neck. I nibbled and licked the sensitive skin as she undulated beneath me, moaning and sighing.

"You're so soft, Marjorie." I continued to the upper parts of her breasts, kissing and licking and nibbling. "I could lick every part of you. You're a feast."

Not just for my eyes and mouth, but her soft sighs and moans were a glorious concerto to my ears. Her scent was warm and intoxicating and comforting, like a fresh-baked apple pie laced with feminine musk. The texture of her skin was like satin against my lips, and her taste... Oh, her taste... Tart apples and citrusy tang and musky arousal. No more delicious creation could possibly exist in the universe.

I moved downward, purposefully avoiding her nipples to tease her. She tensed beneath me, and they stuck out so hard and inviting that I nearly caved. But I held firm and continued downward, kissing the top of her vulva and the inside of her firm thighs, the scent of her musk only inches away. I slid my tongue over her scar at the top of her right thigh. She tensed beneath me for a few seconds, but then trembled and sighed softly.

I salivated, aching to slide my tongue into her, but I held back and continued down her legs, the skin pulled tautly over their shapely musculature. When I got to the tops of her feet, she squirmed. I ignored her silent protest and skimmed my lips over them and then kissed each pretty toe.

"Turn over, baby," I said gruffly. "I want to kiss the rest of you."

"You're killing me," she said softly, but she obeyed, turning over.

I kissed the bottoms of her feet and then proceeded upward, along her muscular calves to the insides of her knees. She giggled a bit, so I pressed my lips there again, tickling her. When I'd teased her enough, I moved upward to her thighs and then to that gorgeous butt. Her narrow hips produced an ass that was just plump enough, and I nibbled at her cheeks. Then I spread them slightly. Her cute little asshole was puckered and pink, and I swiped my tongue over it as it tightened, winking at me. She didn't flinch. Was she experienced with anal? I loved anal play, but I'd never actually penetrated a woman there with anything other than a finger.

Damn. I'd love to sink my cock into Marjorie Steel's tight little asshole. I'd never gone there with anyone. Had she? Could we be each other's first?

I'd never know.

It would be too much to hope for this one time.

Still, I stayed at her ass longer than usual, pinching and kissing, licking and biting. Her posterior was a damned work of art.

I finally forced myself away from her bottom and moved upward, sliding my lips over her gorgeous back. Her dark hair fell over her back in a soft walnut veil. I pushed it to the side to bare her silky neck. I kissed the soft flesh, and then whispered in her ear, "You're the most beautiful thing I've ever seen. Every inch of you."

She smiled against the comforter but said nothing in response. I gently turned her over so she lay on her back once more. Her tits stuck out, and her nipples were deliciously hard. I flicked my fingers over them. She jolted, gasping, and then she opened her eyes wide.

"When are you going to take your clothes off, Bryce? Please. Let me touch you."

Part of me hesitated. If I stayed clothed, I could stay at a distance. Leave her perfection untainted. After all, I'd touched and tasted every centimeter of her amazing body. I'd kissed her glorious mouth, eaten her delicious pussy.

And once, I'd been inside that heat. I'd worn a condom, but still, I'd been there.

If I left now, I could feel less guilt.

But hell, the guilt was already eating me alive. Why not take what she was offering? The guilt would be there either way.

I should say something. Make sure she understood this was one time only, could never happen again, for her own good.

I opened my mouth. "Marj—"

She touched two fingers to my lips. "Stop. Don't say anything. Just make love to me, Bryce. Please."

# CHAPTER THIRTY-ONE

## Marjorie

He was thinking about walking away. I could tell by the tension radiating off him, the look of painful determination in his eyes.

No way.

No way was I letting him go. Not until I'd given his body the same treatment he'd bestowed on mine. A tiny part of my mind flew to the scar on my upper thigh.

*No. Can't ruin this moment.*

"Marjorie..."

"Please," I said urgently.

He sighed. "I want to more than I've ever wanted anything."

"Then do it. I want it too. Take off your clothes, Bryce. Let me touch you."

Finally, he stood and began to disrobe. First his shirt, too damned slowly, his fingers unbuttoning each button as if it were permanently attached. Finally, he parted the two halves of his shirt, and I beheld his chest and abs, tan and muscled with light-brown hair scattered over his pecs. His nipples were a coppery color, and they looked delicious. I slid my tongue over my bottom lip as my mouth watered for a taste of him. He slid the shirt over his shoulders, baring them in their broad glory, and tossed it to the floor.

I stood. I couldn't help myself. I had to touch that marvelous flesh. I skimmed my fingers over his shoulders, relishing their muscled tautness. I trailed my hands over his chest, fingering his nipples that hardened further under my touch. I couldn't help a slight smile.

Yes. I affected him as much as he affected me.

I continued down his abdomen, touching each indentation of his six-pack. So beautifully masculine and perfect.

Then, I smoothed my fingers over the trail of sandy hair leading to...

I grabbed his belt buckle.

His hand covered mine, stopping me.

"Let me," I said. "Please."

He moved his hand away with a sharp intake of breath, sighing. "Okay."

I smiled again while I unbuckled his belt and then unbuttoned and unzipped his jeans. His bulge was covered by his light-green boxer briefs. Light green, except for a darker pearl-sized spot. I wet my lips and slid the jeans and boxer briefs over his hips quickly.

His cock sprang out at me, the tip glistening. I glided my tongue over it to lick up the wetness.

He sucked in a huge breath. "Damn."

"You didn't think I'd let you go without giving you a taste of your own medicine, did you?" I teased.

I slid my lips over his cockhead and sucked gently.

Another swift intake of breath.

He tasted of salt and man.

And I wanted more.

A lot more.

I let the head drop with a tiny pop and then kissed along his shaft, all the way to his balls, which had already tightened up against his body. Downy light-brown hair covered them, and when I inhaled his musk and kissed them, he gasped.

"Damn!"

I licked his inner thighs and then made my way back to the main course, his magnificent cock.

*Bryce Simpson, you're about to get the blow job of a lifetime.*

I slid my wet lips over his cockhead and most of the way down his thick shaft, controlling my gag reflex.

I was good at giving head. All my past lovers had said so, and even though I'd gone over a year now without having sex, it was like riding a bike.

In this case, a really big bike with thick tires.

Bryce was massive. I already knew how he felt inside me. Now I wanted him in my mouth, his seed drizzling down my throat.

I squirmed. I was wet and ready.

Did I want him coming in my mouth or in my pussy? Did I need to make the choice? Right now, I wanted to suck his dick, so that was what I'd do. I pulled back and then took him nearly to the base. Damn, he was huge.

"Fuck. Marj. Don't."

I smiled—or as much as I could with my mouth full of cock. Not stopping. No way.

I added my fist so I could get down all the way to the base of his shaft and began sucking faster.

"You're going to kill me," he gritted out.

Didn't care. By the end of this, he'd no longer associate me with pink and yellow unicorns. No way in hell.

"Can't," he panted. "Can't."

*You can, Bryce. Oh, yes, you can.*

"Don't. Want. This. To end. Yet."

Neither did I. And I wanted him in my pussy more than I wanted him to come in my mouth. I wanted us truly joined.

I let him go, stood, and then pushed him until he was sitting on the bed. He removed his boots and socks quickly and then slid his jeans and boxers off and onto the floor. Once he was completely naked, I resisted the urge to stare at him, pushed him flat on the bed, and straddled him.

Slowly I sank down onto his cock.

God. So full. So completely full. I sat there a moment, just savoring how he filled me, how he eased the empty ache.

He closed his eyes. "You're so tight, baby."

I leaned down and kissed him, tracing his lips with my tongue, and he opened. We kissed deeply while he pistoned into me and I moved with him. We found our perfect rhythm, and we kissed as we made love.

So good. Nothing had ever been like this—this true completion. I broke the kiss to inhale a necessary breath. He cupped my tits and thumbed my erect nipples.

"Touch yourself, baby. Touch yourself, and come with me."

I slid my fingers over the swell of my breasts, down my tummy to my clit. If I touched it, I'd explode, and I wasn't ready to end this yet.

"Please. I'm going to come. Come with me."

I sighed and fingered the hard nub. Within seconds, waves of pleasure began to spark over me.

"That's right, baby. That's right." He pushed his hips up, slamming harder and harder into me. "I'm going to come. I'm going to— Fuck!"

We climaxed together in glorious harmony.

Then my body went limp, and I collapsed on his chest.

"Amazing," he whispered.

"More than amazing," I replied.

We lay together for a moment, still joined, until I rolled off him and curled into the crook of his shoulder.

He tensed, as if ready to rise.

"Don't," I said. "Stay with me for a little while."

"But I—"

"Please."

"Okay." He relented, tightening his arm around me.

I closed my eyes, inhaling the scent of our sex that hung in the air.

If this would be all I'd ever get of him, I was going to enjoy every single second.

# CHAPTER THIRTY-TWO

**Bryce**

I opened my eyes to darkness.

Marjorie still slept beside me, cuddled in my arms. The sun had gone down, obviously. How long had I been here?

I kissed the top of her head and eased my arm out from under her.

I stood, found my jeans, and pulled out my phone.

Midnight? We'd been sleeping for hours. My mother hadn't called or texted, so that was good news. No issues with her or Henry.

I eyed Marjorie's still-sleeping body and shook my head.

I'd slept, and I'd slept well—better than I had since this whole thing with my father had come out. No nightmares, no night sweats, no insomnia.

Just sleep. Pure, basic, deep sleep.

And I'd needed it.

The sun had still been shining when we fell asleep, so the time must have been around five o'clock at the latest.

Seven hours of sleep!

Amazing.

My eyes adjusted to the dark room, and I stared at her. Still so beautiful and so innocent-looking in slumber.

Marjorie Steel was far from innocent. She'd made love

like a pro. No mistaking her for a little girl anymore. Nope. No more pink and yellow unicorns. No more toddler trotting after Joe and me as teens.

Thank God.

Still, though, she deserved so much better than I had to offer.

Just thinking about her had my dick hardening again. She was here. I was here. Technically this could count as the same time. I could wake her gently and slide my cock into her once more.

She looked so serene and peaceful, though. How could I wake her just to get my rocks off? That'd be pure selfishness.

Then again, this entire evening had been pure selfishness. I'd slept with her knowing very well that it would never happen again, that I'd never be able to have a relationship with her. I'd slept with her when I should have been home with my mother and my son after Ted Morse had shown up at our home. I quickly texted my mom, apologizing for the late hour. I breathed easier when she texted back that everything was fine.

I sat down on the bed and trailed my hands over Marjorie's sleeping body. She stirred, opening one eye.

"Bryce?"

"I'm sorry. I didn't mean to wake you."

She sat up abruptly. "What time is it?"

"A little after midnight."

"Oh my God," she said, jumping from the bed. "The boys. Talon. Jade. Their dinner. Crap!"

"I think they probably ate without you," I said.

"But I make dinner for them. That's part of how I'm helping while Felicia's gone. I'm supposed to— Shit. Where's my phone?" She turned on the light.

We both flinched against the visual intrusion. She pawed through the clothes on the floor until she came up with her smartphone.

"Three texts from Talon. He's wondering about dinner."

"I'm sure he figured something out. He's a big boy."

"What am I going to tell him? How could I be so selfish?"

"You're living your life for your brother and his family. You are the least selfish person on the planet. We all know that."

"But the boys. Jade. They were counting on me."

"You're not an indentured servant, Marj. They made do."

"But—"

I went to her and gathered her into my arms. "It's okay."

She melted into me. How could this amazing woman even consider herself to be selfish? *I* was the selfish one. I'd taken everything she'd given me, knowing full well I couldn't return it. I kissed the top of her head once more.

Then her hand clamped around my erection.

"Marj…"

"I'm sorry." She let go. "I feel like a piece of crap right now, having let my brother and the others fend for themselves, but you're hard. You're so hard. And I want you." She dropped to her knees.

"God." I clenched my teeth.

She wrapped those beautiful lips around my cock and slid them back and forth. Then she moved away. "I'm doing it again. Being selfish."

Selfishness be damned. I was ready to say anything, do anything, to get her mouth on me again.

*That* was truly selfish.

The problem? I didn't give a fuck at the moment.

I pulled her to her feet and took her lips with my own.

She opened, kissing me back, and I pushed her against the wall, grinding my cock into her belly. She went limp against me, her kisses hard and passionate, her body sticking to mine as if we were glued together.

I reached the light switch and flicked it off, still kissing her, still reveling in her, still wanting her with an insatiable hunger.

Without thinking, I lifted her against the wall and set her onto my hard cock, wincing as I tunneled into her, her tightness the perfect sleeve for me.

She gasped into my mouth, but our lips didn't part all the way. Just enough for each of us to breathe, and then our amazing kiss continued.

I pushed into her, the wall stabilizing her body, and thrust harder. Again and again and again.

And only moments later, when I released again inside her, I knew the blazing, undeniable truth.

I'd never get enough of her. No matter how many times we did this, I'd always want more.

I'd never tire of her perfection, of her sweet sighs, deep kisses, silky fingers on my skin.

I'd never tire of her spicy fragrance, her rosy flesh, her full red lips.

I'd never tire of her perfect pussy around my fingers, around my cock.

Which meant only one thing.

This could never, never happen again. I'd live on the ranch, I'd see her, but I had to resist her. I couldn't be alone with her. Not again.

Not ever.

And now?

I had to leave.

# CHAPTER THIRTY-THREE

### Marjorie

Bryce picked up his clothes and began to dress. I sighed. He was right. We'd crossed a line. I'd let my family down for a romp in the hay—an amazing romp in the hay, but still. I couldn't let that happen again.

I followed his lead and put my clothes on. Without words, we walked out of the bedroom, down the hallway, and out the front door to Bryce's car. Without words, he drove the short distance to the main house. Without words, he stopped, letting the engine idle.

I leaned into him, but his demeanor was icy. No goodbye kiss? No thanks for a lovely evening? No...anything?

"Good night," I said softly. "And..."

And what? I'd been ready to say "thank you," but why should I thank him? I didn't need to thank a man for sex, and he didn't need to thank me. It was a consensual act between the two of us. If we were giving thanks, it should come from both of us.

"...see you around," I finished.

He nodded without smiling. "Yeah. See you around."

I closed the car door as gently as I could. I doubted anyone could hear it out here, but I didn't want to take the chance of waking anyone inside.

*See you around.*

Sounded like we were the athlete and the nerd in high school who were wildly attracted to each other and had just fooled around under the bleachers but couldn't acknowledge each other in public. What the hell kind of craziness had I just allowed to occur?

I turned around to have it out, but Bryce was already backing out of the long driveway.

I sighed. Another time.

I walked into the house stealthily and went straight to my bedroom.

Though tempted, I didn't let any tears fall.

I set the alarm on my phone. I'd be up early to do my duties. I'd let Talon and Jade down enough for now.

★ ★ ★

Talon was up first. I'd spent my entire shower trying to figure out what lie to tell him about where I'd been last night, but I ultimately decided to just apologize for not being here for them and offer no further explanation. I was a grown woman, and I certainly didn't have to account to my big brother where I'd been.

He accepted it with pursed lips. "As long as you're okay."

"I'm fine," I replied as nonchalantly as I could. "Just had to take care of a few things. I should have called."

"Yeah, you should have. We were worried."

I said nothing. He was right. "What do you have going on today?" I asked.

"Meetings mostly. The three of us need to get the financial staff up to speed with Bryce taking over."

I nodded, trying not to let the tension I felt show. He had to mention Bryce, didn't he?

"How about you?" he asked.

"Not much. The usual."

"Aren't you going to call Colin?"

"Colin?" Right. "Yeah, sorry. I forgot. I'll give him a call and set up a time for him to talk to Jade."

"Good. I still don't like the idea of me not being there."

"We'll be fine. I'll be there. I'll look out for Jade." I'd been looking out for Jade long before Talon came into her life, but I left that unsaid.

He nodded, sipping the last of his coffee before he set down the cup and stood. "I have to look in on the hands in the field before I begin the meetings. I'm going to go kiss the boys and Jade goodbye."

"Okay. I'll be in to roust the boys in a few."

He nodded again, walking out of the kitchen.

Whew! That wasn't pleasant, but he seemed to accept that I wasn't going to offer up any details to my whereabouts the previous evening. I hadn't slept a wink once I'd returned, but I felt okay since I'd slept for seven hours in Bryce's arms.

Seven wonderful hours. Granted, I had no memory of them since I was asleep, but I felt oddly refreshed this morning, both physically and mentally. Emotionally? Not so much.

I missed Bryce. I wished we'd ended it on a better note.

But I had other fish to fry today, beginning with taking care of my nephews.

I woke them and pulled them out of bed to come to the kitchen to eat. Even Donny was quiet this morning. The skies were gray, unusual for a Colorado morning, and the boys were feeling it.

An hour later, I'd dropped them at the bus stop and returned. I went in to check on Jade.

She was up and showered, a good sign.

"Starting to feel better?" I asked.

"A little less nauseated. Believe it or not, that's a good thing. I've been feeling so sick that the 'little less' part actually feels good."

"Feel like breakfast?"

"Yeah, actually. Maybe just some scrambled eggs and dry toast."

"You want me to bring it in here?"

"No. I'll come out to the kitchen."

Oddly, she didn't interrogate me about last night.

But it was coming. I knew Jade too well.

Once she'd sat down at the table and I'd placed her breakfast in front of her, the questions began.

"You going to tell me, or what?"

"Tell you what?"

"Yeah. Play coy," she said sarcastically. "That always works."

"I'm a grown woman, and—"

"I get it. That's what you told Talon. He told me. But it won't fly with me. Since when do we have secrets, Marj?"

"I'm really sorry if I worried you guys."

"I know you can take care of yourself, but Tal was a little worried. I mean, after all we've been through and all."

"I know. I'm sorry," I said again.

"Obviously you're fine, so spill it."

Words began tumbling out of my mouth in what I hoped was coherent speech. I held back the tears that threatened. For me, being strong meant no crying. I'd grown up with three brothers, and crying was for girls. Yeah, I was a girl, a girl who once liked pink and yellow unicorns, but I always vowed to be as strong as my brothers were.

I vowed that to this day.

Jade didn't interrupt my jumbled speech, just nodded a few times.

Finally, I stopped talking.

Nothing more to say.

"He just left," I said. "He said, 'see you around.'"

"Sounds like you said it first."

"Well, yeah. What else was I going to say? I wasn't going to thank him."

"How about something like, 'I had a nice time'?"

I stayed silent. "I had a nice time" seemed so light and airy and noncommittal, so nonspecific. We hadn't had a "nice time." We'd had some intense lovemaking, the kind of lovemaking that doesn't come along all that often. It went so far beyond "a nice time."

At least *I* thought it had.

"If you want something more with him, tell him," Jade urged.

"Like you told Talon?"

"Talon was different. He told me up front that he couldn't love me. I accepted that."

"Not so different. Bryce has basically said the same thing. And as I recall, you kept going back for more Talon, no matter what he said."

"He let me come back, though," Jade said.

"Bryce let me come back," I said. "This was our second time, after he'd told me it could never happen again."

"Then accept it. Accept that all you can have is sex right

now. Maybe it will turn into something more for him. It did with Talon."

"What if he doesn't come back for more?" I asked, almost in a whine. I hated whiny women.

"I think he will."

"But what if he doesn't? I don't want to go to him. I can't throw myself at him any more than I already have. I'm not used to being the aggressor"—I smiled—"at least not until we actually get to bed."

"If he doesn't, he doesn't. It is what it is, Marj. There are other men out there."

"Where?"

Jade shook her head. "Everywhere."

"Not in Snow Creek."

"Are you kidding me? We have hundreds of men right here on the ranch."

"Fifty-year-old ranch hands who've been around since I was born? I don't think so."

"They're not all fifty years old. A lot of them are young and hot, Marj, with amazing muscles from the outdoor work. Plus, check out some of the guys in the marketing department. Or that new guy Ryan hired to help with creating the wines. Wowza."

"Aren't you married to my brother?"

"And that means I can't look? Men don't become less hot just because you get married. Plus, I've been feeling so sick, ogling men is one of the few pleasures I have these days."

That got a giggle out of me. "You've never been an ogler."

"Maybe not. But I can still appreciate male beauty. There's a lot of it here on the ranch."

"You've hardly left your bedroom for the last couple months."

"True. But I haven't always been pregnant. I've lived here for almost a year now."

"Are you kidding? You haven't had eyes for anyone but Talon since you got here."

"Okay, you got me. You're right. But there are plenty of hot young men right here for you to choose from."

"What am I supposed to do?"

"Choose one. Go on a date."

"Who's going to want to date me?"

"A beautiful ranch heiress? Who *isn't* going to want to date you?"

I laughed. A date. What a concept. I hadn't been on a date in a while. With Bryce, we'd gone straight to bed. No dates. No just having fun being with each other.

I actually missed dating. I wanted to date.

Problem was, I wanted to date Bryce.

I opened my mouth to say as much but was waylaid by my phone. A text. From Talon.

*When are you and Jade*
*meeting with Colin?*

# CHAPTER THIRTY-FOUR

**Bryce**

My mother hadn't questioned my whereabouts last night. She'd made breakfast for Henry and me, smiling.

She smiled more now, thank goodness. After we'd learned the truth about my father, she'd gone into depression. My sweet son had brought her out of it. A one-year-old little boy had done what I, her son, couldn't. So I'd stepped aside, let her take over with Henry. She needed him more than I did.

I missed him, though. He still smiled and said "Da da" whenever I held him and played with him, but those moments were becoming fewer. I was gone more often, and even when I was here, I was mentally absent. The feeding, the diaper changing, the day-to-day caring had fallen to my mother, who didn't mind at all.

Not that I would've minded.

I'd told myself time and again that this was what was best for my mother because Henry had brought her out of her depression. I'd told myself time and again that it was also best for Henry, since I was not fit to be a father at present.

I wasn't lying to myself.

But I wasn't being entirely truthful either.

I missed my son, so much sometimes that I physically ached. He'd become such an integral part of me, and when I was without him, I almost felt like I'd lost a limb. Only that wasn't even close to the loss I felt.

I wasn't what Henry needed, though. I was a fucked-up mess, and the last thing I wanted was to turn my son into another fucked-up mess.

A knock at the door startled me. "I'll get it," I said to my mother.

Outside, a truck was parked in front of the house, and three men stood wearing brown uniforms. "May I help you?"

"Montgomery packing and moving. Weren't you expecting us?"

Was I? "No. I'm sorry. We're not quite ready to pack up yet."

"That's what we're here for. Just go about your business, and we'll get everything packed up for you. Someone will need to be here, though, to tell us what goes to the new house and what goes into storage."

My mom came to the door, wiping her hands on a dish towel. "Hi, I'm Evelyn. This is my son, Bryce. I'm sorry, honey. They called yesterday while you were...out."

"Oh." Being out of the loop was a fact of life for me these days. "Will you be home today?"

"Of course. Where else would Henry and I be?"

A stone hit my gut. Where else indeed? She was here, taking care of my son, while I was...anywhere *but* here it seemed. "Come on in, I guess." I held the door open for the three men.

"I'll show you where to start." My mom led them into the house.

And just like that, I prepared to leave the only home I'd ever known. I'd lived on my own from time to time—during college and then when I had a job in Denver for a while—but Snow Creek had always seemed like coming home.

I wasn't actually leaving Snow Creek, only leaving the town to live on a nearby ranch. In a completely furnished guesthouse with four bedrooms and a pool and hot tub in the back.

"Mom," I said, "the guesthouse is furnished, but I want to take my own bed."

I wasn't sure why I said that. My bed was a queen—a ten-year-old queen—and the master bedroom at the guesthouse had that luxurious king-size bed. I was being stupid. In fact, it was stupid to even put my old bed in storage. It should be sold, or better yet, tossed.

"Never mind," I said to her when she turned to face me. "The bed at the house is better."

"Anything would be better than your old mattress. It was mine and your fa—" She stopped and hurried away.

The queen mattress had gone into my room when she and my father bought a king.

I looked around the house. We hadn't yet decided whether to sell or rent. Either way, we'd have a hard go of it. Who would want to buy or rent a house vacated by a psychopathic child rapist?

Maybe we couldn't get rid of the house, but we could at least get rid of everything my father ever touched. Would that purge us of his evil?

And did I even want to be purged?

Because that was the cold, hard truth.

He had been my father, and he had been a good father, even though he'd turned out to be the embodiment of evil.

So what did that make me?

The spawn of evil?

The spawn of evil who had nothing but pleasant memories of his father for nearly the whole time he was alive?

My father had brutalized men, women, and children. Raped them. Tortured them. And then he'd come home and spent time with me. Read to me. Helped me learn long division. Taken me camping and fishing with Joe. Taught me how to hit a baseball. Shown me how to throw a perfect spiral. Taught me how to shoot a gun.

Taught me how to be a man.

A shudder ran through me.

What kind of man was I if he had been my inspiration, my role model?

My father?

Yes, I wanted to purge this house—my life—of everything he'd touched.

But I didn't want to just as much.

Because as much as my father had been a truly evil man, he'd also been a good father.

Reconciling those two facts was impossible and the biggest reason why I was a fucked-up mess at the moment.

"Tell them to only pack the personal items in my room," I told my mother. "The bed and other furnishings can be burned, for all I care. Everything he touched can be burned." Then I left the house.

★ ★ ★

An hour later, I arrived at the agreed-upon café in Grand Junction to meet with Ted Morse. He was already there, sitting in a booth. The hostess pointed him out to me.

I approached him and cleared my throat. "I'm Bryce Simpson."

He stood. "Mr. Simpson. Ted Morse." He held out his hand, but I didn't take it. "Please. Have a seat."

I resisted the urge to blurt out an apology for what my father had done to his son. *I am not responsible for the sins of my father*—a mantra I tried, but more often than not failed, to live by.

Silence stretched for an unbearable few seconds that seemed like hours. He'd invited me here, and I'd agreed to come to gather information for the Steels. I had nothing to say to him other than the apology on the tip of my lips. I kept them tightly closed. I would not start this conversation out by putting myself in a vulnerable position. I owed the Steels better.

Ted finally opened his mouth, but we were interrupted by our server, a middle-aged woman with graying hair. "Good morning," she said to me. "What'll it be?"

"Just coffee," I said. If I tried eating while facing Ted Morse, I might spew.

"Coming right up."

Alone again, facing the man whose son my father had ruined. I owed him nothing, especially after he'd tried to blackmail my best friend. Still, guilt gnawed at me.

I cleared my throat again. "So, Mr. Morse, what did you want to talk to me about?"

"Ted, please. And I'll call you Bryce."

"Okay. Fine." Though I didn't really see the point. We weren't friends. We weren't colleagues. We weren't anything, really.

"I've already told you that the FBI is still working the case."

HELEN HARDT

I nodded. I had no idea if he was telling the truth, but I'd hear him out. I'd made a promise to the Steels.

"What you might *not* know is that they've identified two more persons of interest."

"And why would I care?"

"Because one of them, Bryce, is you."

# CHAPTER THIRTY-FIVE

**Marjorie**

"Talon wants to know when we're meeting with Colin," I said to Jade.

"Good question. When are we?"

"I don't know yet." I texted Talon back as much. "I guess I'll call him now."

"Hey, Marj," Colin said into my ear.

"Hey. Jade has decided she'll talk to you."

"Oh? She got the Neanderthal to agree?"

"This conversation is going to be over really quickly if you're determined to dis my brother."

"Right. I get it. Sorry." Though he didn't sound sorry at all. "When?"

"Whenever. But I'll be coming with her."

"That wasn't part of the deal."

"There is no deal, Colin. And if I don't come, Talon will. Your choice."

He paused a few seconds. Then, "Fine. This afternoon?"

"It has to be sometime before three o'clock. The boys get home from school around three thirty."

"I'm still in Snow Creek. How about two at the smoothie shop?"

"Hold on." I turned to Jade, muting the phone. "Are you

feeling up to going into town? Two at the smoothie shop?"

"Yeah. I'm okay today."

"Fine," I said into the phone. "Jade and I will see you then."

Jade bit her bottom lip. "I...don't know how to feel about this."

"There's no right or wrong way to feel."

"I mean, he humiliated me so terribly, but now...he's been through so much more than anyone should ever have to go through. Makes what he did to me seem like a minor pebble in my shoe, you know?"

"Yeah, I get it. But just because he's been through hell doesn't negate what he did to you. Remember that."

She nodded. "I know."

"You feel like doing something?" I said. "If you're up for it, we could go into town early. See if Candy has any openings for manis and pedis or something?"

"You know?" Jade stood. "I've showered and gotten dressed. Why waste it? Let's go."

★ ★ ★

Jade and I had just sunk our feet into the warm aromatic water at the nail salon when both of our phones buzzed simultaneously with a text.

Jade gasped. "It's the school. Something's wrong with Dale."

I read the same text. "Talon probably got it too." I pulled my feet out of the water. "Sorry. We have to go. It's a good thing we're here in town."

Jade frantically called the school while I dried off and

put my shoes back on. Ten-year-old Dale hardly spoke unless spoken to. If the school was calling, this was important.

"They took him over to Dr. Robbin's office," Jade said after ending her call. "They couldn't tell me much else."

Luckily, the doctor's office was only two blocks from the nail salon. The glories of a small town. Rather than get into the car, we walked—very quickly.

"He's in the back," the receptionist said as soon as we walked in.

Jade and I hurried back into the exam room, where Dr. Robbin Shaefer was examining Dale.

"Baby!" Jade said. "Are you okay?"

"He was hyperventilating," Dr. Robbin said. "I got him calmed down, but he nearly passed out at school."

Dale said nothing.

Dr. Robbin had been a classmate of Joe's. I'd known her my whole life. She'd taken her dad's place as our doctor when he retired.

"Dale," Dr. Robbin said, "the only way to deal with what's bothering you is to tell us about it."

Silence.

Jade took his hand. "Please, honey. We're here to help you. Auntie Marj and I are here, and the doctor is here."

He shook his head.

"Please, sweetie," I said. "We want to help you."

"I saw a man," he whispered meekly.

"Where?" Jade asked.

"While I was at recess on the playground."

"Was it someone you recognized?"

He nodded.

"Who was it?"

Silence.

I swallowed. This couldn't lead to anything good. The Feds had shut down the trafficking ring, but had they caught everyone involved? According to Ted Morse, they were still investigating.

Could someone from Dale's past be here in Snow Creek?

Why? Coming here made no sense. Why go somewhere someone might recognize you?

"I won't let him," Dale said.

"Won't let him what?" Jade asked.

"Hurt Donny. I won't let him hurt my brother."

My heart ached, and Jade's eyes glistened. We'd known for a while that Dale had taken the brunt of the abuse to spare his younger brother. They'd even made a suicide pact with each other, one Donny had nearly brought to fruition.

"Dale, the bad men have been caught," Jade said. "Is it possible you imagined it? Maybe saw someone else who looked like someone you remember?"

He shook his head.

"Are you sure?"

"Jade..." I began.

She nodded. "I'm sorry, honey. I just want to protect you. I don't want you to be scared. Daddy and I will never let anyone harm you. I promise."

It was a hefty promise to make but one she and Talon would keep no matter the cost.

"Has anyone called the police?" I asked.

Robbin shrugged. "I don't know. The school didn't say."

"I'll take care of it."

"Marj," Jade said, "he may not be ready to talk to the police."

"You've got to try, Dale," I said. "If you think this man might want to hurt you or your brother, the police need to know." I quickly made the call. "They're sending someone over here."

Dale's skin had gone white.

"You have to try to talk to the police, honey." Jade held his hand.

The boy nodded.

I checked my watch. We had an hour before our meeting with Colin. Plenty of time for Dale to talk to the police. But then what? Would he go back to school? If he couldn't, Jade and I would need to stay with him.

No matter. Dale was the priority. Colin would have to wait.

# CHAPTER THIRTY-SIX

**B r y c e**

*Because one of them, Bryce, is you.*

I remained calm, at least on the outside. Inside, my guts were churning like cream into butter. No way would I let this moron know that.

I was innocent. Completely innocent.

"Really? And who is the other?"

Ted's face stayed noncommittal. "Jonah Steel."

Joe. My best friend, Joe. Joe, who this idiot had already tried to frame and blackmail for what my father had done to Colin.

My guts continued their tumbling as anger took hold. I was determined to keep my cool. I had no reason to believe anything this asshole said.

"Why would they be investigating the two of us? We're innocent."

"I believe you are," Ted said.

"There's no belief required. It's a damned fact." *Keep cool, Bryce. Keep fucking cool.*

Joe was about to become a father. Did he know anything about this? The Steels had connections almost everywhere. If Joe was any kind of target of a federal investigation, surely he'd be aware.

"I'm just trying to give you a heads-up," Ted said.

"And I suppose you'd like to be compensated for this information?"

He scoffed and looked to the left. "If I wanted compensation, I'd have gone straight to Steel myself."

Right. Straight to Joe, who he'd already tried to blackmail. I wasn't buying it. But I wasn't quite ready to let Ted know that yet.

"Good call," I said. "Because you know I have nothing."

"Not true. You have a house."

"A house no one will buy because of my father's exploits."

"Maybe so." He sipped his coffee. "I'm here solely as a Good Samaritan, to let you know."

"And how do you know all this?"

"Easy. The Feds talked to me. To me and my son. They asked a lot of questions about the two of you."

*I am not responsible for the sins of my father.*

My mantra.

As much as I'd had to convince myself it was true, now Ted Morse was telling me it wasn't. Why else would anyone ask about Joe and me?

"A *Good Samaritan*?" I said.

"Yes."

*You're bluffing.*

But I didn't say the words aloud.

"They've spoken to Colin as well, you say?" I asked.

He nodded.

The server arrived with my coffee. I let it sit undisturbed. If I tried to put anything in my mouth, I might puke. Keeping this normal tone when I was raging inside was taking its toll.

"What kinds of questions did they ask the two of you?"

"I'm not at liberty to say. I'm taking a chance just telling you this much."

"I see." Though I didn't see at all.

"You don't believe me." A statement.

This time I took a sip of my coffee—a small sip—and let it trickle down my throat. All for show. "Why should I?"

"What ulterior motive would I have?"

"I don't know. Maybe you've got some"—air quotes— "*friend* in the FBI, someone who could bury this *investigation*. For a price."

"If I wanted money, I'd have gone straight to Steel. Wait. I already said that."

"Then what the hell do you want, Morse? Because the way I see it, the Feds can turn over every rock in my life, and they'll never find any evidence that either Joe or I are connected to the trafficking ring. Not one tiny shred."

"I mean no disrespect," Ted said, "but you're being naïve, Bryce. Incredibly naïve."

My knuckles whitened around the handle of my coffee cup. Maintaining a level head was becoming increasingly more difficult.

"And you're being incredibly transparent."

"How is that?" he asked. "Aren't you aware of Jonah Steel's history?"

"I'm very aware of Jonah Steel's history. He's been my best friend nearly my entire life."

"Then you know he paid off prison guards to beat Larry Wade?"

I swallowed, keeping my expression noncommittal. I did *not* know that. But I knew Joe, and he had a hot temper. Larry Wade was his half uncle and one of the men who'd tortured and raped Joe's brother. Could I see him ordering a beating?

Yeah, I could.

"Ah. So you didn't know."

"Joe wouldn't do that." The lie tasted good. Actually good. I'd defend Joe with my life.

"I assure you he did. See? Something you didn't know about your best friend of all these years."

"You think prison guards are paragons of virtue? If Wade got beaten in prison, he probably had it coming, and even if he didn't, a couple black eyes are nothing compared to what he inflicted on innocent children over the years. Joe didn't order anything, but even if he did, Wade got what he deserved. You know what those men were capable of as well as I do."

That last part was a cheap shot. Ted's son had been brutalized at the hands of my father. I never forgot that. But right now, he was trying to implicate Joe and me, so I'd defend us both.

"Jonah Steel is a loose cannon," Morse said nonchalantly. "You're his best friend and the son of Tom Simpson. Why *wouldn't* they be investigating you?"

"Well, for one, because we're innocent."

"Are you? What happened during those camping trips your father took you and Joe on, Bryce?"

The camping trips? The ones Joe and I looked forward to more than anything? We foraged, fished, hunted. Only the three of us ever. No one else would know anything about—

*Oh, God.*

I'd nearly forgotten.

Just once, we hadn't been alone.

Just once.

I stood and threw a couple bucks on the table to cover my

coffee. "This meeting is over."

I walked out the door quickly, and when I was out of eyeshot of the café, I called Joe and left a voicemail.

"We need to talk. Now."

# CHAPTER THIRTY-SEVEN

**Marjorie**

Jeans, a gray hoodie, and a black beanie.

That was all Dale could tell the officer about the man who had spooked him. The officer wanted to speak to some of the other children who'd been on the playground at the time, but the school principal forbade it without getting their parents' permission first.

Who could blame the principal? No more information to be had, though. Dale didn't want to go back to school, so I texted Colin and canceled our meeting. Jade and I picked up Donny early and headed back to the ranch.

Dale was quiet the rest of the afternoon, though that in itself wasn't unusual. Jade and I both made sure he knew that he could talk to either of us or to Talon when he felt ready. In the meantime, he retreated to his bedroom.

Donny played outside with the dogs.

Jade's nausea had returned, so I made her a cup of peppermint tea and brought it down to the family room, where she sat in one of the recliners.

"Thanks," she murmured, taking the mug of hot liquid.

"You okay?" I sat down on the couch next to her chair.

She took a sip. "Not even slightly. I tried to put on a strong face for Dale, but I'm completely petrified. What if he truly saw a face he recognized?"

"In Snow Creek?"

"Tom Simpson lived in Snow Creek for decades, and so did Larry Wade. That's two of them. It would make sense that they had others here."

"Or it would make sense that they didn't. Snow Creek was their *other* life."

"I need to get back to work," she said. "My leave of absence ends now."

"Jade..."

"I'm the city attorney, for God's sake. This town needs me, especially now."

"Your *sons* need you," I said. "Especially now. You hired the acting city attorney yourself. You know she's qualified."

"Yeah, but she's not personally involved here."

"All the better," I said. "You know that. As an attorney, you *shouldn't* be personally involved."

"Larry ended that the day he gave me Talon's case to work on."

"Larry was unethical. Hardly the standard you want to live up to."

"True." She sighed and took another sip. "I feel like I should be doing something, especially if Dale is right and there is another psycho on the loose."

"You're still technically the city attorney, just on leave. You still have access to all the files, right?"

"Technically, yes, but I can't access the server from here." She shook her head. "That was my idea. After finding out Wendy and the others had hacked into so many files, I had the city install a superpowered security system. What was I thinking?"

"You were thinking you were doing your job, and you were. You can always go into the office to do research. Especially now that you're feeling better."

"Yeah, but I don't want to step on Mary's toes."

"You're Mary's boss. How would you be stepping on her toes?"

"I don't know." She exhaled. "All I know is that I feel utterly useless at the moment."

"Useless?" Talon entered the family room. "Blue eyes, stop talking like that. Is Dale okay? I got here as soon as I could."

"He's in his room," Jade said. "He was spooked something awful. I'm scared, Talon."

"I won't let anything happen to any of you," he said. "Count on that."

She smiled. "I know. Still..."

Still... I agreed. I wouldn't go soft for Jade's sake, but I was pretty spooked myself.

Talon kissed Jade's lips. "Count on that," he said again. "I'll go talk to Dale." He left.

"Your brother is strong," Jade said, "but he's not invincible."

"You think he doesn't know that? He was tortured and abused. If anyone knows he isn't invincible, it's Talon."

"He was a child then. He went off to war and tried to get himself killed, but he came back."

"Doesn't make him invincible."

"I know that. I'm saying he *thinks* he is." She took another sip and then set the mug down on an end table. "He'll do anything to protect me and those boys, and if anything happened to him..."

"Nothing will happen to him." I tried to make my voice sound calm and reassuring.

But I wasn't convinced.

"He's in there talking to his son," Jade said, "and I'll bet you anything when he comes out, he'll be going on a full-force manhunt to track that hoodie guy down. You watch."

I didn't have the heart to try to disagree.

Jade was right. Talon would get Joe and Ryan, and the three of them would sniff this guy out or die trying.

The latter was what concerned Jade and me.

I swallowed my fear. "Well, if the guy is someone from Dale's past, he *should* be found. We don't want him hurting anyone else."

"Of course we don't. I just thought..."

She didn't have to complete her sentence. I understood. She'd just thought what we all thought. The FBI had raided the compound, the bad guys were dead, and this nightmare was finally over.

And now we had to face the fact that perhaps it wasn't.

Donny came in, and I made him a quick snack. Talon was still speaking to Dale in the bedroom. He'd been gone a half hour when he finally emerged. He ruffled Donny's hair and smiled, and when the little boy retreated back outside, he turned serious.

"I need to talk to Joe and Ryan."

Jade and I exchanged a worried glance.

Again. It was all starting again.

# CHAPTER THIRTY-EIGHT

**Bryce**

I sat in Joe's office—not his home office but the office in the ranch business building. That had been my choice. I wanted privacy. Not that Melanie wouldn't give us our privacy, but I didn't want the chance of anyone walking in. I'd even managed to convince Joe to let his assistant and secretary leave early.

His dark eyes were heavy-lidded and troubled when we finally sat down together—alone—in his office.

Even then, I was freaked. Was this office bugged? I still wasn't sure Ted Morse had been straight with me. He could be playing games, trying to get a payoff. I had no idea. But at this point, given the vague memory that had popped into my head, I couldn't chance it.

"What is it, Bryce?" Joe asked. "You've got me a little on edge."

Joe on edge was not a pretty sight. He had a hot head and a quick temper. I'd seen it in action many times, and I needed him to remain calm.

"Can we get out of here?" I asked.

"What? You just made me send my staff home so we could speak privately. There's no more private place on this ranch right now."

I couldn't say anything more, not here. My whole body

tensed and tingled, as if myriad eyes and ears were watching and listening. Probably in my mind, but given what Joe and I needed to discuss, I wasn't willing to take the chance.

"I need a walk." I coughed into my hand to relieve the lump in my throat. "Now."

"What the—"

"Please," I said softly, looking toward the door.

Joe stood quietly, seeming to understand. I sighed in relief. We walked out of the office together.

"Where to?" he said.

"Outside. It's a decent day. Sun's out."

He nodded and we left the building. Once we were a couple hundred feet from the building, he turned to me, his gaze serious. "Tell me what's going on. Now."

"I met with Ted Morse."

"Yeah?"

"I don't know what his angle is, Joe, but he claims the Feds are investigating the two of us."

"You and me?"

"Yeah. Now I don't know if it's true. Whether it's the Feds or if it's Ted pulling something, which I wouldn't put past him, but he mentioned the camping trips you and I took with my dad."

Joe's face reddened. Yup, here went the hothead.

"Joe…"

"Fuck." He grabbed a fistful of his long hair. "Fuck, fuck, fuck."

"I know. So you remember?"

"Did Morse mention that time?"

"I'd forgotten, honestly. What was it? Nearly thirty years ago now? We couldn't have been more than eight or nine."

"Fuck."

"I told him we were always alone with my dad. And we always were..."

"Except for once," Joe said.

"He claims my phone and my house are bugged. That's why we needed to get out of there. He didn't say anything about your office, so I originally thought we'd be safe there. I mean, you have the best security and all. But these are the Feds."

"It's only the Feds if Morse is telling the truth."

"True. But how would he know about the camping?"

"Fuck if I know." Joe paced in circles.

"Does anyone else know? Your brothers?"

"I never told anyone. I trusted your dad. And like you, I'd forgotten until now. It was pushed back in my head, a nonissue, you know?"

"Yeah. Nothing ever happened. The family moved away. I mean, I assume they did. Hell, I can't even remember his name, can you?"

"Justin? Or Dustin?"

A memory sparked in my mind. "Justin. You're right. Justin... What was his last name?"

"I can't remember. I feel like it's in my brain somewhere."

Recall came trickling back. Justin had been a new kid in town. He was nothing special, but for some reason, he never quite fit in. He didn't blend. He was quiet and always alone, and...

"Whose idea was it, anyway?" Joe asked.

"It was mine," I said, thinking. "I asked my dad if we could bring him along."

"Damn. Do you think your father...?"

"I don't know." This time I paced in circles. "I'm afraid to even think about it."

"We have to think about it, man. We *have* to."

"Whether he did or not, it shouldn't have anything to do with us," I said. "We were nine. We're innocent."

"Morse is bluffing," Joe said. "He has to be. How could he even know anything?"

"I don't know. He's got money, though. Not Steel money, but enough to dig up any dirt there is. And he might have done just that."

"He seriously can't think he can take us on," Joe said. "Like you said, he doesn't have Steel money."

"I don't have *any* money."

"But he has to know that we've got your back."

"Why would he know that?"

"He'll know if he tries anything."

"I can't—"

"Don't even," Joe said. "You're an honorary Steel brother. You always have been. Whatever you need, bro. Always."

I already felt like I was taking advantage of the Steels by accepting their generous offer. My only solace was that I knew I was qualified and would do a damned good job for them. "Thanks, man."

"You know it." He shoved his hands into his pockets. "I'm going to talk to Morse."

"I'll come with you."

"I should go alone."

Hell, no. If Joe went alone, he might do something hotheaded and stupid. He'd been ready to blow Ted Morse away once before. With good reason, but still. Joe and I were good for each other. We kept each other level-headed.

"I'll go with you. He came to me with this. I'm already involved."

"Good enough." He pointed to his ankle. "But Rosie's coming along."

I nodded. "No problem there. I'll be packing as well." If I was there to stop him, Joe wouldn't cross the line. But I was absolutely fine with him scaring Morse a little, and since I'd learned the truth about my father, I'd carried my own concealed weapon.

"Funny," I said. "My dad is the one who taught us how to be such good shots."

Joe started to reply but stopped when his phone dinged. He pulled it out of his pocket. "Text from Talon. He needs to talk. I guess I'm going over to his house. Come with me. We have to tell them—"

I widened my eyes. "No, Joe. Not yet."

"You're right," he said. "This has stayed between the two of us for thirty years. A few more days won't hurt. We see Morse first."

I nodded. "You were going to have those PIs sweep my house for bugs. We need to get all your properties swept too before we even mention this anywhere inside."

"Good call," Joe said. "Let's go."

# CHAPTER THIRTY-NINE

**Marjorie**

Dinner for ten at the last minute. No problem when you lived on a beef ranch. Burgers for all. Jade's nausea had lessened some, and she helped me get everything together.

Melanie arrived before Joe, and I couldn't help smiling as I hugged her. She looked so beautifully radiant, her skin glowing, her belly in the third trimester. She was clearly enjoying her pregnancy and had little difficulty.

Which made me feel even worse for Jade.

I could tell Melanie felt a little guilty when she was around Jade, but she hid it well. The two of them weren't overly close. Melanie was much closer to my other sister-in-law, Ruby Lee Steel, who arrived moments later. The two of them had been each other's maids of honor at their respective weddings. They set to chatting, so Jade and I went back to work in the kitchen.

Jade sighed. "I'm trying to be happy for Melanie. I really am."

"I know it's hard," I replied.

"I'm trying to concentrate on the fact that my baby is okay. That's what's important."

"It is. And it'll be over in less than six months."

"She'll have a baby before I do."

"True, but she may only have this one chance because

239

of her age. Remember that. You're young. You can have lots more."

"After this?" Jade shook her head. "I'm not sure I can go through it again. Plus we have the boys to think about as well. I can't be spread too thin. And right now? This stuff with Dale? I'm scared, Marj."

"It'll all work itself out," I said, hoping I sounded convincing. I was every bit as frightened as she was.

I carried a tray of raw burgers out onto the deck for Talon to grill. I looked around. Everyone was here.

Everyone, that was, except for Joe and Bryce.

Joe had texted Talon back that he was with Bryce and that Bryce was coming along. Even now, my body still tingled from our time together.

I wanted to see him.

And I wanted not to see him.

I turned, and—

"Oh!" I gasped, my knees trembling.

Bryce grabbed my arm and steadied me. "Sorry. I didn't mean to startle you."

I wasn't startled so much as...hyperaware. His body so close to mine sent me into shivers—shivers that raced along my spine and landed between my legs.

"Where's Joe?" I asked.

"Should be right behind me," Bryce said. "Jade sent us straight out here."

"I need to get back to the kitchen," I said weakly.

Still, he held on to my arm.

"Okay?" I pulled out of his grasp.

"Oh, sure. Sorry." His cheeks reddened.

I turned quickly and raced to the kitchen, where Jade was

HELEN HARDT

mixing up the salad. I set to work slicing tomatoes and onions, the latter making my eyes water.

Just what I didn't need.

Joe walked up the stairs from the family room, carrying two martinis. "Hey, Sis," he said halfheartedly, and then he walked outside.

Huh. Joe seemed a little off, as if his thoughts were somewhere else.

I had too much else to think about, though, so I slotted it into the back of my mind and continued preparing the condiments for the burgers. When I was done, I grabbed the tray, took it outside, and set it on the table.

Talon was finishing up the first batch of burgers, and Ryan popped open a few bottles of his house red.

"Come and get it," Talon said.

First in line was Donny, of course. The little boy loved to eat. I looked around for Dale. He'd been out here earlier. I went back in and walked back to the boys' room. The door was open, so I knocked gently and walked in. "Dale?"

"Yeah?" He lay on his bed, his nose in a book.

"Dinner's ready."

"I'm not too hungry."

"It's your dad's burgers," I said. "The best around."

He didn't reply.

"All your aunts and uncles are out there. They want to see you."

"They're not really my aunts and uncles," he said sullenly.

I lifted my brows. This was new. Though Dale hadn't taken to his new family quite as quickly as Donny had, he'd come around. Where was this coming from?

"Of course they are. And next week, we're going to court—"

"None of it matters. My real mom is dead. And my real dad is... I never had one."

"Dale—"

"Just go away. I don't want any supper, okay?"

I sighed. "I know you had a rough day, Dale. I'm sorry." I left the room quietly, leaving the door as it was. I'd send Talon in. Talon had been the best at getting through to Dale.

Or maybe Mel. She'd been working with him.

I sighed again. I didn't know what the heck to do. Best get Talon. He was back at the grill, and who was standing next to him? Bryce.

Of course.

I touched Talon's arm to get his attention. "Dale's in his room. He's upset."

Talon nodded. "I'm there. Can you man the grill?" he said to Bryce.

"Sure, though I'm hardly a chef."

"Marj can help you. She can cook anything."

Great. As much as I loved cooking, I never thought it could be used against me. Then again, Talon didn't know what had gone on between Bryce and me. I'd sworn Jade to secrecy. "Yeah. Sure. I'll help."

"What do I do?" Bryce asked after Talon had gone inside.

"You know? You don't have to stay here. I'll take care of the grill. I can do it in my sleep."

"He asked me to do it, so I'll do it," Bryce replied almost tersely.

Okay, then. "It's easy. Just keep your eye on them. When you see the edges start to brown, flip them over."

"Then what?"

"Then you wait until they feel done."

"What is that supposed to mean?"

I touched my middle finger to my thumb. "For medium rare, it feels like this. Press the spatula to the burger."

"Huh?"

"I don't know how else to explain it. You'll get the hang of it. The second side only takes about three minutes. Just let me do it."

"Nope."

Such stubbornness! Until it dawned on me. Maybe he wanted to talk to me. Be with me.

Problem was, I had no idea what to say. Until I spied Joe by himself, looking...strange, sipping his martini. An empty glass sat next to him on the table. Had he brought out both drinks for himself? I'd assumed one was for Bryce.

"What's up with Joe?" I asked Bryce.

"Joe's fine," Bryce said, again tersely.

"Since when does he start with two drinks?"

Bryce cleared his throat. Tersely. "You'd have to ask him."

"I'm asking you. You were with him today. He doesn't seem like himself." As a matter of fact, Bryce didn't seem like himself either. Not that I could tell, really. He'd been an enigma since his father died.

"He's fine. And I'm fine."

"I didn't ask about you."

He huffed and looked down at the grill, poking the edge of the spatula into the burgers. Red juice flowed out.

"Don't do that," I admonished. "They'll dry up. You want the juices trapped inside."

"But you said—"

"I said press the flat part of the spatula against it to gauge the feel of the meat. Don't cut into it."

"Fine. You just take over." He huffed again and handed me the spatula.

Then he walked toward Joe.

# CHAPTER FORTY

## Bryce

"Your sister's asking questions."

Joe finished his second drink. "Like what?"

"She says you're not yourself," I said quietly. "Which means we both need to put on an act."

"How am I not myself?"

"I don't know. She's *your* sister. She specifically mentioned the two drinks, though."

"Oh."

"That's it?"

"What do you want me to say? I've got a lot on my mind. We both do."

"True enough, but if we're going to keep this to ourselves until we have more information, we're going to have to act our parts."

"Meaning I need to untense myself? How the fuck am I supposed to do that when I'd like to go off on that bastard Ted Morse?"

"Joe, come on," I said. "I'm freaked too, but for all we know, this deck is bugged somehow. So ease up."

"Fucker."

"I know. Go talk to Ryan or something. I'm going to go inside and get a drink."

I walked back past Marjorie, who was removing the cooked burgers from the grill. They'd no doubt be perfect. Just as well that she'd taken over. I'd have probably turned them into shoe leather. I made my way down to the bar and poured myself some of Talon's Peach Street bourbon. Good stuff. I took a sip and let the smokiness linger on my tongue before I swallowed its warmth.

I walked back upstairs and ran into Talon, who was returning from Dale's room.

"He's not coming out?" I said.

"Not right now, but he's okay. Just a little scared."

"Why?"

"Oh, you don't know yet, do you? He saw a man on the playground he thought he recognized from when he was in captivity."

My heart dropped into my gut, but I took a sip of bourbon to hide my surprise. "Oh?"

"It's probably nothing. I used to see all sorts of shit after my...experience. But he's scared, and it's bringing up a bunch of other stuff."

"Like what?"

"He's feeling like he's not really a Steel. That he's a bother to us."

"Oh. Jeez."

"I know. I reassured him that he's a valuable part of the family and we all love him. He's okay, but he needs his alone time, and I totally get that. I was his age when..."

He didn't finish. He didn't have to. We both knew what he didn't say.

"That Peach Street?" Talon gestured to my drink.

"The one and only. You want one?"

"Yeah."

We walked back down to the bar, and I poured Talon two fingers. "More?"

"Nope. That'll do for starters. What are you doing in here, anyway? Didn't I leave you in charge of the grill?"

"I turned it over to Marj. I think we'd all rather not sample my cooking."

Talon chuckled, and we walked back upstairs and out onto the deck. Everyone had found a seat around the large table, so we joined them. I loaded up a burger with all the fixings and then wondered how I was going to choke it down.

Joe was still being quiet. Not overly odd for Joe, but he was normally a little more talkative when he was with his family. I met his gaze, mentally telling him to get a grip, when something sparked in me.

I'd seen Joe look that way before, one morning as we stood along a riverbank.

Thirty years ago.

★ ★ ★

*"Daddy, can Joe and I invite a friend to go camping?"*

*My father raised one eyebrow. "A friend? Haven't we always said these trips are for us?"*

*"You let Joe come along."*

*"Joe's your best friend. He's like your brother. That's what you've always said."*

*"Yeah."*

*"And now you have a new friend?"*

*"I have lots of friends, Daddy. Joe's just my* best *friend."*

*"Who do you want to invite, son?"*

*"Justin. He's new at school."*

*"Why do you want to invite him?"*

*"He got beat up by Taylor and the other bullies. Joe and I had to rescue him."*

*"You know I don't want you getting into fights."*

*"We didn't. Joe and I are the biggest kids in third grade, so we told Taylor we'd crush his skull if he ever bothered Justin again."*

*My father smiled then but quickly changed to a stern expression. "Maybe Justin should fight his own battles. You and Joe won't always be there to bail him out."*

*"We weren't there, Daddy. We found out about it later. That's when we told Taylor to leave him alone."*

*"Let me think about it, Bryce."*

*"Please?" I'd already told Justin he could come along, so I had to get my father to agree.*

*"I said I'd think about it. I'll let you know tomorrow."*

★ ★ ★

I well-remembered Taylor Johns and his band of bullies. The rest of them didn't seem to have names. I'd known them at the time, but Taylor, as their leader, overshadowed the rest of them. They were just brawn. Nine-year-old brawn. I couldn't help a chuckle. They'd left me alone because I was Joe's best friend, and no one messed with a Steel. Of course, it helped that we were the biggest boys in the class too.

*We told Taylor we'd crush his skull if he ever bothered Justin again.*

Crush his skull? Where had I learned a phrase like that at nine years old? Not from a video game, as children these days might. From a movie? Possibly.

Or perhaps from a conversation I'd overheard once...

Damn. The memory was a sliver on the rim of my brain, trying to push its way in. I was young, so young, and the words had come from...

Damn.

My father had relented the next day and allowed Justin to accompany us. It was the only time another child had ever come along on one of our trips. The trips had begun when Joe and I met in first grade, and they had continued through high school, until we both went off to college.

My father had taught us how to shoot a pistol and a rifle, had shown us how to track animals and hunt them, had taught us how to fish.

Had taught us how to be men.

We'd learned the value of hard work and prosperity from Joe's father, Bradford Steel. I'd spent many summers helping on the ranch, earning more than my allowance and building muscles along the way.

But the things all little boys should learn from the men in their lives? How to defend yourself and live off the land?

Those skills had come from Tom Simpson.

My father. The man whose DNA accounted for half of me.

Bringing Justin camping had been my idea. Joe and I had felt sorry for him, had wanted him to have something fun after being such a target for the school bullies. Camping and fishing with my dad was the highlight of the week for Joe and me. We went some weekends, with two longer trips each year in spring and fall.

We could do something nice for someone. After all, that was what my mom always taught me to do.

So we'd brought along the new kid, the scared kid, the kid who'd been ripe for the picking. The kid who was the perfect prey for bullies.

And though I hadn't known it at the time, my father was the biggest bully in Snow Creek.

# CHAPTER FORTY-ONE

**Marjorie**

Bryce sat directly across from me, deliberately not meeting my gaze. Not that I expected him to. Oddly, he was keeping his eye on Joe, who was still acting strangely.

Talon and Jade were quiet as well, but I expected that after Dale's issues. They were at least themselves. Quiet, but themselves.

I watched Bryce and my oldest brother.

Something was going on.

If only Jade and I had been able to talk to Colin, maybe we'd know more. Bryce was supposed to talk to Ted Morse today, and if he had, whatever was going on with him and Joe was most likely related.

Bryce had hardly touched his burger, and though Joe was eating, he wasn't making eye contact with anyone, and he answered in one-word replies when someone spoke to him. Melanie and Ruby sat next to each other and were chatting animatedly, to the point where Mel didn't seem to notice that her husband was acting strangely. That wasn't like her. Ryan was his usual self, laughing and talking to whomever would listen. He sat next to Donny and kept him engaged.

That left me to sit quietly and eat my burger.

I felt like the little girl who had to sit alone at lunch with everyone watching her.

In truth, though, no one was watching me.

I was the last person on anyone's mind at the moment, so after I finished eating, I began clearing the table as others finished.

No one noticed.

I went inside to clean up in the kitchen. Dessert was ice cream, and they could all serve themselves when they wanted to. I was done for the night. I went to my bedroom to relax a bit. No one would miss me.

Until a soft knock at the door startled me.

"Yeah? Come in."

I jerked when Bryce entered the room. "Hey," I said.

"I'm taking off," he said. "I just wanted to say thanks for dinner."

"Oh? I thought you'd stay to talk to the guys about what went down with Dale today."

"I thought about it, but it's not really my place."

"Sure it is. You're as involved in this as any of the rest of us."

"Don't remind me." He rubbed at his chin. "So are you, though. Why aren't you in there?"

"They're not going to talk about anything I don't already know. To be honest, I need a break from it all. It's been a rough day."

"I know, and I'm sorry. How did your talk with Colin go?"

"It didn't. The timing overlapped with Dale, so we canceled."

"Oh." He gazed around my room absently, as if trying to zero in on something but not quite finding it.

"Honestly," I went on, "with this new development with

Dale, I'm not sure talking to Colin is the best thing for Jade."

"You might be right."

I lifted my brow. I hadn't expected that response from Bryce. He'd been all in on getting information from the Morses previously. "Oh?"

"Yeah. I'm not sure the Morses have anything of value for us."

"That's right. You talked to Ted today. It didn't go well?"

"He's just looking for a payoff," Bryce said. "He doesn't know anything."

"Oh. That's good, I guess. We don't need anything else going down right now. Not with Dale being troubled and Jade still having a rough pregnancy."

"Yeah." He cleared his throat.

Now what? He made no move to leave. I wanted to spend time with him, but I could hardly make a move when my entire family was in the house. "So...uh...you're welcome."

His forehead wrinkled. "For what?"

"You came in to thank me for dinner. Remember?"

"Oh. Yeah." His cheeks went pink.

Damn, he was so good-looking! I wanted to cup those rosy cheeks, let his sandy stubble prickle my fingertips. Kiss those firm lips, touch those broad shoulders.

He still didn't move.

I bit my lip. "Well...good night."

No words, and no movement.

"Bryce?"

He turned and met my gaze, his blue eyes sparkling. "I can't get you out of my mind."

My skin tightened around me as I warmed all over. I bit my lip once more.

"Nothing to say?" he asked.

"What do you want me to say? You've made it clear that there can't be anything between us."

"Yeah."

"So there's nothing to say."

He walked toward me, taking my hand. "But there is."

I gulped. "Then...what?"

"I want you to remember. I want you to remember everything. How it felt when we kissed, when we touched each other. How you felt, Marjorie, when you came in my arms."

Another gulp. "You're not making this easy," I said.

"Damn it." He pulled me close, meeting my gaze, his own on fire. "I don't want to make it easy. I want it to be hard for you. As fucking hard as it is for me."

Third gulp. "It is."

"Is it?" His fiery gaze made me hot all over. "Is it?"

I nodded.

"Because from where I stand, I could walk away from this house, this city, this state, and you'd go on as if nothing had happened between us. As if we hadn't made explosive love twice. Twice, baby. Twice. And it was earthmoving."

"How can you—" I stopped, gathering my emotions before I let them get the best of me. "How can you say that?"

"You let me walk away."

"You walked away on your own, Bryce. Do you really think I have any control over what you do? I made it clear for you that I was falling for you, and—"

His mouth came down on mine ferociously. I tried to hold back, honestly I did, but my lips opened anyway, inviting him in.

Inviting him in as I always would.

Feelings coiled in my belly, feelings I'd denied for the sake of my own sanity. Bryce wanted me yet didn't want me, but this kiss... This amazing, heart-pounding kiss... All our kisses had been magical, but this one had turbulence jolting through me, making my skin hot and cold at the same time. Arrows of passion and desire catapulted through me, landing in my pussy. Already I was wet and near orgasm.

Already I was prepared to shed my clothes and fuck him hard. Hard and fast.

I moaned into his mouth, moving my legs around his hard thigh, finding the friction I craved.

Then—

He pulled away urgently. "I can't."

I didn't speak. Couldn't speak. I was too busy panting. When I finally caught my breath, I rubbed my lips. "Fine," I said.

"Fine?"

"What do you want me to do, Bryce? Throw myself at you just so you can tell me again that it won't happen? Let you fuck me again so you can leave? I'm sorry, but it's getting old."

I hoped he believed my lie. One more kiss like that, and I'd let him do whatever he wanted. Tie me up. Dress me like a nurse. Make me call him Daddy. I didn't care.

"I... You..."

"You're going to have to finish a sentence," I said.

He nodded. "I should go."

"Yeah, you should."

He didn't move.

"Tell you what. We'll both go. Let's go see what my brothers are talking about." I looked quickly in the mirror above my dresser, finger-combed my hair, and then left.

# CHAPTER FORTY-TWO

**Bryce**

I followed her.

She was falling for me.

She'd as much as said it.

I was at once elated and crushed. I'd fallen for her long ago, when I'd seen how good she was with Henry. I just hadn't been able to admit it to myself. All the "baby sister" stuff had gotten to me, and then, once I found out about my father...

She deserved better.

The guys were in Talon's office, and we knocked before entering.

"Hey," Joe said to me. "We thought you'd left."

"I was going to, and then I ran into Marj and she suggested we join you."

"Of course," Talon said. "We had assumed you both would."

"We're just talking about what happened with Dale," Ryan said. "How we can find out who this guy is who spooked him."

I nodded and sat down in one of the leather chairs. Marj sat next to me.

"We're going to contact Mills and Johnson," Ryan continued. "They seem to be able to ferret out anything."

I nodded again. Trevor Mills and Johnny Johnson had

been integral in helping the Steels solve the mystery of Talon's abduction. They were high-paid mercenary PIs. The cops called *them*. Joe had already suggested getting them to check my house for surveillance.

Oh, shit...

I looked over to Joe. He was deliberately not making eye contact with me.

I understood why. The last thing he and I needed was Mills and Johnson poking around. If they uncovered what Ted Morse allegedly had, Joe and I would have a lot to answer for.

Answers that wouldn't make us look good.

We were innocent. We both knew that. We'd been little kids, for God's sake.

But we weren't nine anymore, and we'd been sitting on a secret for thirty years—a secret that could have outed my father long ago and saved so many, including Talon Steel, from physical, sexual, and emotional torment.

How had we forgotten? How had my father made us forget?

"Why not have the cops investigate?" I asked. "Why spend the money on PIs?"

"That's what I've been saying," Joe said, finally meeting my gaze. "My brothers won't hear of it."

"I agree with Tal and Ry," Marj said. "Why trust the cops to find the guy when we know the best PIs out there?"

"It's a lot of money," I said, knowing the argument would fall on deaf ears. Since when did the Steels have to worry about money?

"It's not your money, dude," Ryan said. "Let us worry about that."

I could say no more. I knew I'd lose this battle. Joe

remained quiet, his lips pursed. He knew as well. Mills and Johnson would be on the case, and soon. If he continued to argue the point, his brothers would get suspicious.

We couldn't have that. Not yet. Not until we knew exactly what we were dealing with.

I cleared my throat. "Have you thought about having this office swept for bugs?"

"Bugs?" Talon said. "Why?"

"I told you why. Because Ted Morse told me that the federal investigation was still open."

"Why would they bug us?" Ryan asked. "We're the victims. And our father is dead."

"Actually," Joe said, "I agree with Bryce. We can't be too cautious. Not after everything that's gone down. They got to Felicia, remember?"

"Yeah," Ryan said. "And those three guys are all dead."

"But if the investigation is still open," I said, "there might be others. And if Dale truly thinks he saw someone he recognized, someone might still be out there. After all, you guys brought them down. Someone might have a bone to pick."

Joe nodded slightly at me but said nothing. He and I knew well how to communicate without words. He wouldn't back up my statement. It would look too obvious. But he agreed.

"Actually," Marjorie piped in, "I think Bryce has a good point. If you're hiring Mills and Johnson, what would it hurt to have them check all of our buildings and homes for hidden bugs?"

"You nervous about something, Sis?" Ryan asked.

"Well...yeah. Dale is totally spooked, and that has Jade and me spooked. We need to protect those little boys above all else."

"Enough said," Talon agreed. "You're right, Bryce. We'll have everything checked."

I resisted the urge to sigh in relief. Joe gave me another of his unspoken "good job" looks.

I couldn't take all the credit. Marjorie had backed me up. If their baby sister was spooked, the Steel brothers would act.

She'd never know how much she'd come to Joe's and my aid. We needed to know if any of the Steel properties were bugged. We'd already discussed checking my house and cars. The house wasn't a huge concern. Mom, Henry, and I would officially be moved out within a few days. But our cars? They needed to be swept.

Mills and Johnson could sweep for bugs better than anyone in the field. The fact remained, though... Once they'd eliminated any bugs, they'd start digging into our past again. I shuddered to think of what they might find. Those details that Joe and I had never known.

I'd talk to Joe and figure it out later. I listened with one ear as the conversation turned back to Dale's purported stalker. Most of me was focused on the woman sitting next to me, the woman I wanted to drag off to bed and ravage more than I wanted my next breath of air.

Wouldn't happen tonight. Melanie, Ruby, and Jade were in the family room talking and drinking nonalcoholic wine. And of course her three big and burly brothers were also here.

Not a problem, as I was interrupted by my phone vibrating against my thigh. I looked quickly.

A text from my mom.

*Come home now. Need to talk.*

★ ★ ★

"What? Is Henry all right?" I demanded as I walked into our home.

I'd tried calling my mother as I drove home frantically, but she didn't answer.

"Henry's fine," she said, clearly on edge.

"Thank God." I sighed in relief. "Then what's going on? Why didn't you pick up the phone?"

"I didn't hear it ring." She glanced at her cell phone sitting on the table and then picked it up. "I'm sorry. I turned it off, I guess."

"You don't turn your phone off after sending a text, Mom." I gestured her to be quiet when she opened her mouth to argue. "Now what's going on?"

"Henry's mother. She's in Denver. And she wants to see him."

A brick hit my gut. Francine "Frankie" Stokes was a Las Vegas showgirl with long legs, fake tits, and a killer smile. My beautiful son was the result of a drunken one-nighter. She'd relinquished her parental rights, and I'd taken sole custody of Henry.

She'd promised to stay out of his life and leave us alone.

"Did you tell her no?"

"Of course not. She's his mother."

"His mother who relinquished all rights to him. He's my son now. Not hers."

"You have sole custody," she said. "Would it be too much to ask for her to see him?"

"Yeah."

"You don't understand. You're not a mother."

"Since when do you have such sympathy toward Henry's mother? What kind of woman gives away her son?"

She sighed. "I don't know. Honestly, I don't want her here any more than you do, but she sounded desperate."

Desperate? I didn't like the sound of that. No way was she coming near my son.

"What's her number? I'll call her and set her straight."

My mom pointed to her cell. "It's on my phone."

"You didn't take down her number?"

"I...guess I wasn't thinking. Everything that's gone on, and I've been packing all day."

"The packers were supposed to take care of all of that."

"I didn't trust them with the breakable stuff. They clomp around here like they own the place, trailing dirt and sand onto the carpet." She shook her head. "I didn't like it. Didn't like having strange men in the house."

My mother had been wary of strange men since my father's death. She was still dealing with what he'd been, and I understood completely. So what did I do? Instead of heading straight home after Ted Morse had come to her house, I'd fucked Marjorie Steel. What the hell was wrong with me?

"Mom, it's okay. I'll call Frankie and take care of everything."

"She's his mother, Bryce."

"Yeah, she is. But have you thought about the big picture here? What if she falls in love with Henry and wants to take him from us?"

My mother gasped, her fingers covering her mouth. "But she already gave up her rights!"

"Do you think that matters? She's his biological mother. The courts favor mothers over fathers. If she decides to pursue something"—I swallowed, the thought killing me—"we could lose him."

"No. Just no." She wrung her hands together.

"Exactly. I will *not* let that happen. She has no rights, so there's no reason we need to let her see him."

"I'm sorry, Bryce. I haven't been thinking straight lately. I don't know what's the matter with me."

I said nothing, just gave her a quick hug. I knew well what the matter was. My father. My psycho father. We were both still dealing with the truth of what he'd been.

I grabbed her phone and hit last call received.

No way was that wayward bitch coming near my son.

# CHAPTER FORTY-THREE

**Marjorie**

My brothers were still in the office, but I'd left after Bryce stormed out so quickly. I had no idea what his problem was, and I tried not to care.

Still, I cared. Maybe I didn't try very hard. Or maybe, more likely, I cared anyway, despite knowing I'd be better off if I didn't.

The clock was nearing nine p.m. when the doorbell rang.

My heart leaped. Bryce had returned! Not that he'd be here to see me, but I couldn't help the way my body responded. My sisters-in-law were still in the family room. I was nearest the door, so I walked through the foyer and opened it without looking in the peephole.

I smiled brightly, and—

Then frowned.

Bryce Simpson did not stand in the doorway.

Colin Morse did.

Colin Morse had come to my home...while all of my brothers were here. Not a good combination.

"Hey, Marj," he said.

"What are you doing here, Colin?"

"After you canceled on me today, I got worried. Is Jade all right?"

"She's fine."

"You didn't give me much of an explanation."

"I told you something came up and we couldn't make it. I didn't owe you anything else."

"May I come in?"

"I don't think that's a good—"

"Who is it, Sis?"

I turned at Talon's voice. This was, after all, his home too.

I opened my mouth to speak, but before I could—

"What do you want, Morse?" Talon asked, not overly nicely.

Colin cowered slightly. He tried to hide it, but his discomfort in Talon's presence was apparent. Talon had pummeled him once, and since then, Colin had been through torture and rape at the hands of Bryce's father.

"Tal..." I pleaded with my gaze. Talon, of all people, knew what had befallen Colin.

"I just want to make sure Jade is okay," Colin said, not meeting Talon's gaze.

"It's late."

"I know, but she and I were supposed to talk today. I was worried."

"She's fine, as I'm sure my sister told you. She'll reschedule your meeting."

"Come in, Colin," Jade said from behind me. "We can talk now."

Talon's facial muscles tensed. "It's late, blue eyes."

"I know, but I'm feeling okay for once, and I'd like to get the talk with Colin over with, honestly."

Colin stepped inside tentatively.

"Fine," Talon said. "I'll be joining you."

"We agreed that Marj and I would talk to him," Jade said.

"Because I was otherwise engaged," he said. "I happen to be free as a bird at the moment."

"Maybe another time," Colin said, his lips trembling slightly. "You're right. It's late."

"You've interrupted us already," Talon said. "If Jade wants to talk to you, you'll talk to her."

"With Marj," Jade emphasized. "Aren't you still talking to your brothers?"

"Yeah, we're working on things." He touched Jade's cheek lovingly. "All right. But Sis, don't leave them alone for a microsecond."

"I won't."

My brother had no idea how truthful I was being. I was every bit as interested as Jade to hear what Colin had to say, and I had plenty of questions for him.

Melanie and Ruby were in the family room, so I led Colin to the formal living room, which we hardly ever used. However, it was quiet and secluded and no way would anyone overhear us from Talon's office or the family room. Not that I cared. I'd tell them all everything eventually. But Colin needed to feel secure if I was going to get the truth out of him.

He walked in tentatively, looking a little scared to sit down on the gold silk brocade sofa. When Jade took a seat, he sat next to her at the opposite end of the couch.

"Do you need anything?" I asked Jade.

"Maybe some peppermint tea," she said.

"You want some?" I asked Colin.

"No. Just some water."

"Okay. No talking until I get back."

I quickly prepared Jade's tea and returned with the cup

and a glass of water for Colin. He sat stiffly on the couch, quiet. Apparently they'd taken me seriously when I said no talking, though I hadn't meant small talk.

I sat in the chair closest to Jade. I was tempted to take the couch between her and Colin, but that felt...strange. I wanted to protect Jade, but I felt I could do it better next to her, where we could both look at Colin. Make it two against one.

I waited a few seconds for one of them to say something, but neither did.

"So why are you here, Colin?" I asked to break the ice.

"I told you. I was worried about Jade."

Again, I waited for Jade to reply. When she didn't, I said, "We're looking for the real reason."

"That *is* the real—"

"Colin, we weren't born yesterday." I met his gaze sternly. "You don't come over to your ex's home—where she lives with her muscled husband—at nine at night to see if she's okay."

Colin opened his mouth, but no words came out. His face had returned to normalcy, handsome and high cheekboned, no longer gaunt from being starved and tortured by Tom Simpson. The only remnants were a few scars on his brow and one on his jawline, which would fade given more time.

Clothes hid the rest of the scars. Joe had told us in detail how he'd found Colin—naked and shaved, skin and bones with bruises and lacerations. He was wearing long sleeves, which made sense in February, but we were having a mild winter. I'd been wearing T-shirts and tanks around the house.

Jade bit her bottom lip, a gesture we had in common. Then she reached toward Colin and laid her hand on his. I stifled the surprised jerk that threatened me.

"I understand what you've been through, and I'm so sorry."

"I don't blame you," Colin said.

His tone was...ambivalent. Was he lying? I couldn't tell.

"Your father does," I said, not in the nicest way. "Even though my brother was the one who rescued you."

Colin reddened...and again said nothing, just fidgeted with the left sleeve of his shirt.

"You need to call him off," I continued. "We're dealing with enough crap right now."

"Marj..." Jade began.

"I'm right, and you know it," I said. "You're pregnant. Melanie's pregnant. You guys don't need more crap coming your way. None of us do. We're all victims here in our own way, and none of us are responsible for what happened to you, Colin."

"I just said I don't—"

"You said you don't blame Jade. What about Talon? What about Joe? What about what your father tried to do to him?"

"I stopped that."

"As you should have. But he's still up to something, and you're going to tell us what it is."

# CHAPTER FORTY-FOUR

**Bryce**

"Please, Bryce," Frankie said through my phone. "I just want to see him."

"No," I said for the third time. "It's not going to happen. You relinquished your parental rights, and I owe you nothing."

"I know that. I just thought, since I was in town—"

"You thought wrong. You have no idea what's going on in my life right now, and you've upset my mother. I can't have that. Henry is fine. He's a happy, healthy toddler. You'll just have to take my word for it."

"But I—"

"This conversation is over, Frankie. Don't call here again." I pushed End so violently that my mother's phone slipped from my hand and clattered to the floor.

Had I been too harsh? I couldn't bring myself to care. Too much else cluttered my mind.

My son. My mother. The Steels. My new position. Ted Morse.

And Marjorie.

At the top of the heap was Marjorie Steel.

I had to get her out of my system.

Just thinking of her had my groin tightening, despite the nerve-racking phone call I'd just completed. Despite my mother wringing her hands a few yards away from me.

"It's taken care of," I told her. "If she calls again, don't answer."

She nodded and walked toward Henry's nursery, presumably to check on him.

Since my father's death, my mother had let me be in charge of major decisions. She'd been a housewife her whole life, leaving such things to my father. Those days were over, and she was going to have to learn to stand on her own two feet. Would she be able to do that living with me on the Steel ranch? I didn't know, and I couldn't dwell on it. For the time being, I needed her help with Henry, and the two of them needed each other. I'd always be there for her, but she also needed to be an individual who didn't depend solely on another person.

I gazed around the house. Only furniture remained. Most of the little things that made the house a home—photos and paintings on the walls, books on the shelves, my mother's collectible cherubs on the mantel—had all been packed up and were probably on a truck somewhere, waiting to arrive at the Steel guesthouse.

I continued toward the kitchen to get a glass of water when a lone picture frame caught my eye. It sat on the floor in the corner of the small nook in our foyer. The glass had been broken and the photo scratched.

My mother and father's wedding photo.

It had stayed in place after my father's death. Many times I'd thought about trashing it, but it wasn't mine to trash. I hadn't existed when the photo had been taken. It was my mother's to do with as she pleased, and she hadn't moved it.

The other photos that had sat in that nook—a few of my baby pictures, one of Henry, and a couple other family photos—

were all gone, presumably packed up.

But this one...

I bent down and retrieved it. I was always amazed at how much I resembled my father. In this wedding pic, he was young, blond, blue-eyed, and handsome. He looked genuinely happy. Genuinely *normal*.

My mother was radiant in her wedding gown, her hair glowing around her shoulders. She was beautiful. She still was, with silver hair and light-brown eyes.

But she'd aged so much in the past year.

We all had.

I looked again at my father's image.

Was he already messed up then? What had caused him to become what he was?

Thanks to the Steels' investigation and the information that had come out when arrests were made, I knew he'd been corrupted by power and money, beginning when he was in high school. Had he already done heinous things by the time he'd wed my mother? Joe would know. The Steels hadn't told me everything they'd found, at my own request. I'd needed to keep my sanity.

But sanity be damned.

If I was to truly make sure I didn't become my father, I needed to know everything there was to know about him— what he'd done and why.

What could make a good man turn bad? Could anything? Or was he never a good man to begin with?

With the photo in hand, I headed into the nursery. My mother was standing at the crib, gazing down at a sleeping Henry.

"Mom?"

She turned. "He looks so much like you when you were a baby."

"I don't know about that." I smiled. "He's so beautiful."

"So were you. Just gorgeous. Just like..." She looked upward wistfully.

*...your father.*

The two words she didn't say.

I'd been told all my life how much I resembled my father. Even his mother—my grandmother, may she rest in peace—had said the same thing, said how much I looked like my father at every age. She'd been gone over a decade now. Thank God she never knew who her son really was.

I cleared my throat and held up the wedding photo. "I found this on the floor in the foyer."

"Oh." She quickly grabbed it from me. "The movers must have dropped it."

"Mom..."

"They must have— Oh, it's no use. You already know I destroyed it."

"I had a feeling."

"Do you know how difficult it is to look at this photo of what has always been the second happiest day of my life?"

"The second happiest day?" I said.

"The first happiest day was the day you were born, Bryce."

I warmed with love for my mother. "I understand. Even though I wasn't expecting him, the day I got Henry has turned into the happiest day for me."

"Children do that. You were so precious to me. We tried, but we never got blessed with another." Then she shook her head. "I used to love to gaze at this photo. To remember how happy your father and I were then, and we *were* happy. At least

I was. I always thought your father was. But now I look at it and I feel sick. It was all a lie."

"Why did you leave the picture on the floor, Mom?"

"That's where I threw it."

"Why didn't you throw it out?"

"I don't know. I wanted to. I was ready to pick it up and hurl it into the nearest trash can."

"And...?"

"Instead I left it on the floor." She shrugged her shoulders lightly. "I don't know why. Maybe I wasn't quite ready to let it go."

"Let go of what? Dad's dead."

"Let go of the memory of what we had." She sighed. "Or rather, what *I* had. I have no idea what he thought we had. I thought I knew him so well, and now... He was the loving husband and father who went off and did unspeakable things."

"I know. All those business trips when I was young."

"He was an attorney then, before he was mayor. He had some high-profile clients. It made sense that he'd travel. I never thought to question any of it. How could I have been so naïve?"

"We were both naïve."

"You were a child, Bryce. This isn't on you."

"Mom, I haven't been a child for the last twenty years. This is on me too."

"Don't do that to yourself," she said.

"I could give you the same advice." I took the photo from her. "What do you want me to do with this?"

She looked to the ceiling for at least a minute, seemingly lost in thought. Then she met my gaze. "Throw out the frame and the broken glass. Keep the picture. Hide it in a book somewhere. I know it's ridiculous, but although I don't want to see it, I can't bear to part with it."

"I understand." I walked to the crib, leaned down, and kissed my sleeping son lightly on his forehead. "I'll take care of this, and then I'm going out for a while."

"At this hour?"

"Yeah. Just back to Joe's. He has some information I need."

"All right. I love you, honey."

I kissed my mother's cheek. "Love you too, Mom."

# CHAPTER FORTY-FIVE

**Marjorie**

Colin stared at his lap for seconds that seemed like hours. Jade seemed to feel sorry for him, and I knew I should as well. He'd been to hell and back, but so had my brother. So had all of us in our own way, and his time to talk was running out. I had no idea how long Talon would allow him in this house. He could storm out of the office any minute and demand Colin leave, and he'd be well within his rights.

Still, I waited for Jade to make the first move.

And I waited.

Until I could wait no longer.

"We're waiting, Colin," I said.

He messed with his sleeve again.

"What's wrong?" Jade asked.

"I got a tattoo on my forearm. It itches."

"What did you get?" She leaned slightly forward.

"It's bandaged up. But it's...nothing really."

Yeah. He got a tattoo. Who cared? "We're waiting," I said again.

He finally met my gaze. "Would you believe me if I told you I have no idea what my father's up to?"

"Not even slightly. Jade?"

"I don't know," she said. "Maybe."

"Jade, we spent seven years together," he said. "You *know* me."

"The Colin I knew was committed to me. He wouldn't have run off and left me at the altar. Do you have any idea how humiliating that was for me?"

"There are things you don't know," he said, looking down at his lap again.

"You're lying," I said.

"I'm not."

"You looked down. It's a classic tell. You left because you were selfish. If you had second thoughts, you should have discussed them with Jade beforehand. For God's sake, you could have told her the day before and spared her the embarrassment. You could have called it off together, made it look mutual. You deserted her, Colin."

"Marj..." Jade entwined her fingers.

"Sorry. I know it all turned out for the best. You and Talon belong together, but that doesn't make what he did okay."

This time Colin met my gaze. "There are things you don't know," he said again.

"Really? Spill them, then. And while you're at it, you can tell us what your father's up to."

"My father doesn't tell me everything he does."

"Did you know he was trying to pin your abduction on Joe?"

"Not at the time he was doing it. No."

"Did it surprise you to find out?"

"Honestly?" He looked down again, shaking his head. "No."

I turned to Jade. "You knew Ted Morse. What kind of man is he?"

"He seemed fine to me. Polite. Always nice, but never overly friendly. Though I did think it was weird, Colin, that you waited until we were engaged to even take me home to meet your parents."

"Yeah, that always seemed weird to me too," I agreed.

"You didn't know my parents," he said. "I did."

"So?" I said.

"Does it matter at this point?" he asked.

"Yeah, maybe it does," I said. "What's up with your parents? Your father?"

"Your mother always seemed detached," Jade said. "Detached from your father, from you. From everything."

"She's a classic trophy wife," Colin said. "Botox and all. She looks the other way when my father has affairs, does questionable business deals."

"So you admit he engages in questionable business deals," I said.

"Does that really surprise you, after he tried to frame your brother?" Colin met my gaze once more.

"What was he thinking?" I asked. "You know what kind of money we have. How could he think he'd get away with framing Joe, who—I'll say it again—rescued you?"

"If I knew what my father was thinking, I'd be able to deal with him a lot better. He doesn't have a lot of scruples, which should be obvious to you by now. He saw dollar signs and was looking for a payoff. It's really that simple."

"Is it?" I asked. "Really?"

"Seems like it is to me." He still met my gaze.

I had to give him credit. He was looking me in the eye and everything. For a few minutes, I stayed quiet, digesting Colin's words.

"Tell me then, Colin. You say there are things I don't know. Why did you leave me alone on our wedding day?"

"Does it matter now?" he asked.

"It matters to me. You told me you were afraid. You had cold feet. But we'd been together for seven years. Maybe I bought it at the time, but it doesn't make any kind of sense."

"I loved you, Jade. I still do."

"She's taken," I said harshly. "And pregnant with my brother's child."

"I'm not here to win her back," he said. "Jesus, Marjorie."

"Why are you here, then?"

He cleared his throat. "To say I'm sorry."

"Too little, too late."

"You don't understand," he said. "I'm sorry for what I did. For what I allowed to happen." He cleared his throat again. "And for what's to come."

# CHAPTER FORTY-SIX

**Bryce**

I texted Joe, and he agreed to leave the meeting with his brothers and meet me at the dive bar in Grand Junction, where no one would see us or hear us. He was already sitting at the bar, nursing a martini and talking to an elderly man, when I walked in. I scanned the room quickly. No Heidi, thank God.

"Hey," I said.

"Bryce, hey." He held up his drink in greeting. "Meet Mike. Mike, my best and oldest friend, Bryce Simpson."

"Hi, Bryce," the old man said. "Any friend of the Steel brothers is a friend of mine."

"Nice to meet you. How do you know the Steels?"

"We seem to cross paths a lot." He set his empty glass on the bar and stood. "It's way past my bedtime, though. I just hate going home to an empty house since my wife passed. See you around."

I turned to Joe. "I hope he didn't leave on my account."

"Nah. He's a good guy, though. Helped me out once. Helped Talon and Ryan as well, as I understand it. He seems to be something like a guardian angel, always around when we need him."

"I wish he'd stayed, then. I could use a guardian angel about now." I quickly told him about the call with Frankie.

"She gave up her rights to Henry," Joe said. "Nothing to worry about. And if she tries anything, we've all got your back."

"I know." I signaled the bartender and ordered a bourbon.

"No beer?" Joe raised his brow.

"Had to grow up sometime."

"So what's up?" Joe asked. "Other than all the shit we've got on our plates already."

I took a sip of the drink the barkeep had placed in front of me. "Harsh stuff."

"They specialize in rotgut here." Joe smiled, holding up his martini glass. "This isn't exactly Cap Rock, but sometimes you need the harsh stuff. It reminds you that life can be...well... harsh."

I nodded. I knew exactly what he meant. Our conversations lately hadn't exactly been Champagne and Bordeaux material. "I need the truth, Joe. About my dad. About what he was into and when."

"You didn't want to know at the time. Why now?"

"My mom all but destroyed her wedding photo today, and it got me wondering about him. He looked so happy in that photo. So innocent. So *normal*. So now I have to know. When did he become what he was? Or was he always that way?"

"I'm not sure of the timing," Joe said. "All I know is that your father, Mathias, and Wade all went through extensive"— air quotes—"*training* to work for the trafficking ring. Training they were very well paid for."

"Training? What do you mean?" Another sip left burning embers in its wake.

"You sure you want to know?"

Was I? Another sip, another flaming throat. "Yeah. That's why I'm here."

"During training, everything they ever did to another human being was done to them."

"What?" I went numb. *What? What? What?*

"Surely you don't want me to get into specifics."

My mouth dropped open.

"Sorry, bro. You asked."

"So my father..."

"Was tortured. Raped. Beaten. God knows what else. Probably starved too, but that would have been the least of his trials."

"When?"

"Like I said, I'm not sure of the timing, but I could get that information if you really want it."

Did I? Had he been going through this when he married my mother? When I was born? When he took Joe and me camping?

And why? Why in hell would he allow anyone to do such things to him?

"Why?" I asked quietly.

"For money," Joe said succinctly. "It could only be for money. They were each paid millions."

"Did they know what they were in for?"

He shook his head. "No idea. Probably not, or they wouldn't have done it. Or maybe they would have. Money had become God to the three of them."

"He was paid to become a monster," I said, more to myself than to Joe.

"So it would seem."

"Then maybe..."

"Maybe what?"

"I don't know. Maybe he wasn't always a psychopath.

Maybe he could have been a normal human being."

Joe met my gaze sternly. "I'm sure you'd like to believe that, man, and I wish it were true for you. But think about it. If someone offered you several million dollars to be tortured and raped so you could then inflict that horror on others, would you do it?"

"Of course not!"

"I think you have your answer, then. They were already messed up. Big-time."

An image seared itself into my mind.

Justin's limp body washed up on the edge of the river where we fished. We'd been looking for him all morning after we'd awoken to find him missing from the tent.

My father had held his fingers to Justin's neck, said he was dead, and had taken him to the nearest police station. Joe and I stayed at camp.

Alone.

At nine years old.

Not a big deal. We knew where we were and what to do. We knew how to start a fire, how to find our own food, how to take care of ourselves. Besides, we were in an isolated area, and while mountain lions occasionally appeared, there were no grizzly bears in Colorado. We both knew how to shoot a rifle.

At nine years old.

My father had taught us.

My father had also warned us, when he returned that day, never to speak of what we'd seen. "It would be too painful for everyone," he'd said. "If I hear either of you ever utter a word, I'll tan your hides. This never happened."

*This never happened.*

After a while, I'd believed it. I'd forgotten, and apparently so had Joe.

How? We were young, but still we had brains that worked. I remembered other things from when I was nine. How had my father made sure we forgot every detail?

"I'm sorry, Bryce," Joe said.

I hurtled back into reality. "About what?"

"That your dad wasn't a better man."

I nodded. Joe had been there when my father had shot himself. In fact, my father had been ready to kill my best friend.

"I'm sorry too, for what he put you through."

"Water under the bridge, man."

I nodded again, though how Joe could be so readily forgiving, I had no idea. Probably had to do with Melanie and his son on the way. Love and a new life had a way of putting things into perspective.

"But we do have to talk about what happened thirty years ago."

Once more, I nodded. "Justin," I said softly.

"Somehow Ted Morse knows. Or he knows something else, but I don't know what it could be. I've racked my mind for the last day and a half, trying to find something else we might have forgotten."

"Me too," I said. "All I can come up with is Justin. How have we forgotten for so long?"

"Your dad told us to. Told us not to mention him at school because it would be too sad for everyone. Told us we'd be in big trouble if we ever said his name."

"And we believed him," I said. "Why did we believe him?"

"Because we were nine." Joe took another sip of his drink. "We were nine fucking years old, Bryce."

"Why is it all so fuzzy? It doesn't make sense." I shoved my hand through my hair. "My father killed him. My father killed Justin." After doing God only knew what else to him, though I couldn't say the words aloud.

"And then threw him into the river, no doubt."

I took another sip of my bourbon and let it burn a new trail down my throat. "Surely the police were called, right?"

"I don't know, man. This is your father we're talking about."

How well I knew. "But Justin's parents..."

"These men got away with everything," Joe said. "None of this should surprise us."

My best friend was right.

"I haven't given him a thought in all this time," I said. "Even now the memories are like a faded dream. But what else could Morse have on us?"

"I have no idea."

"We were nine. We're innocent. I don't know what he thinks he's going to accomplish. He says he doesn't want money, but what else could he be after?"

"He'll get none from me," Joe said. "Not a fucking penny, not after he tried to blame me when I rescued his son."

"Do you remember Justin's last name?" I asked. "I know it's in my head somewhere, but I can't bring it to the surface."

Joe shook his head. "We should be able to find it, though. He attended school in Snow Creek. There'd be records."

"How do we get them?"

"Jade is the city attorney. She has access."

"To school records? Minors?"

"I assume so, and if she doesn't, Mills and Johnson can find it."

"That means we have to tell either Jade or Mills and Johnson why we want the information," I said.

"No fucking way." Joe let out a huff. "I'm worried they'll

find it anyway. I guess it's up to us, then."

I downed the last of the brown swill in my glass. "I guess so."

If we could find Justin's last name, we might be able to locate his family and discover whether Ted Morse or anyone else had contacted them recently.

Or...

We could be walking into a giant trap.

# CHAPTER FORTY-SEVEN

### Marjorie

I eyed Colin, anger rising. "Say what?"

Jade fidgeted, twirling her thumbs together. "For what's to come? What does that mean, Colin?"

"That's all I can say."

"You absolutely do *not* waltz into our home, drop a bomb like that, and then leave us hanging," I said, my cheeks warming with rage. "Not fair, Colin. Not fair at all."

Jade stood, her face paler than it had been seconds ago. "I'm not feeling very well. Oh, shit!" She ran out of the living room.

"Now look what you did." I balled my hands into fists. "Talon's going to come in here, really pissed, and once I tell him what you just said, you'd better watch out."

Colin stood. "I need to leave."

I rose, blocking his exit. "Think again. My brothers are just down the hallway. All three of them. They'll hear me if I scream."

"You have no idea what I've been through," Colin said.

"Maybe I don't. We're all truly sorry about what Tom Simpson did to you. But that doesn't give you the right—"

He held up his hand. "I can't say any more. My father will..."

"Will what? What will your father do?"

"Let's just say he'll make everything worse if I do."

"You said you didn't know what he was up to."

"I don't. But I suspect he's up to something. I honestly don't know what, Marj. You've got to believe me."

"Then why did you come here?"

"I already told you. To tell Jade I'm sorry. For...everything."

I finally let him pass. "Go. Get the hell out of here. And thanks for nothing."

After Colin left, I checked on Jade in the powder room. She had her heaving under control and assured me she was fine, so I trekked to Talon's office. The door was open, and Talon and Ryan were talking.

"Where's Joe?" I asked.

"He got a text from Bryce about an hour ago and took off," Ryan said.

The mention of Bryce's name sent a quick shudder through me. "Is everything okay?"

"He didn't say otherwise," Ryan said. "How'd it go with Colin?"

I filled them in. "Jade got so upset she had to leave. She's in the bathroom."

Talon stood quickly. "I'll take care of her."

"She's okay. I just checked on her."

He left anyway.

Ryan stood then. "I should go. It's late."

"Ruby's still in the family room with Mel."

"She didn't go with Joe?"

"Guess not. Any idea what Bryce wanted?" I asked, trying to sound sufficiently disinterested.

"Not a clue," Ryan said. "I'll take Melanie home. Night, Sis."

"Good night."

I stood alone in Talon's empty office. Where had Joe and Bryce gone? Was Bryce okay? My tummy churned, and a slow wave of nausea wound its way up my throat.

I was worried.

Really worried.

Neither Joe nor Bryce had been acting like themselves earlier, and now Colin's enigmatic words disturbed me as well. Something was up, and I was going to find out what. I pulled my phone out of my pocket. I could text Joe.

Yes, that would be the logical thing to do. Joe was my brother.

My fingers had other ideas. They tapped on Bryce's number.

*I need to talk to you.*

★ ★ ★

I waited impatiently, biting my lip and grinding my teeth, at the guesthouse behind the main house. Bryce had texted me back within minutes, telling me he couldn't talk but would meet me there as soon as he could get away. Was he still with Joe? He didn't say, and I couldn't even begin to guess.

Everything was imploding around me.

Our tough times were supposed to be over, weren't they?

I took a drink from the glass of ice water I'd poured myself. Even the kitchen of the guesthouse was stocked. Bryce and his mom wouldn't have to bring anything when they moved in. By the time I drained the glass, Bryce still hadn't arrived, so I went outside to the deck, complete with an enclosed hot tub. The

February night was mild, around forty degrees. The whir of the hot tub's motor drew me closer, and I removed the cover. Steam rose from the warm water, and I inhaled the crisp scent of bromide.

Still no Bryce.

What the heck? I went back into the house and into the master bedroom to get a towel. Instead, I found a cushy white robe that must have been Ruby's. I undressed and wrapped the robe around my body.

A soak in the hot tub would relax me.

Over an hour had passed since I contacted Bryce, and he hadn't responded to my more recent text. Had he decided not to come? Probably. I'd take a long, soothing soak. He wasn't going to show up anyway, and if he did? Well, he wouldn't see anything he hadn't seen before.

I poured myself another glass of water—had to keep hydrated in the hot tub—and walked back out onto the deck. In the distance, soft lights shone from the main house. Thanks to the redwood enclosure around the tub, I wouldn't be seen, though frankly I didn't much care at the moment. In the midst of another looming crisis, I deserved a little relaxation. Sure, I could have drawn a hot bath in my own room or used our much larger hot tub at the main house. But I was here now, waiting for Bryce.

And if he showed up, I kind of liked the fact that he'd find me naked.

I stepped into the water, letting it encase me in its soothing warmth. The steam rose like night fog around me. I sat, and the water covered my breasts. I closed my eyes and inhaled a relaxing deep breath.

Then I giggled. What if I started playing with myself, a la

a romance novel? Then the hero would certainly catch me in the middle of my self-service and take over. I'd read it a thousand times. I cupped my breasts and thumbed my nipples, making them harden even within the heat of the water.

I giggled again.

Couldn't do it. Just too damned cliché.

I drained my glass of water and checked my phone, which was sitting on the ledge. I'd been soaking for nearly fifteen minutes, and my body temperature was on fire. Time to get out.

I stepped out of the tub, the cool air chilling me slightly, and wrapped the fluffy robe around my shoulders.

Then I turned—

I held back a gasp. Bryce stood in the doorway leading into the house. I'd locked the front door, but he no doubt already had a key. I'd expected a text if he actually showed up, which I'd pretty much given up on...until this moment.

"Hey," he said.

"Hey back. I didn't think you were coming."

"I'm sorry. I couldn't tell Joe where I was going."

"Why not?"

"I..." He paused a few seconds. "I don't know. I just didn't feel like I could. He'd ask a lot of questions, want to know why you wanted to see me."

"Do you know why I want to see you?"

"The same reason I want to see you, I hope." He grabbed me and pulled me to him.

"Bryce..."

"God, don't talk. Just kiss me. Please." His lips came down on mine.

This honestly hadn't been my plan. Kissing Bryce was

always in the back of my mind, but I'd truly needed to talk to him about... About...

My thoughts melded together until they were an incoherent blob. Didn't matter. None of it mattered. All that mattered was Bryce and this kiss.

Our lips slid together, and desire welled inside me, beginning in my core and shooting outward until my clit was pulsing with need. Every part of my body quickened under the fluffy robe, my nipples hardening.

Bryce deepened the kiss, exploring every inch of my mouth with his tongue. With one swift movement, he could brush the robe from my body. I wanted him to, was silently begging him to as I returned his kiss. Instead, he pulled me through the doorway and into the house.

He grabbed one of my hands and led it to his crotch. "Feel what you do to me."

I squeezed gently, and he sucked in a breath. Before I could speak, he swept me into his arms and carried me down the hallway to the spare bedroom, where we'd made love previously.

Finally, he ripped the robe from my body and pushed me down onto the bed. "You're so beautiful, Marjorie. I've never seen a more beautiful woman."

I sighed softly. I hadn't expected this, but I wasn't about to stop. We could talk afterward, though I'd forgotten my intended subject.

The end of my ponytail was wet from the hot tub, and the rest of my body was covered in shiny perspiration left over from the heat. I wasn't looking my best, but he didn't seem to mind.

"I didn't think you were coming," I said.

"I told you I would."

"But it's been nearly two hours."

"I know. I'm sorry. Joe and I..."

Questions tugged at me. A lot of them. But not now. Not while I was naked on a bed with Bryce Simpson staring down at me like I was tonight's main course.

Everything else could wait.

"It's okay. Come to me. Please. Make love to me, Bryce."

His blue eyes were on fire. "Damn. You make me insane. I want you so much. In all my life, I don't think I've ever wanted anything more."

"I'm right here," I said. "I'm right here, and I'm yours."

# CHAPTER FORTY-EIGHT

**Bryce**

Such breathtaking beauty. Marjorie Steel was long legs with curves in all the right places. Her dark eyes were deep and smoky, her breasts swollen, her nipples hard and taut. Her flesh glistened and was tinted pink from the heat of the tub.

Luscious. Delicious. A temptress.

She was all those things and so much more.

Emotions coiled through me, feelings I wasn't ready to face yet. This woman meant so much to me, and I wasn't even close to worthy.

I banished those thoughts from my mind. She was here. I was here. And she was offering herself to me. No strings—at least none that I knew of.

I couldn't offer her strings of any kind. Not now, and maybe not ever. I'd vowed to stay away, but I could offer her the next few hours.

I was so hard right now that I had to get inside her. After I took the edge off, I'd love her until morning. I'd force every ounce of pleasure I could out of her.

But now...

I undressed as quickly as I could and lay down next to her, spooning her. I kissed the soft silk of her shoulder and pushed my cock against the crack of her ass.

"Please," she said softly.

I thrust into her wet heat.

"God, yes," she said, her voice a sweet, soothing breeze in my ears.

She wrapped around me in a perfect sexual hug, a glove for my cock in the most intimate way. For a moment, everything else—the past, the lies, the situation Joe and I needed to deal with—disappeared, and I escaped into her embracing warmth.

If I could only stay here, encased within her welcoming body forever, I could be complete. Complete and happy.

I let those warm thoughts float around the mess inside my mind as I pumped into her quickly. In. Out. In. Out. Her moans were my reward.

"Can't last long," I panted into her ear.

"S'okay," she said. "Feel good. I want you to feel good."

Her unselfishness unmanned me, and I pushed once more into her and released into an exploding star. The pulses spread through me like torpedoes, and I gripped her hips, trying to push farther and farther into her, trying to make it last, make it last, make it last...

"Mmm," she said in her angelic voice.

"I'll make this up to you," I said against her earlobe.

"S'okay," she said again.

"No, it's not. Give me a minute, and I swear to God I'll make you come like you never have before."

She smiled into the pillow. I couldn't see her lips, but just the slight movement of her facial muscles clued me in. That was how well I knew her already, knew the responses of her body. Man, how could I ever give this woman up?

*Not going to think about that now.*

Instead, I inhaled, breathing in the coconut scent of

Marj's still-damp hair. I eased the holder from her ponytail, letting her hair flow down her back. So beautiful.

I trailed my lips along the side of her face and then over her neck and shoulder, my cock finally sliding out of her. I was still semi-hard, and already my dick was showing signs of new life. Just being next to this woman, kissing her smooth flesh, inhaling the fragrance of her hair mixed with the raw scent of our sex that hung in the air...

As much as I wanted to take her to another plane of passion, part of me wanted to lie here, just be next to her, and pretend, if only for a moment, that this was normal.

My normal life.

If only I were worthy of such a thing.

As much as I was not worthy, she was. She deserved so much more than just me getting my rocks off inside her.

Time to show her what true pleasure was.

I moved slightly, placing her supine on the bed, and then I positioned myself between her legs, lifted her hips so her knees were snug against my shoulders, and dived into her sweet center.

She was wet, and my semen drizzled out of her. Her clit was swollen into a hard pink knob, begging for attention, attention I was happy to bestow. I massaged it with my fingers.

"Oh!" She jerked against me.

I rubbed it tenderly again and then with more force, and finally I closed my lips around it and sucked.

"Bryce!"

Yes, she was more than ready. Just a few swipes of my tongue and lips and she was nearly at a climax.

It would be the first of many tonight.

# CHAPTER FORTY-NINE

**Marjorie**

His lips were so warm on my pussy, and then—

"I'm coming!" I flew into the orgasm so quickly I surprised myself. Just a suck on my clit, and then, when he forced two fingers into me, my entire body quivered with unbridled passion.

*Bryce, Bryce, Bryce. I love you, Bryce. I love you.*

But I could only say those words inside my head, as much as I longed to utter them to the man with his head between my legs. I knew I was falling for him, and perhaps realizing I was in love during an orgasm wasn't true love.

But damn, I felt like it was.

*I love you.*

*I love you.*

*I love you.*

Higher and higher I flew, into another and yet another climax. Bryce trailed his hands over my abdomen, up to my breasts, and circled his fingers around my hard nipples. More jolts shattered me, as if his fingers were electric nipple clamps sending buzzing tingles into my already blazing body.

*I love you.*

*I love you.*

*I love you.*

"Damn, Marjorie. You're so hot," Bryce said against my vulva, pushing his fingers into me once more. "Come for me. Come for me again and again."

As if in response to his command, I soared once more, bolts shooting from my breasts to my pussy and then outward, as if I were on fire with desire.

Which I was. I so was.

My silent declarations of love continued as my head spun and, I came again. Then again.

My body shuddered, and my mind whirled. And finally... finally...

He moved his fingers out of my channel, moved his head back.

And gazed at me.

"So pink and beautiful. You're amazing." He buried his head again, pulling my labia into his mouth and tugging.

I had no more climaxes to give... No more...but still he licked me, ate me, tugged at me, and it all felt so good, as if every corner of emptiness I'd ever felt in my body had been miraculously filled. I closed my eyes, basking in the afterglow and loving the touch of his mouth on my most sensitive place. He moved his tongue downward then, licking my ass.

"Mmm. Beautiful," he said again against my forbidden hole. "Beautiful and delicious."

Desire swept through me, desire so profound that needed sating now. Right now.

"Please," I said, not sure what I was asking for. "Please, Bryce."

"Easy, baby. Let out a breath."

I obeyed, and a new feeling sucked me in. His finger. His finger, wet with my juices, had breached the tight rim of my ass.

"God, if you could see this," he said. "Fucking gorgeous."

He moved his finger in and out slowly at first, and then more quickly, the invasion morphing from a slight pain to an unbelievable pleasure. And then...when his lips touched my clit once more...

A climax so profound hit me like a thunder crash.

"That's it, baby. I knew you had one more. Give it to me. Give me your orgasm. It's mine. All mine."

All his.

It surely was.

As was I.

I was still coming when he removed his finger and climbed up my body, crushed his lips to mine in a searing kiss, and pushed his giant cock back into my pussy.

He pumped into me, mimicking with his tongue what his cock was doing inside me.

I was all out of orgasms, but that didn't matter. The feel of him, the completeness of us together, overwhelmed me in the best way.

He kept kissing me as he released a second time. Kept kissing me as he held himself inside me for several timeless moments, kept kissing me... Kept kissing me.

And I knew my orgasmic declarations of love had been real.

I was in love with Bryce Simpson.

Completely and hopelessly in love.

# CHAPTER FIFTY

### Bryce

After staring at her for as long as I could and choking back a tear that threatened, I covered Marjorie's sleeping body.

*I love you.*

Had she meant to say the words aloud? They'd come out on a soft sigh during one of her many climaxes, and though I'd yearned to return them, I hadn't.

I couldn't go there. Not yet. Not until...

Not until I'd dealt with the demons that plagued me... including the long-buried secret from Joe's and my past that threatened us now.

I had to move on, make her understand that we couldn't ever be. I dressed quietly and then walked out to the desk in the kitchen. After finding a notepad and pen, I scribbled down some words.

Noxious words that I didn't mean but had to say. She needed to move on, and I needed to help her. I walked back into the bedroom where my perfect angel still slept. I kissed her cheek lightly. She moved slightly but didn't awaken.

I wanted to remember her like this—soft and innocent and beautiful. So fucking beautiful.

*I'm sorry,* I said silently. *I'm sorry I can't be what you deserve.*

One more light kiss to her silky forehead.
Then I laid the note on the nightstand next to her.
I walked out of the bedroom.
Out of the guesthouse.
Out of Marjorie Steel's life.

# CHAPTER FIFTY-ONE

**Marjorie**

The note was callous.

The words were cruel.

Even the sheet of paper was crisp and unsympathetic.

Bryce Simpson was heartless.

I'd fallen in love with a heartless man.

My purse sat on a chair on the other side of the room. Still naked from our night of passion, I rose and grabbed it. Inside the hidden pocket was something I kept, even though I'd promised Mel I'd trashed it.

It was a reminder.

It was a security blanket.

Right now I needed it.

*Stop.*

I could walk to the kitchen. Open the refrigerator. Let the blast of cold air ease the unpleasantness from my mind.

Yes, it would be easier.

Much easier than...

I unzipped the pocket slowly and withdrew the sharp razor blade. I sat back down on the bed and regarded the scar on my upper thigh. It was still red, but it had healed. If I left it alone, it would eventually turn white and then gradually fade over the years.

Slowly, I lowered the blade to my flesh.

# EPILOGUE

I shine my knife. I polish my gun. Always keeping one eye on you.

And I remember.

You will pay.

You will *all* pay.

# EXCERPT FROM
## *MISADVENTURES WITH A ROCK STAR*

Why was I here again?

I stifled a yawn. Watching a couple of women do each other while others undressed, clamoring for a minute of the band's attention, wasn't my idea of a good time. The two women were gorgeous, of course, with tight bodies and big boobs. The contrasts in their skin and hair color made their show even more exotic. They were interesting to watch, but they didn't do much for me sexually. Maybe if I weren't so exhausted. I'd pulled the morning and noon shifts, and my legs were aching.

Even so, I was glad Susie had dragged me to the concert, if only to see and hear Jett Draconis live. His deep bass-baritone was rich enough to fill an opera house but had just enough of a rasp to make him the ultimate rock vocalist. And when he slid into falsetto and then back down to bass notes? Panty-melting. No other words could describe the effect. Watching him had mesmerized me. He lived his music as he sang and played, not as if it were coming from his mouth but emanating from his entire body and soul. The man had been born to perform.

A true artist.

Which only made me feel like more of a loser.

Jett Draconis was my age, had hit the LA scene around the same time I had, and he'd made it big in no time. Me? I was still a struggling screenwriter working a dead-end job waiting tables at a local diner where B-list actors and directors hung out. Not only was I not an A-lister, I wasn't even serving them. When I couldn't sell a movie to second-rate producer Rod Hanson? I hadn't yet said the words out loud, but the time had come to give up.

"What are you doing hanging out here all by yourself?"

Susie's words knocked me out of my barrage of self-pity. For a minute anyway.

"Just bored. Can we leave soon?"

"Are you kidding me? The party's just getting started." She pointed to the two women on the floor. "That's Janet and Lindy. Works every time. They always go home with someone in the band."

"Only proves that men are pigs."

Susie didn't appear to be listening. Her gaze was glued on Zane, the keyboardist, whose gaze was in turn glued on the two women cavorting in the middle of the floor. She turned to me. "Let's make out."

I squinted at her, as if that might help my ears struggling in the loud din. I couldn't possibly have heard her correctly. "What?"

"You and me. Kiss me." She planted a peck right on my mouth.

I stepped away from her. "Are you kidding me?"

"It works. Look around. All the girls do it."

"I'm not a girl. I'm a thirty-year-old woman."

"Don't you think I'm hot?" she asked.

"Seriously? Of course you are." Indeed, Susie looked great with her dark hair flowing down to her ass and her form-fitting leopard-print tank and leggings. "So is Angelina Jolie, but I sure as heck don't want to make out with her. I don't swing that way." Well, for Angelina Jolie I might. Or Lupita Nyong'o. But that was it.

"Neither do I—at least not long-term. But it'll get us closer to the band."

"Is this what you do at all the after-parties you go to?"

She giggled. "Sometimes. But only if there's someone as hot as you to make out with. I have my standards."

Maybe I should have been flattered. But no way was I swapping spit with my friend to get some guy's attention. They were still just men, after all. Even the gorgeous and velvet-voiced Jett Draconis, who seemed to be watching the floor show.

Susie inched toward me again. I turned my head just in time so her lips and tongue swept across my cheek.

"Sorry, girl. If you want to make out, I'm sure there's someone here who will take you up on your offer. Not me, though. It would be too...weird."

She nodded. "Yeah, it would be a little odd. I mean, we live together and all. But I hate that you're just standing here against the wall not having any fun. And I'm not ready to go home yet."

I sighed. This was Susie's scene, and she enjoyed it. She had come to LA for the rockers and was happy to work as a receptionist at a talent agency as long as she made enough money to keep her wardrobe in shape and made enough contacts to get into all the after-parties she wanted. That was the extent of her aspirations. She was living her dream, and she'd no doubt continue to live it until her looks gave out... which wouldn't happen for a while with all the Botox and plastic surgery available in LA. She was a good soul, but right now her ambition was lacking.

"Tell you what," I said. "Have fun. Do your thing. I'll catch an Uber home."

She frowned. "I wanted to show you a good time. I'm sorry I suggested making out. I get a little crazy at these things."

I chuckled. "It's okay. Don't worry about it."

"Please stay. I'll introduce you to some people."

"Any producers or directors here?" I asked.

"I don't know. Mostly the band and their agents, and of course the sound and tech guys who like to try to get it on with the groupies. I doubt any film people are here."

"Then there isn't anyone I need to meet, but thanks for offering." I pulled my phone out of my clutch to check the time. It was nearing midnight, and this party was only getting started.

"Sure I can't convince you to stay?" Susie asked.

"Afraid not." I pulled up the Uber app and ordered a ride. "But have a great time, okay? And stay safe, please."

"I always do." She gave me a quick hug and then lunged toward a group of girls, most of them still dressed, thank God.

I scanned the large room. Susie and her new gaggle of friends were laughing and drinking cocktails. A couple girls were slobbering over the drummer's dick. The two beautiful women putting on the sex show had abandoned the floor, and the one with dark skin was draped between the legs of Zane Michaels, who was, believe it or not, even prettier than she was. The other sat on Jett Draconis's lap.

Zane Michaels was gorgeous, but Jett Draconis? He made his keyboardist look average in comparison. I couldn't help staring. His hair was the color of strong coffee, and he wore it long, the walnut waves hitting below his shoulders. His eyes shone a soft hazel green. His face boasted high cheekbones and a perfectly formed nose, and those lips... The most amazing lips I'd ever seen on a man—full and flawless. I'd gawked at photos of him in magazines, not believing it was possible for a man to be quite so perfect-looking—beautiful and rugged handsome at the same time.

Not that I could see any of this at the moment, with the blonde on top of him blocking most of my view.

I looked down at my phone once more. My driver was still fifteen minutes away. Crap.

Then I looked up.

Straight into the piercing eyes of Jett Draconis.

**This story continues in**
***Misadventures with a Rock Star!***

# MESSAGE FROM HELEN HARDT

Dear Reader,

Thank you for reading *Breathless*. If you want to find out about my current backlist and future releases, please like my Facebook page and join my mailing list. I often do giveaways. If you're a fan and would like to join my street team to help spread the word about my books. I regularly do awesome giveaways for my street team members.

If you enjoyed the story, please take the time to leave a review on a site like Amazon or Goodreads. I welcome all feedback. I wish you all the best!

Helen

**Facebook**
Facebook.com/HelenHardt

**Newsletter**
HelenHardt.com/Sign-Up

**Street Team**
Facebook.com/Groups/HardtAndSoul/

# ALSO BY HELEN HARDT

**The Steel Brothers Saga:**
*Craving*
*Obsession*
*Possession*
*Melt*
*Burn*
*Surrender*
*Shattered*
*Twisted*
*Unraveled*
*Breathless*
*Ravenous* (Coming Soon)
*Insatiable* (Coming Soon)

**Blood Bond Saga:**
*Unchained*
*Unhinged*
*Undaunted*
*Unmasked*
*Undefeated*

**Misadventures Series:**
*Misadventures with a Rock Star*
*Misadventures of a Good Wife* (with Meredith Wild)

**The Temptation Saga:**
*Tempting Dusty*
*Teasing Annie*
*Taking Catie*
*Taming Angelina*
*Treasuring Amber*
*Trusting Sydney*
*Tantalizing Maria*

**The Sex and the Season Series:**
*Lily and the Duke*
*Rose in Bloom*
*Lady Alexandra's Lover*
*Sophie's Voice*

**Daughters of the Prairie:**
*The Outlaw's Angel*
*Lessons of the Heart*
*Song of the Raven*

# ACKNOWLEDGMENTS

Readers clamored for Marjorie's story from the beginning, so I had my work cut out for me. I hope it meets and exceeds your expectations. I worried about writing it, but once I started, the words flowed better than they have in a while. Not since *Craving* have I enjoyed crafting a story so much. I loved revisiting the Steels, and we're only just beginning. You'll see more of Marj and Bryce in *Ravenous*, coming soon!

As always, no book is ever the result of only the author. Massive thanks to the following individuals whose effort and belief made this book shine: Jennifer Becker, Audrey Bobak, Dana Bridges, Haley Byrd, Yvonne Ellis, Jesse Kench, Robyn Lee, Jon Mac, Amber Maxwell, Dave McInerney, Michele Hamner Moore, Keli Jo Nida, Jenny Rarden, Chrissie Saunders, Scott Saunders, Celina Summers, Kurt Vachon, and Meredith Wild.

Thanks also to the women and men of Hardt and Soul. You all are my rock!

To my family and friends, thank you for your unwavering support.

And most importantly, thank you to my readers. None of this matters without all of you.

# ABOUT THE AUTHOR

#1 *New York Times*, #1 *USA Today*, and #1 *Wall Street Journal* bestselling author Helen Hardt's passion for the written word began with the books her mother read to her at bedtime. She wrote her first story at age six and hasn't stopped since. In addition to being an award-winning author of contemporary and historical romance and erotica, she's a mother, an attorney, a black belt in Taekwondo, a grammar geek, an appreciator of fine red wine, and a lover of Ben and Jerry's ice cream. She writes from her home in Colorado, where she lives with her family. Helen loves to hear from readers.

Visit her at HelenHardt.com